DISCLAIMER

Hello, this is the author, Britton Bean. I would just like to let you know that this book is not the best book ever written. I just wanted to get that out of the way. This book pales in comparison to the writings of Richard Paul Evens, or Brandon Sanderson. I am aware of my faults and imperfections in writing this book. I just ask you to look past those faults and imperfections, and enjoy the story and characters of this novel.
Thank You.

Learning to Fly

This Book is dedicated to Rosina Bean

Britton Bean

Special Thanks to Porter Butterfield and Kennedy Snow
I couldn't have done it without them.

Learning to Fly

Prologue
Chapter 1
Chapter 2
Chapter 3
Chapter 4
Chapter 5
Chapter 6
Chapter 7
Chapter 8
Chapter 9
Chapter 10
Chapter 11
Chapter 12
Chapter 13
Chapter 14
Chapter 15
Chapter 16
Chapter 17
Chapter 18
Chapter 19
Chapter 20
Chapter 21

Britton Bean

Chapter 22
Chapter 23
Chapter 24
Chapter 25
Chapter 26
Chapter 27
Chapter 28
Chapter 29
Chapter 30
Chapter 31
Chapter 32
Chapter 33
Chapter 34
Chapter 35
Chapter 36
Chapter 37
Chapter 38
Chapter 39
Chapter 40
Chapter 41
Epilogue

Learning to Fly

Prologue

"Sir, there's someone here for you." Marcus poked his head into the office. He was the butler, but the man didn't like that word. He just called him Marcus.

"Send him in." The gruff voice sounded from a chair. He was extremely bored and would let anyone in. Unless it was…

"He's a reporter." Marcus clarified.

"Ugh, didn't I tell them I'm not doing exclusives?" The gruff voice said as he stood up from his chair. A reporter was the one person the man did not want to see. He hated reporters. He thought they were all overly dramatic and plain dumb.

"He is really adamant, sir," Marcus added, not wanting to deal with another one of these reporters himself.

"Aren't they all?" The gruff voice responded, trying to make a joke. Marcus didn't laugh. After an awkward silence, the rough voice continued, "Fine, I'll deal with this myself." He *was* really bored.

"Yes, sir."

***

"What's your name, son?" The gruff voice sounded as he fiddled with some papers, trying to look busy. He actually had nothing to do ever since he'd declined the position.

"J-Justin Woodwind, sir." A small young man stuttered from a chair opposite a big desk. He couldn't have been taller than five feet. The young man, who called himself Justin, had blue eyes and blond hair and carried himself like a scared, lonely puppy. He wore a tan suit with a white shirt. Not the best look. *Perfect reporter material.* The man thought to himself.

"You work for a newspaper company, I assume." The man said, already regretting his decision to let this man in.

"Uh-h...yes, sir. The Present." Justin stuttered.

"What do you not get?" The gruff voice asked, annoyed and standing up from his chair to look out the window. "I made a public announcement that I am not doing any exclusives. Did you not see it?!" Then he muttered to himself, "It's all over the news."

The small man steeled himself; this would be harder than expected, and he'd expected it to be hard, "I'm different, sir."

"How?" The gruff man turned and looked Justin straight in the eyes.

While intimidated, Justin continued strongly, "I'm not looking for why you turned down the position. I'm here for your story. The story that I know is in there."

Justin grew more confident, "The story of our country's past. Of your past. Because I know that you did something that changed the world, and I think you deserve credit. And I need your help to fill in *the gap*. The gap of more than six years in our history books."

"You have the wrong person, son. Nothing happened. That's why it's called the gap." The gruff voice lied as he sat back down. He had underestimated this reporter. Something big *had* happened in those six years. But the man didn't go around bragging about it. It was something he didn't even want to think about.

His confidence only growing, Justin continued, "Then how would I know that you were the last of the six? That the other five are dead. And that you and five other people changed our world." Justin paused, waiting for a response. None came. The man simply stared at Justin. So, Justin sighed and said, "So what will it be, sir? Kick me out, or tell me your story?"

"You're quite the kid, aren't you?" The gruff voice responded, thoroughly impressed. Some wall inside him broke. He thought of his story. The man sighed. He had to tell it eventually. He wasn't getting any younger. Now was the time.

Britton Bean

The gruff voice opened a drawer and took out a worn and torn book.

"You see this book? This is my story. The story of my life. This book contains one of the *only* first-hand accounts of the gap. And the *only* account of how the Great Flash came to be."

"Well, let's start then," Justin nodded, breathing a sigh of relief and eagerly taking out his notepad. He was old-fashioned in that way.

"Alright, where do you want me to begin?" The gruff man asked as he flipped through the worn, dusty pages of the book. He hadn't opened it in decades.

"The beginning. Any good story starts at the beginning."

Chapter 1

The Fall of the USA

April 20th, 2023. That's when it happened. That's when the first nuke was launched. The war started before that, though. April 12th, 2023.

The war in Ukraine has been going on for a while, but when Russia "accidentally" hit a power station in Poland, the North Atlantic Treaty Organization or NATO fought back. NATO included the USA, UK, Germany, France, and other democratic nations.

Everyone knew that Russia had allies, but no one knew they would react so quickly. People came to the conclusion it had been planned. North Korea destroyed South Korea so quickly that no one even knew what happened. South Korea was taken in under 48 hours. China took the entire northern tip of Taiwan. America deployed forces to Taiwan and the Eastern front of Russia. NATO abandoned South Korea seeing the country as "Doomed from the start."

Americans were cocky. It was just their nature. They had the most powerful army, air force, and navy. Heck, they were so powerful they even had a Space Force. What could go wrong? But something went very, very wrong.

Eight days after Russia attacked Poland, Russia did something bold. According to American intelligence, Russia had been working on a stealth bomber for a while. But no one knew it was air ready. The bombardment of the USA began.

Why America or Taiwan didn't see them, no one knows. Many people thought it was because of incompetence. But once they were in the air, there was nothing NATO could do about it.

12:04 am, April 20th, 2023, Russian bombers and their fighter escorts made a line 900 miles long above China and part of Japan. About as long as the California Coastline. Even though Japan had surprisingly declared neutrality, Russia put its planes in Japanese airspace. Japan did not stop them—another crucial error.

These weren't any ordinary aircraft. These aircraft were flying at 120,000 feet in the air. They were nuclear-powered and carried some kind of huge, new missile that deployed over 200 regular-sized bombs when launched. And each bomber had

Learning to Fly

ten of these missiles. No one knows the exact numbers of the aircraft. Estimations roll in at about 1,200 to even 3,000. It was an insane force.

Once America finally found them, they sent up all the fighters they could muster. Only one problem: American fighters couldn't hit them. They couldn't even reach them. So, NATO tried missiles. The USA and Taiwan fired at least 120 ballistic missiles at the bombers. Some were even fired directly from B-2 bombers. None of them reached their targets. To this day, no one knows why. We may never know. The mysteries surrounding the aircraft seemed limitless. NATO knew almost nothing about them. The bombers seemed untouchable.

So as American forces struggled to find something, anything to stop them, Russia started launching the missiles. It was estimated that they used 200 of the bomb missiles on Taiwan. Taiwan was reduced to ash. Fiji: Gone. And they didn't stop there. Hawaii was destroyed. And what was worse, they weren't stopping.

But when all hope seemed lost, America played its last card. Their last hope.

The bombers started bombing California and some of Oregon. The first time America had ever been attacked on their mainland on such a large scale since the War of 1812. Because no fighter jet could reach 120,000 feet, the USA pulled out their best, most secret spy planes. And they strapped as many missiles and guns onto them as possible until the USA had 20 birds in the air. They called them SR-72s. Or, as they were known by the public, Ravens.

Britton Bean

Not much is known about the planes. The planes were top secret per US standards. The only thing the public knew for certain was the aircraft could fly to space. They were big enough to carry 150 of the US's smallest missiles. They were also powered by nuclear reactors. But we didn't learn that until it was too late. The public didn't even know their top speed. Nothing was clear about the jets. No one ever got a picture or even saw the jets. All the public knew was that the US was fighting back with spy planes.

The USA sent in their best pilots, their Top Gun. After a valiant, nearly impossible effort by the US Ravens, most of the bombers and their escorts were destroyed. Most. There were ten bombers and 18 escorts left. Ravens: one.

The pilot was LT. Steven Glade. He had no missiles left, no way to attack, only an airplane. Steven did something that no one had ever done. He did something that changed the world. Saved is a better word. Or maybe, he destroyed it.

To understand this, you must know some basic nuclear reactor knowledge. In a nuclear reactor, there needs to be a cooling system. Sometimes this is water, but in airplanes, lead is most often used. So smart interceptors would aim for the back middle, where the lead or nuclear reactor was. Damaging the cooling system would make the reactor go supercritical and die or explode. This was a confirmed kill, no matter the luck.

Lt. Glade knew this and decided to take hits on purpose in that region. His cooling system was compromised. So right before he blew up, he pushed his engine to the max, pushing the reactor to overload levels, and rammed one of the bombers.

This set off the biggest explosion ever. Anything within 20 miles of the air was vaporized. The shockwave ruptured an estimated 3,000 eardrums of personnel in the area. The light permanently blinded many of them as well. But in the end, that didn't matter.

After the initial shock of the explosion, the USA started to regroup and create a new strategy. The economy took a huge hit. Many coastal states to the west, including California, Washington, Oregon, Utah, Nevada, Idaho, and some parts of Montana and Colorado were demolished.

Citizens couldn't comprehend it all. Half of the USA had been destroyed, and the people were wondering why the USA didn't try harder. But they just didn't understand the situation. There were revolts in the streets just 20 minutes after the attack. It was anarchy. People attacked stores, malls, and even restaurants. Companies' stock value plummeted, while the stocks of military suppliers increased tenfold. The Dow dropped 20 points in a matter of minutes. Food and bottled water prices suddenly skyrocketed, but nobody was buying them.

People started looting stores, killing anyone they thought was a threat, and most assumed everyone else was. People boarded up their doors and windows – anything to shut out the outside world. But that didn't stop the military from preparing for a strike. They didn't get far, though.

Britton Bean

It is unknown how the nukes started or who even fired first, but only one hour after the bombardment stopped, the first nuke since Nagasaki began gaining altitude. The news stations, podcasts, live streamers, and radio stations were throwing out conspiracy theories even when there were only 20 minutes left to live. It was insane.

There were two main theories. The first was that the USA had gotten desperate because of the chaos and decided to end it all. An "if I can't have it, no one can" situation.

The second, more likely theory was that hackers had hacked Russia's launch codes. It made no sense for Russia to launch a nuke themselves because they were winning.

Once the public knew the nukes were flying, anyone who hadn't gone crazy went crazy. People ransacking gun shops, shooting people on sight. And why not? Who's going to punish them? People were drinking in the streets, doing drugs openly, and police stations were overrun with criminals.

Priests were preaching in the streets and throwing out every line in the Bible. They were preaching that this was the Second Coming. Or that it was Armageddon. Or Qiyamah. They all were preaching that this was the end.

 Commercial and private pilots started trying to outfly the nukes. All air traffic controllers ran when they heard the news, so as various aircraft were taking off as fast as they could, airplanes collided on the runway and in the sky, creating even more chaos for the people on the ground. Wreckage was raining down from the sky, and jetliner debris crushed entire buildings.

Cars were going almost 150 mph on roads. Drag races ensued, with people showing off their vehicles one last time.

Learning to Fly

There just wasn't enough space for all of it. Cars were crashing head-on at 150 mph. More people were estimated to die in the chaos before the blast than in the explosion itself. But who can really know? And then it was all over. It's funny how much damage one person can do.

Chapter 2

My School Blows Up

Now to my part of the story. I'm a 14-year-old that lives in St. George, Utah. The name's Britton Bean. Or, as I'm more commonly known – Bean. The only people that call me Britton are my family and my best friend, Hunter. Hunter was my very first friend and liked Britton better than Bean.

I'm in eighth grade, the shortest in the grade by a long shot, with a height of four feet eight inches. You could say the nickname Bean just fits. I have short brown hair with a big cowlick right in the middle front of my hair that makes my hair look like a wave. I don't bother to comb it. I have brown eyes and am well-built for my size.

Learning to Fly

I love planes. I've always wanted to be an Air Force pilot when I grew up. I'm pretty smart. A 4.0 was expected in my family. To me, failing was a B+. I like engineering and electronics. I want to work with my hands. Everything just feels easier with them.

I've always believed that everything should be done fast and efficiently. I finish things quickly. I figure them out as I go. I think that experience is always the best teacher.

But now to the bombing, the start of my portion of the story. St. George was spared most of the damage because of the geography. The valley helped prevent most of the bombs from hitting us. That didn't mean that none hit. City halls, power stations, and other public places were hit. The bombers also put the airport out of commission. And schools were hit. My school was just one of the many.

I remember the moment exactly. We had heard of the war, but word hadn't reached the school yet to evacuate. And why would it? We were in St. George, Utah. In the middle of nowhere. A quickly growing town, but nonetheless, a small one. Why would someone attack a small town in the middle of the desert? But they did.

I was in second period, P.E. It was about ten. We were outside playing soccer when we heard the sound. A loud, electric droning coming from the sky. Everyone kinda just looked up, confused. I looked at my friend, Hunter, and said jokingly, "They found me!"

Hunter was average-sized and well-built. He was good at almost any sport he played. He loved football with a passion.

Britton Bean

He had short brown hair and brown eyes like me. He had two cowlicks in his hair, making it look like two hurricanes fighting for space. He was a tough guy. No nonsense here. His favorite phrase was, "You suck!" emphasizing the "ck." The phrase really just meant, "C'mon on man."

Hunter really wasn't all that smart. He got all A's but wasn't in any honors classes. Hunter was really just street-smart. He also wanted to be a pilot. You can see why I was friends with him.

Hunter chuckled but was still confused. And then I saw the worst sight anyone can see. I watched to the south as St. George was blown to bits. That's when people went crazy. The line of fire and explosions were just coming closer to the school. Teachers tried their best, but kids ran.

The issue was that the north wing couldn't see the impending doom approaching them. They were blocked by the south wing. I ducked as bombs exploded all around me. The explosions and banging made my ears start ringing. Surprisingly, I did *not* die. Maybe it was fate.

When I looked up, I wasn't prepared for what I saw. All around me were bodies. A soccer goal had crushed a group of kids. I heard groaning and crying. Craters littered the field. A fire burned in the high school which was across the street. Not the greatest sight for a 14-year-old kid, let me tell you. I had no idea so much fire was possible.

When I looked at my school, I was surprised to find some parts of the school still standing. It looked like it had been spared. People were still running out of the building bleeding through. I turned around, remembering Hunter. I saw him unconscious about 50 feet from where he last was.

I ran over to him and knelt by him. I started screaming frantically at him, yelling his name over and over again, "HUNTER! HUNTER! HUNTER, HAWS WAKE UP!" He didn't move. I slapped him in the face over and over again. "C'mon, Hunter!" I pleaded to no one in particular.

"Please, Hunter. Please…" And then came an answer to my plea. Hunter's eyes burst open, yelling, "AHH-oooo, what the heck just happened?!" Hunter said as he looked around.

Relief flooded over me. There was my Hunter. I tackled him to the ground and yelled at him, "Don't you ever do that again!"

"Hey, I didn't do anything?! I'm just wondering what is going on!" Hunter responded defensively. He pushed me off of him. Hunter looked around more. "Holy moly. This is new."

My smile faded as I remembered everyone inside the building.

"What is going on?!" Hunter repeated more urgently.

"No time, just follow me," I said quickly as I ran towards the building. I still saw people running out bloody, which was confusing because the school looked intact. I ran into the building, turning around to ensure Hunter was with me. He was. And that's when I realized why everyone was bloody.

A bomb had exploded in the courtyard. All the courtyard-facing walls of the school were rubble. Then I heard a groan. I turned to see who it was. No one was next to me. I turned to Hunter and asked, "Did you just groan?"

"No," Hunter responded, confused. "Why would I groan? Will you explain what I just saw?" He motioned with his hand at the building and out at the courtyard.

That's when I realized the groan...was the building. The building was about to collapse in on itself!

Hunter realized it, too, "Oooh crap. That's our queue." Hunter grabbed my arm, and we ran. I looked back to see the ceiling collapse just where I was. And then the school folded in on itself. Hunter was still pulling me when I saw Kai.

Kai was one of my best friends. He had curly black hair and was really chill. Kai didn't look chill then, though. I saw him sprinting as hard as he could, trying to make it out. I tried running to help, but Hunter was too strong. I watched as Kai reached out his hand, but no one was there to grab it. And the building came down on him. I still have nightmares to this day about that moment.

There was a loud boom as the building came down, and dust enveloped me. After what seemed like forever, Hunter and I made it out coughing. I was sobbing. One of my best friends just died right in front of me. How could I not?

And what was worse was that I felt I could have helped him. I felt I hadn't done enough. I was angry at Hunter that he had pulled me out. I was angry that I hadn't tried harder. I was angry at the explosions. I was angry at Kai that he didn't run faster. I cried into Hunter's shoulder.

Then I felt the pain. The unimaginable pain rocked me. At that moment, I wished I was dead. That Kai was alive and that

Learning to Fly

I was dead. I felt Hunter pressing hard on my leg, but the pain I felt was deep in my soul.

I cried till there were no tears left to cry. It felt like someone had pulled out my heart, smashed it with a hammer, and smashed it back in. After all the adrenaline wore off, I started to feel the pain in my leg. I had built up the courage to look at it. I wished I hadn't. The pain increased when I did. Hunter had tied a piece of his shirt around the wound as a tourniquet. A piece of glass was stuck just above my ankle. This time the pain was physical. But it was like a bee sting compared to the aching in my chest.

I don't know how long we sat there; everything was a blur. I remember seeing Rockwell and Ezra come over.

Ezra and Rockwell were twins. Not identical by a long shot. Ezra was tall, very tall. Ezra had brown hair and hazel eyes. His hair was short and always combed. Rockwell was short, about my size, at four feet ten inches. But Rockwell was older than Ezra, and we never let Ezra forget. Rockwell also had brown hair, which was a bit longer than mine, coming down his neck. I couldn't tell if they were hurt or not. As I said, I wasn't paying much attention.

Eli and Porter found us next. Eli had blond hair with blue eyes and was also short. He was a jokester and was almost always sarcastic. He was skinnier than me and less bulky. Porter was like Eli except taller. Porter had short blond hair and blue eyes. Sometimes he grew his hair out, and occasionally he buzzed it. He was pretty average overall.

We huddled together for a while. We were just shocked. Hunter told them what had happened. I don't know how we concluded this, but we started to move. All I could think was that I should have done better.

The boys helped me get to Hunter's house since it was the closest, where Rockwell wrapped my leg. We also got painkillers. Everyone started asking questions.

"Where are the emergency crews?!" asked Ezra, visibly angry.

"Probably dealing with all the other damage," Hunter muttered.

"Well, we need to find somewhere to hide. It's not safe here. If they come around a second time, we're toast." Ezra commented.

"Who's 'they'?" Porter asked.

"I don't know, but we need to go somewhere," Ezra confirmed.

"Well, where do we go!?" I yelled, sitting up. Rockwell pushed me back down onto the table.

"My place," Porter said quietly. "My house was built during the cold war, and the basement doubles as a bunker. My family keeps it well stocked."

"Wait, wait, why not just go to the hospital?" Eli challenged Porter.

"He's not wrong. Let's go." Hunter said. "We can take the golf cart."

After limping over to the golf cart, Hunter started it and began making his way to the hospital. The golf cart was not

Learning to Fly

designed to carry six kids. More like four. They decided to lay me down on the back of the cart. Rockwell was back there, holding onto a pole to keep from falling off. Rockwell really wasn't on the cart. He just had his feet on and leaned out while holding the bar. Ezra sat up front with Hunter at the wheel. Eli and Porter squeezed into the back seats.

The roads were bumpy and had seen better days, but they were still drivable. Potholes littered the ground around the area. Several cars had stopped on the streets and weren't moving. People were just looking up and around them, stunned.

We sat in silence, most of us numb. After 15 minutes of driving, Hunter stopped the cart. I heard a gasp. Rockwell let go of the bar and stepped onto the ground. I sat up and saw a hill. A hill that should have had a hospital on it. Instead, there was rubble. A single wall was still standing. Nothing more.

"They blew it up." Hunter gawked. "Isn't that, like, against the law?"

"According to the Geneva Convention, it is," I mumbled dully.

"What's that?" Hunter asked.

I sighed and asked him, "Do you know anything?"

"So, what now?" Eli asked before Hunter could answer.

Hunter had just opened his mouth when we heard the gunshots of an automatic weapon. Everyone ducked and put their hands over their heads. I turned my body away and put my head down. Rockwell jumped back on the cart.

"DRIVE HUNTER!!" Ezra screamed.

Britton Bean

But Hunter was way ahead of him, pushing the golf cart engine to the max. I smelled burning rubber, and the wheels spun. We were going way faster than the cart was designed to go. I turned my head, and my eyes widened as I looked behind and saw several men in a truck following us and shooting at us.

"HUNTER, GO FASTER!!" Rockwell yelled, gripping the pole for dear life.

Hunter turned hard, putting the golf cart on two wheels and almost flipping it. We heard the car turn, too, and bullets sprayed over the cart, putting several holes in it. I looked down to see a liquid coming out of the cart. Gasoline.

Knowing we wouldn't last long like this, I tried to think quickly. I sat up and looked around me. I searched the area, looking for a way we might be able to escape them. Nothing. We were on a main road that didn't have any turns for a while. The closest one was at least a mile away. By then, we would be dead. We were coming up on several store parking lots, but there were no turns. I looked around the cart, looking for something, anything that would work. That's when I saw the matches. A box of matches sitting on the dash. Then I had an idea.

"Hunter, pass me the matches on the dash!" I yelled urgently.

He threw them back, which was a risk in and of itself, but I reached up and caught them. I took one out. I tried to light it. The match broke under the pressure. I tossed the remnants away and tried to calm myself down. I heard more shots fly past me. It's not the easiest thing to calm yourself down when you're being shot at. But at last, fire grabbed hold of the match. Then, ensuring it didn't go out, I dropped the match onto the leaking gas.

"Turn, Hunter!!" I screamed.

Hunter turned hard into a store parking lot while everyone instinctively leaned the other way to prevent us from flipping. The fire grabbed hold of the gas and followed it toward the car. It was almost as if the gas was saying, *"This way, this is where the bad guys are."* It sure felt like it.

The flame went right under the car and caught the fuel. As luck would have it, the flame caught the full fuel tank, blowing the back of the vehicle forward. It looked like a rocket ship gone wrong. The car flew forward, then hit the ground windshield first and flipped. It kept flipped six more times before it finally came to a stop. No one moved inside the car.

Everyone turned around to see what the explosion was about. Eli smiled faintly and commented, "That was a big brain moment Bean."

"At least school taught me something," I responded bitterly and laid my head back on the hard plastic, and breathed a sigh of relief. Hunter tried the gas, but the engine sputtered, and it died.

"Out of gas?" Rockwell asked.

"Yup," Hunter confirmed. "Where to now?"

"Wait, are we just going to ignore the fact that some full-blown-army-looking dudes just started firing at some kids in a golf cart!?" Ezra screamed.

"Yeah, is anyone else concerned?" Eli agreed.

"Hunter, turn on the radio." I turned and said to Hunter.

Hunter immediately turned it on.

A loud beeping and a monotone voice rang out, "Find shelter immediately. Nuclear Missile incoming. Please find shelter immediately. Nuclear Missile incoming."

"That... Can't... What?!" Porter said, astounded.

Remembering Porter's house, I said sternly, "Porter, how close is your house?"

"A m-mile from here." Porter stuttered.

"Then what are we waiting for? Let's go! Our lives *literally* depend on it!"

Everyone had the same idea and got out, except me, of course, and started pushing the golf cart. It began to pick up speed, and when my friends couldn't go any faster, they jumped on. This repeated for a mile.

We arrived at Porter's house in about five minutes and ran to the door. Hunter helped me out of the cart. Porter pulled out a hidden key from inside a bush and opened the door. Porter led the way as we all ran downstairs.

Sure enough, a bunker door was on the bottom of the stairs.

"Everyone in, let's go!" Porter screamed as he opened what looked like a vault door.

When we walked, it looked like a supermarket. Cans of food everywhere. Bottled water packages took up half of the shelves. The other half was food. Canned and food mixes. There was a shelf full of board games, cards, and two CD players with what looked like a thousand CDs. In the southeastern corner, there was an entire library that was bigger than our school library. And every shelf was full of books. Porter wasn't kidding. His family really did keep the house pretty well stocked.

There was a 1,000-gallon tank labeled FLAMMABLE. In the northwest corner was another big machine with several tanks of oxygen strapped to it and several more on the side. There was an entire kitchen in the middle of the bunker, with a table that could seat six. There were four bunk beds to the east, and I could even spot an electric generator next to the bunks with a pipe connected to the tank labeled FLAMMABLE to the west. There were rectangular LED lights on the ceiling. You know, the ones you see in school gyms. This place was like an entirely new world.

"Woah!" Rockwell said, astonished.

"Quite the preppers," Eli mumbled.

"Bet you like that now," I told him.

"This place is sick!" Hunter said while helping me into the room.

Then we heard Porter close the bunker door and lock it. Four solid steel locks slid into place in all corners of the vault door. We were officially locked in.

"You can look at it in a second, but someone, please turn on the radio," Porter said, pointing to the CD players. Eli ran over and grabbed one, plugging it into a socket on the wall. I was surprised it turned on. I thought the power would be out by now. He turned it on to the news radio.

Britton Bean

"Nuclear impact in three minutes. Find shelter immediately. Nuclear impact in two minutes. Find shelter immediately." A monotone voice sounded repeatedly.

Hunter brought a chair over for me to sit down and asked what everyone had been wondering. "Can this thing protect us from a nuke?"

Porter responded quietly, "I don't know."

"Well, goodbye, everyone," Rockwell muttered.

I have to admit, I kinda agreed with him. This was like something out of a dream. But at least I would die surrounded by my friends. I can't imagine being alone when I die. I just hoped that my death wasn't today.

Everyone seemed to go quiet after that. It must have been a while, too, because the deafening sound of the nuke explosion brought me out of my thoughts. Everyone covered their ears instinctively. Then we heard the destruction of the building above us and the cracking of wood and plaster. After what seemed like forever, the sounds of destruction died down. But the end of one world was only the beginning of another.

Chapter 3

Bunker Life

Life in the bunker was pretty nice, actually. I'll walk through an average day. Everyone wakes up to Hunter's alarm on his watch at eight a.m. His watch was the only time that we had because everyone else's smart watches died pretty quickly. We would wake up and take turns for who makes breakfast while the rest of us would do a morning workout. It was Hunter who had started this, and everyone kinda followed. And we really didn't know what to do in the mornings.

I didn't do the workout for the first week because of my leg, so I was kinda behind in strength. I was always behind on strength. I was never the strongest person. The workout usually consists of 20 laps around the bunker (which we had measured was a mile on Rockwell's smartwatch before it died). After that, we would do 40 push-ups, 60 sit-ups, 50 arm curls (for which we used big five-gallon water jugs filled with two gallons of water), and 50 squats with full five-gallon water jugs attached to a broom. Every Friday, we would do a push-up contest, and the winner got bragging rights for that week. I got close, but never won.

Then we would have breakfast, usually consisting of pancakes or waffles, because we had a lot of mix, and we really didn't have many other options. I mean, once Porter tried to make our faces in the pancakes. We wasted a lot of water that day cleaning up.

After that, we would have quiet time, which was basically home school. That might come as a shock, but we kids are responsible sometimes. And, I'll give you this: Monopoly gets real boring real quick. We really didn't do anything for the first four days. But soon, the gang agreed that we needed some kind of education. And again, we were bored. Almost all the things we did, was because we were bored.

Everyone would choose a subject to research. Ever since the pancake incident, Porter started looking into cooking. And eventually, we were begging him to cook the pancakes and waffles. But he still made us cook sometimes just for the experience. We still don't know what his secret was. And believe me, we tried to get him to confess. We held a full interrogation.

Learning to Fly

***

We tied Porter to a chair, and Hunter and I interrogated him.

"Alright, Porter, we know you got the information," Hunter said intensely while I shined a flashlight in his eyes. "So, we can do this the easy way or the hard way. Your choice."

"You're not getting anything out of me," Porter said, playing his part. He *was* in the theater before the nuke.

"So, this is how we are going to play it…" Hunter said. And then he slapped Porter. And it wasn't a fake slap. It was a nice, crisp slap. "Give us the information!" Hunter screamed in his face. I heard Rockwell squeak out a laugh from behind Porter.

Reeling from the blow, Porter turned to Hunter, "You can't make me talk." And then he spit at Hunter. This time, I held down laughter. Ezra giggled a little.

Hunter jumped back from Porter. "Eww! Gross! That was too far!"

"You're the one who slapped me," Porter had wiggled out of the tape by now.

"Touché," Hunter said. I just smiled. I looked at Rockwell and Ezra, also smiling. It was moments like those that kept us sane.

Britton Bean

***

Ezra was the fittest out of all of us and was a real calorie guzzler. There was a rumor that he purposely lost the push-up contest once to make Hunter feel good. Ahh, but it was only a rumor. I'm pretty sure Ezra might have started it. There was a rivalry between Ezra and Hunter. After all, they were the strongest in the group. Ezra didn't really research anything. He just read novels.

Now Hunter was, well, as his name implies, a hunter. He loved guns and hunting. Hunter even made a shooting range next to the bunks, which was not the safest thing in the world. He read up on hunting techniques and traps you could make. Why? No one knows. He also read up on survivalist things. And he wasn't a big fan of reading. Still, he spent most of the research time shooting a rifle. He was like our Scout Leader. He also learned a little first aid from Rockwell.

That brings us to Rockwell, who was big into medicine. He was the smartest out of all of us and was the doctor. Like one time, Porter burned his hand badly while baking, and Rockwell had to treat it. He could just absorb information. He also stitched up my leg when we first got to the bunker. It wasn't his finest work, but it did work.

Now there's Eli. Eli was the mom. And I know that sounds weird, but hear me out. Eli was a fun sucker. Now don't get me wrong, Eli was awesome. We respected him more than anyone else. What he said went. He just made sure we didn't die. For example, Hunter said that if I lost Monopoly, he could shoot in the shooting range while I was there.

Now Hunter was a perfect shot and could hit a dime from 50 yards. I knew he wouldn't hit me. And Hunter was really bad at Monopoly. So, what were the chances he won? Against all odds, I lost.

So, as I was lining up down the shooting range, Hunter joked, "Any last words?" But before Hunter could shoot, Eli came over and broke it up.

"HEY!!" Hunter yelled as Eli ran over and forced the gun upwards.

"'Hey?!'" Eli mocked, "You could have killed him, you idiot!"

"I wouldn't have killed him. I wouldn't have suggested the bet if I wasn't confident in my abilities. And what if I had pulled the trigger and then you hit the gun. That would have killed him."

"You pointed a gun at Bean! Don't you know anything about gun safety?!"

"FINE!" Then Hunter muttered, "Fun-sucker."

I just stifled a laugh with everyone else. Until I saw Eli coming over to me. I got quiet real quick.

"What were you thinking!?!" Eli yelled at me.

"I lost a bet," I muttered quietly.

"You and Hunter with your bets." And then he walked away, shaking his head. I looked at Hunter, who had the look of, "That's your fault." I had that way with Hunter. Almost telepathy. Just one look could transmit so much information.

Britton Bean

Eli was the person we needed in that bunker. He did inventory checks on food and water and ensured everything worked, like the oxygen recycler and the electricity generator. He was immensely needed. So, during quiet time, he usually chilled and ensured nothing was wrong. Sometimes he took a nap, or read novels, or played solitaire.

Now there's me. I loved science. But my main research topic was electricity. Anything electric. I loved working with machines. I took apart Rockwell's smartwatch and put it back together again. Does it work? We may never know. We just didn't have the charger for it. Chargers for that stuff were made of a very different charging system.

After quiet time, we would have a snack for lunch, then go into free time. Usually, we would work on whatever we wanted, like projects or learning new skills. Everyone had something. We could do whatever we wanted.

Then after that, we would eat dinner and have game time. Whether it was Texas hold 'em, Risk, or even some P.E. game, we always did something fun. And everyone was very competitive. This was when Eli did most of his "mom" work. We even did capture the flag once. Keyword: "once."

***

The teams were Hunter, Rockwell, and me versus Eli, Ezra, and Porter. We used some handkerchiefs we found as

Learning to Fly

flags. We divided the bunker into two sides. It was divided directly at the center of the dining room. The west side and the east side. We were on the east side with the library, bunks, and shooting range.

"Alright, guys, here's the plan," I said in the huddle with Hunter and Rockwell. "We got to sneak someone over there. Someone small, someone agile, someone cool." I looked at Hunter and Rockwell.

"And let me guess," Hunter rolled his eyes, "That someone is you." He pointed at me.

"I'm honored, but that's what they are expecting. They are expecting me to go get it when in reality, Rocky's going to." I pointed at Rockwell. "We'll both sneak in, but I'll be slightly less sneaky. They'll think I'm the only one and forget about Rocky."

"Ohh." Hunter said, tapping his temple with his finger, "That's thinking."

"Yeah, and then Hunter will defend," Rockwell said.

"What?!" Hunter exclaimed, "No, I will not!"

"Hunter calm down," I said, "We need someone to do it."

"You know I don't defend Britton! Never!"

"Shh! You'll be fine."

Hunter shook his head rapidly, making his eyes wiggle in their sockets.

"You guys ready over there?!" Eli said. "Or are you still arguing?"

I rolled my eyes and turned to him, "Yeah, yeah, yeah. One second." I turned back to Hunter, "You're defending."

Britton Bean

"Mannan!" Hunter exclaimed. "You suck!"

The game started, and Eli and Ezra imminently rushed in to get the flag. We really hadn't established many rules. If you got touched with both hands, you had to go touch your flag.

Rockwell headed left while I ran right. I snuck behind a shelf. Hunter quickly moved to get Eli. He got him and sprinted over and got Ezra right after. They didn't even get close to the flag.

On their way back, they spotted Rockwell and I. They yelled to Porter, who came and tagged me, despite my best efforts. Rockwell dashed in but was tagged by Eli. I went to the flag and said to Hunter, "Don't tag 'em. We need them trying to get the flag. That takes two guys off Rockwell and me." I motioned with my head, "Just keep them away from the flag."

"Huh?" Hunter asked, confused.

I groaned, "You'll figure it out. You just got to give us a chance." I didn't wait for a reply, and Rockwell met us at the flag.

"What's the plan?" Rockwell asked, gathering his breath.

"Same plan. We got this." I said quickly, "Let's go, Rocky." I nodded to Rockwell.

"Alright." Rockwell shook his head, visibly skeptical.

Rockwell and I split up. I headed left this time, and Rockwell went right. I hid behind the table Rockwell had hidden behind. Then I dashed to a shelf filled with bottled water. Porter saw me. I saw him jog over to me, leaving the flag wide open. I glanced at Hunter. He was defending the flag from Ezra and Eli. They tried to reach the flag, jumping back whenever Hunter swung at them.

Porter came opposite the water shelf. I walked right every time he walked to the left, putting us in a stalemate. "Oh, Bean, are we really going to do this?"

"I don't know, are we?" I commented slyly. "We don't have to; all you have to do is give us that flag."

"You're sooo funny, Bean,"

"I know, right?" I saw Porter steal a glance at the flag. The handkerchief was unmoving in its normal spot. What he didn't see was Rockwell crouched behind a shelf three feet from the flag. Porter started to get too comfortable and started to look around. I acted like I was going to bolt for the flag, and Porter quickly jerked back. I gave him a side smile as I saw Rockwell grab the flag out of the corner of my eye.

"Porter!" Ezra yelled as he saw him. Porter spun around and saw Rockwell sprinting hard for our side. But Porter had a better angle and would reach Rockwell before he crossed the line. I quickly thought of a solution.

"Rockwell!" I poked my head around the water shelf. I reached my hand out. Porter was already in full sprint. Rockwell saw me, and a wide grin grew on his face. He threw me the handkerchief. I caught it and sprinted towards our side. But Eli was sprinting towards me. There was only the table in between us. The line was right there. All I had to do was get across it. But I couldn't get caught in a stalemate again. I would definitely lose. Porter and Eli would just corner me. I would have to jump over Eli.

Britton Bean

I ran towards the table in a full sprint. Eli got to the table first. Porter came in right behind me. No stopping now. I planted my left foot on the table and pushed hard into the air. Surprised, Eli ducked. I soared over Eli and headed for our side. But I'd misjudged it. I was headed right for a shelf!

My shoulder crashed into the shelf hard, knocking the entire rack of food to the ground. Cans flew all over the place. I landed hard on the metal shelf. I landed on one of the metal bars, knocking the wind out of me. I rolled onto my back and groaned.

Before I knew it, faces appeared in my vision. "You good, Bean?" Ezra asked.

I smiled and groaned, "Did we win?"

Hunter smiled and confirmed, "Oh, we did. We won with style."

We lost 56 cans of food that had opened and spilled and couldn't be used again. Eli was *livid.* We never played Capture the Flag again. On the bright side, the bunker always smelled like peaches.

***

Another time when we were playing Monopoly, Hunter accused Ezra of being a corrupt banker. Hunter thought he saw Ezra stealing money. There was yelling and name-calling. We even had a court case on it.

Learning to Fly

"Order!" Eli said as he banged a spoon on the table. "Prosecutor, your statement."

Keep in mind we really didn't know what we were doing. I stood up from the table. "Your honor, I will represent Hunter in this situation. My client believes-"

"Knows!" Hunter whispered harshly beside me.

"Objection!" Rockwell stood up. "Speaking with the client during statement!"

"That's not a rule!" Hunter argued.

"He's right. Overruled!" Eli agreed.

I continued, "As I was saying, my client *knows* that Ezra stole money during the game of Monopoly." I acted like I was straightening my tie, "I would like to call Hunter to the stand."

"Alright," Eli said. Hunter stood up and walked over to the head of the table. "Come here." Eli motioned with his hand.

Hunter walked over, and Eli took Hunter's hand and put it on the table. "Do you, Hunter Haws, blah, blah, blah, speak truthfully, blah blah, blah, blah, amen."

"Amen." Hunter nodded.

"Go ahead then."

"So, you see, I was playing the game like a good boy, and then I saw that Ezra had a new 500. And I was like, 'Wait, hold up, something ain't right.' And I thought, 'Ezra only had three 100's, so how would he have a new 500? No one had landed on him. And I was like, 'Ezra's the banker, right? Which means he's the closest one to the money, right? So, he must have gotten tempted and stole a 500, trading in his three 100s, thinking no one would notice. So that's when I accused Ezra of cheating." Hunter walked back to his seat proudly.

"I see," Eli said, rubbing his chin. Then he turned to Rockwell, "Your response."

"Yes, sir." Rockwell stood up, straightening his own fake tie. "While all this may be true, Hunter failed to mention the location of the pieces." Rockwell motioned to the board, which was on the table. "As we can see, Ezra had just passed 'Go.' Which means he would have gotten 200 more dollars, bringing his total up to 500. Then he simply traded in three one hundred's and got a 500. Not a crime."

"I see." Eli said, "Your rebuttal." He nodded to me.

Before I could speak, Rockwell cut in, "If I may your honor, I would like to accuse *Hunter* of cheating."

"Excuse me?" Hunter asked.

"Huh?" Ezra said, clearly not knowing anything about this.

"This just got interesting," Porter said with a smile. He was the jury, after all.

"That's not the focus of this trial." I said, "You can't do that." We all looked at Eli.

Eli stroked his chin, feeling way too powerful, and said, "I'll allow it."

"Oh my gosh." I put my head in my hands.

Rockwell smiled and continued, "As I was saying, Hunter is the one that cheated. I would like to call him to the stand."

Hunter stood up and walked to the front again. He walked over to Eli with his hand up.

"I'm not doing that again," Eli said. "Just speak the truth."

Learning to Fly

"Alright." Hunter turned and faced us from the head of the table.

Rockwell started pacing repeatedly, "You bought Boardwalk two turns ago, correct?"

"Objection! Leading the witness!" I stood up.

"Overruled because I have no idea what that means." Eli pointed at Rockwell. "Please continue, Rockwell."

"Thank you." Rockwell turned to Hunter, "Did you not?"

"Yes, I did. I bought Boardwalk." Hunter said, getting annoyed.

"And how much money did you have after the purchase?"

"Two 50's and a 20."

"And did anyone land on you in the past two turns?"

"No."

"And you only passed go once, correct?"

"Yes."

"And did you land on Take a Chance or Community Chest?"

"No. Where is this going?"

"I'm getting to that. So, here's my last question. How did you get a 500?" Hunter bit his bottom lip. The room went silent. I covered my head with my hand. Rockwell continued, "Your honor, that is all I have to say." Rockwell high-fived Ezra and sat down.

Porter stood up and clapped. I shook my head and smiled at Hunter. He looked at me. I looked at him. He smiled back, and his eyes said, "So close."

Britton Bean

"Well done, Rocky," Hunter said. "Well done." Hunter started clapping. I just shook my head and thought to myself, *Idiot Hunter.*

Overall, Eli wasn't the person we wanted, but he was the person we needed. As I grew older, I saw more and more how much we needed Eli. We had great respect for Eli. We obeyed his rules. And, in time, we knew he had made the right call. In reality, we needed Eli more than anyone else. Everyone knew that. We just never said it. I wish we did.

Anyways, life in the bunker was pretty chill... for about a month. Eli talked to me privately and told me the others were getting antsy. Boredom and frustration filled the bunker. We needed something new. So, I called the gang together.

"Alright, people, I think it's time," I announced.

Everyone looked confused, and Hunter asked, "Time for what?"

"It's time to leave." Eli sighed.

Everyone was surprised to hear that.

"He's right." I agreed. "We've been here for a month, and let's be honest, I think it's time to go. All the deadly radiation from the blast should have dissipated by now. And we have been running low on supplies."

"How much stuff do we have left?" Ezra asked.

"Three days of water left, two days of food, and we are in reserves for gasoline," Eli noted, looking at a clipboard. "We were supposed to have more food." Eli glared at me. I gave him a smug grin.

"That's a bit dire. Didn't you think of telling us that a while ago?" Hunter said incredulously.

"Well, I never could find a good time," Eli responded. Then he mumbled under his breath, "'Dire' is a big word for you, Hunter."

I stifled a laugh but kept it to myself, "Alright, guys, calm down. That gives us a few days to get ready to move out. We need to prepare backpacks and fill them with all the food and water we can. Hunter's on ammo and guns. We don't know what could be out there. Ezra can help carry the supplies and guns. You guys' figure that out. Porter and Eli will be in charge of the food and supplies. Rockwell, we need as many medical supplies as we can carry. I will help carry guns and supplies. We will start preparing tomorrow. Then the day after that, we leave. Any questions?"

No one had questions, and Porter started preparing food. We ate dinner in silence. Then we went to bed early that night. After all, we did have two big days coming up. The only question on my mind was, "What's out there?"

After a whole day of preparing, we all stood there at the door waiting. I got everyone's attention.

"Alright, people, this is it. I would like to share a poem I wrote."

Everyone groaned. I was kinda embarrassed by the poem too, but I pushed forward.

"Ugh, not a poem!!" Hunter complained.

I ignored him, pulling out a piece of paper, and told myself I would not cry, "Today, we embark on a journey; a journey that will prove if we are worthy. Worthy for the hardships, the trials, and the grief. Worthy for happiness, joy, and relief. And to the people who survived, to the people who died, to families broken, we give you this token." And I took out a nail and hammer. And with one stroke, I hammered the nail into cement.

    I gave in. I tried not to think of my family because I knew if I did, I would cry. But I couldn't not. My mom. My dad. My brother, my sister. All gone. Everything I'd ever known was gone. And so, I teared up. I felt a tear snake down my face. And I didn't wipe it. I let it hit the ground. And then, in a voice that was firm and strong, in a voice that we needed, "Alright, boys, let's change the world." I turned the crank and opened the door.

Learning to Fly

Chapter 4

I Jump Out of a Plane

We stepped out and surprisingly saw the stairs were still there. But the house wasn't. But more surprises were coming. We stepped outside into the bright morning sun. That was unexpected. We thought it was the afternoon. At least, that's what Hunter's clock had said.

I turned to Hunter, "You said that watch was correct!"

"It must have gotten reset or something, I don't know," Hunter responded quickly, defensively putting his hands in the air.

But what was even more surprising was the wasteland that we stepped into. Everything was gone. And I mean everything. There wasn't a single tree, vegetation, or building in sight. Just destroyed wasteland. You would have never guessed there was once a busy city where we stood. We climbed a hill to see if anything was on the other side. It wasn't much better. We could see where the city hall used to be. Now it was gone.

"Where do we go now?" Porter asked.

"Well, if I was a survivor, where would I go?" I asked.

"The airport, maybe?" Rockwell suggested.

"That would make sense. If someone was smart, they would go farther from the impact zone. And the airport is on a hill."

"How far away do you think it is?" Asked Ezra.

"From where we are, about five miles and 300 feet increase in altitude." Answered Hunter.

"You just know that off the top of your head?" I said more like a statement.

"I *have* lived here all my life, you know."

So, we started the trek. It took us about three hours to get to the airport. Along the way, we looked for some sign of life or anything. We saw a few birds, but that was it. As we came up the hill, we looked at the airport. It was in pretty good shape, actually. Not too many potholes in the runway, and the buildings look pretty intact. But it wasn't the airport that surprised us. It was the view.

A barren desert with a few tumbleweeds here and there. That was my town right there. The hot summer sun beat down on the land like a hammer. You could clearly see where the blast happened. The farther you went from the blast zone, the more rubble remained. I couldn't help but look where my

Learning to Fly

house would have been. Just more rubble. I could see some homes on the outskirts of St. George. That area seemed relatively unharmed.

"Look over there." I turned towards everyone else. "It looks unharmed. Let's head over there. What is that, Santa Clara?"

"Yeah," Hunter confirmed.

Eli groaned and took the backpack off, tired from carrying the food for so long. "Ugh, we just got up here. We should try to find a ride."

"Yeah, that's probably a good idea. Let's go see what we can find."

We searched the terminal and some of the hangers that weren't destroyed. We found airplanes but no people. That's when I saw the Cessna 182.

I thought to myself, *hey, maybe I could fly one of these.* I had flown planes before. I had even taken off in one. I had been in this program called Civil Air Patrol or CAP, where they teach you how to fly planes. It was basically military for teens. The Cessna 182 was the plane I had been taught in.

And then I saw the parachutes. I thought, *you know what? We need something to wake us up.* My brother had gone skydiving before, and I was in the plane when he jumped. I also watched the skydiving instructional video. I thought it was stupid at the time, but now I'm glad I watched it. I smiled to myself and shrugged. *What's there to lose?*

I ran outside and got everyone rounded up.

Britton Bean

"Alright, guys, hear me out" I started using my hands to represent what I meant. "We get in a Cessna, we fly it off the runway, we get to Santa Clara, we jump out of the airplane, and we fly down using a parachute to the ground." I grinned.

They looked at me like I was crazy. And maybe I was.

And then Hunter spoke, "Britton, let me ask you a question, and I want you to answer honestly. Are you INSANE?!?"

"Bean, I think you spent too much time in that bunker." Ezra gave me a worried look.

"Guys, guys, we need to have some fun in our life. We've been cooped up for a month. We're kids; let's have some fun!!" I said happily.

"Do you even know how to fly a plane?" Rockwell asked incredulously.

"I know how to fly and take off, but I don't know how to land, and last time I checked, that's unnecessary."

"Are you kidding me?" Hunter asked as he covered his head with his hands.

"Guys, c'mon. Let's get back to our childhood. Let's do something crazy. Let's have some fun. Let's make the best of the worst."

There was a long silence after that.

"Alright." Hunter relented, breaking the silence. "Let's do this thing, Britton. What do we have to lose?"

"That's what I thought!" I motioned to Hunter.

"You are crazy, Bean." Porter said, "But in the end, so are we."

Learning to Fly

Everyone else reluctantly agreed. So, we started pushing the airplane onto the runway. Now the first part of this plan was making sure everyone was informed. I didn't tell them that I'd never skydived. So, after everyone put their vests on and the Cessna was lined up on the runway, I explained how to skydive…from a video I'd watched three years ago. This was crazy.

"Alright, guys, when you jump, you'll want to flatten yourself out to create as much drag as possible. Now to the people with guns, you'll want to strap your guns to your chest or just keep them in the plane. Also, to the people with backpacks, you're not going to take your backpacks."

Porter looked like he was going to kill me. "And before you get mad at me, this is what we are going to do: in the Cessna, there are several compartments to put your stuff in. You're going to put the backpacks in there. I'll drop all the fuel so there won't be a fire. We are going to crash the plane."

"Excuse me?" Eli said.

"Okay, maybe 'crash' isn't the right word. Forcibly, land is a better description. It should glide down pretty easily. The backpacks should be fine. You are going to want to pull your parachute earlier than later. I would suggest way early. We will be about 10,000 feet up, so I'd wait about 45 seconds. Just pull when everyone else does. Then you will want to lean back and slide onto the ground on your butt. Everyone good?"

No one said anything. I think they were too scared to talk. "Alright, let's do this thing," I said, trying to hide my fear.

Britton Bean

As we all got in the Cessna, I realized that the runway was kind of destroyed. Hunter, who had climbed into the co-pilot's seat next to me, realized too.

"Ummm, Britton, the runway is more like a dirt road. A dirt road with potholes every six feet."

"Then this will be a bumpy ride, won't it," I replied.

"No, Britton, let's not do this."

"Too late," I said as I started up the engine.

"No, Britton. It's not too late." Hunter said more sternly. "You can just turn the engine off and…" The engine drowned out Hunter.

"Hold on, everyone!"

"BRITTON!!" Hunter screamed.

Hunter brought the seat belt across his chest and put his hands together in prayer. I revved the engine and checked my instruments. My heart was pounding. My mind was racing. I hadn't felt this alive in months! Years even! I looked ahead of me and saw all the potholes. I thought *this will be an adventure and a half.*

I looked over at Hunter. He looked more scared than I had ever seen him. I smiled to myself. I'd done the impossible. I'd made Hunter scared.

I looked ahead at the world in front of me. I thought of the life I had ahead of me. I looked at the destroyed, forgotten ghost town. We would have challenges for sure. We would have fights. But boy, would we change the world.

And we had two options. We could stay where we were or go full steam ahead. I increased the throttle to maximum

Learning to Fly

power. The plane started moving, and soon we were powering down the runway. I was dodging potholes with the rudder. I could feel the entire plane shaking. I could feel the power underneath me struggling. I could hear the wheels screeching. I watched my speedometer, waiting for 60 knots. Takeoff speed. I was getting closer and closer. But the number went down every time I turned to avoid a pothole. Then I saw it. The end of the runway. I didn't have the speed. I was only at 52 knots.

"HOLD ON GUYS!!" I screamed as I pulled back on the stick. The nose pitched upward.

And the aircraft started violently shaking as we went through dirt and bushes. Then I felt the entire aircraft shudder, and the left side sank. The left gear had gotten ripped right off. Luckily, the rotors didn't hit the ground.

Then we went off the edge and started falling. I pulled up as hard as I could. I could feel my muscles straining. And the aircraft pulled up. I immediately pushed the stick down a little to keep it from stalling.

And I guess I have the bomb to thank for this. Because we would not have made it if there were buildings there. We were only three feet from the ground. I felt my right gear get torn off. As I flew into the sky, I assessed the damage. We had lost two of our wheels. But everything else was good.

"Did we lose anyone?" I asked. I looked back and laughed. "Wasn't that fun?"

Their faces said it all. No. They did not have fun. A big smile crossed my face. It crossed Hunter's face next, and then all of them. They were all shaking their heads and laughing with relief.

"Oh my gosh, Bean. Don't ever do that again." Porter breathed hard. Everyone laughed.

I climbed and climbed. The aircraft went up and up. Until all you could see was the sky. The deep, dark, blue sky. It was beautiful. I ascended to 10,000 feet and put the plane on autopilot. I also dumped all but one gallon of fuel. I lowered the airspeed as much as possible.

With the low fuel warning blaring, I said, "Alright, guys, we are over the drop zone. You ready?"

Porter finished putting the backpacks in a compartment near the back. "Let's go," he said.

Rockwell looked at the backpacks and asked, concerned, "Are you sure those packs will survive?"

"Pretty sure," I replied. Rockwell turned and looked at me sternly. "I'm positive." I clarified.

I opened the sliding door. Alarms started going off in the cockpit. Apparently, you're not supposed to open the door while you're flying. Then another warning came on, and the engine began to die.

"Alright, guys, that's our cue. Let's go."

"Who's going first?" asked Hunter.

"You are."

"What?"

"Let's go, Hunter; we don't have all day."

"Alright, alright."

Learning to Fly

Hunter stepped up to the edge and looked over. That was a mistake.

"Any last words, Hunter?" I asked.

"How about…. no."

"I wouldn't have chosen those exact words, but you do you," I said. And then I pushed Hunter out. I had never heard him scream so loud. I turned back to everyone. They were stunned. They all looked terrified at the ground and then back at me. I smiled, "Alright, who's next?"

Sadly, I didn't get to push anyone else out. I went last, and the exhilaration I felt when jumping was incredible. It was like you were hair in a hair dryer. Except it was cold. But the adrenaline rush made it feel like I was on fire.

The view was wonderful. You never know how beautiful something is until you see it from the sky. It was like a whole new world. It was my world. This wonderful place of St. George, all to me and my friends.

I fell for about 45 seconds, and I pulled my cord. My parachute flew out and yanked me up. It hurt. I didn't know that it would cause such a big whiplash. I reached up and rubbed my neck. I counted five other parachutes, which made me happy. In fact, one had already landed. I aimed for the one on the ground, but I couldn't do much. Of course, I overshot it. I landed perfectly, pulling my legs up and sliding on my butt. I soon came to a stop. I took my parachute off and jogged to Hunter to see if he was okay. I got one big slap in the face.

"Bro, what the heck!?!?" I yelled.

"ME? You pushed me out of a plane!!" Hunter screamed in my face.

"I knew you'd survive," I commented, waving him off.

"No, you didn't! What if I died, huh!? What would you have done then!?"

"Well, then you could have slapped me."

"I'D BE DEAD!!"

"Good point Hunter. I didn't think that far ahead." I tried to joke. Hunter wasn't having it. "Hunter, I understand you're mad, but I had to make a statement to everyone else. And I knew that if anyone could handle it, it would be you. And yes, I am sorry I pushed you out of a plane."

Hunter was still fuming.

"You couldn't have done anyone else? You could have talked people into it. Why did you push *me* out of a freakin' PLANE?!?! And how do you know our supplies didn't go up in flames? You don't know anything for certain!"

"You're right, Hunter. I don't. But... if we are going to be the only ones in the city...let's have some fun. Who cares? Let's take risks. Take chances. Let's stop thinking about tomorrow and start thinking about the present. Who knows what we'll find?"

Hunter just shook his head and said, "Idiot." But he said it in a way that made me think he had forgiven me.

So, I wrapped my arm around his shoulder and said, "Shall we get some lunch?

Learning to Fly

***

We gathered the supplies from the crashed Cessna. Just like I said, it was secure and safe. We gathered our guns and started walking to Santa Clara. We entered the city of Santa Clara, Utah, around noon. It had looked unaffected, but now we could clearly see that every single window had been destroyed. Some wooden buildings had collapsed, but the new buildings looked pretty good if you didn't include not having any windows. Of course, the first thing we did was search for survivors. But we knew we wouldn't find any. It was an eerie thing. It was like everyone had just disintegrated.

"It's like Thanos just snapped." Remarked Ezra.

I chuckled, "Yeah, except it was more like everyone instead of half."

After searching for a while, we decided we were hungry and wanted food. We ate some chicken noodle soup. And since we really couldn't heat anything up, we put the cold soup in a pot and out in the sun. It was summer in St. George. It had to be at least 110 degrees outside. We figured that the sun would heat the pot.

We chilled under a tree for about an hour, playing all kinds of games like eye spy, sticks, shotgun, shadow boxing, rock, paper, scissors, and other games like that. We called them the "Bored Games." We played them when we were bored. Pretty clever, I know.

Britton Bean

Surprisingly the soup actually got pretty warm. We ate all of it and continued heading into Santa Clara. We arrived on main street and started exploring, trying to find anything fun. Eli had the best luck.

"GUYS!" Eli shouted from a big three-story house. The owner must have been rich because the thing was huge. I was closest and, thinking he was in trouble, I ran over with my gun raised. I kicked open the door like an FBI agent. Ignoring how cool I felt, ran around the corner and almost killed Eli.

"AHH," I screamed as I ran into him with my gun raised, pointing at his chest.

"Ouch!!" Eli said, clutching his chest where I had hit him. "Dude, what the heck. That hurt, man. Is there another bomb or something? Why are you being so stupid? Calm down, man."

"Sorry, I thought you were in trouble," I said, getting my breath back. "Bro, did you see how I kicked down the door? That was sick."

"Yeah, yeah, yeah." Eli said quickly, "Where's everyone else? I want to show you guys something."

Seconds later, the others ran inside the house, also thinking Eli was in trouble. When they realized he wasn't, they weren't happy about it.

"What the heck was that scream?" Hunter said, catching his breath.

"See, I'm not the only 'stupid' person!" I added sarcastically.

Learning to Fly

Eli responded defensively, "Alright, so maybe it was a little weird scream, but that doesn't matter. You guys have to see this."

Eli led us to the garage door and opened it. What I saw blew my mind. Three rows of supercars. Four cars in each row. Some cars had seen better days, with one looking like it had been broken into, but everyone still went crazy. Eli ran over and manually opened all the garages. I ran to a McLaren and yelled, "I call this one!!"

I wasn't the only one calling out what car they wanted. I hopped in and looked for the keys. I found them in the cup holder and started up the car. The car roared to life, and I backed up out of the garage. I went too fast and nailed the mailbox.

"Whoops!" I exclaimed.

But then I saw the problem. We would have to back out every single car to get the vehicle closest to the wall out. So, we did. We wanted to drive all the cars. We lined them all up, and I thought it looked like those illegal drag races. That gave me an idea.

After a while, we gathered up in our cars, and that's when I heard Rockwell ask, "Should we be doing this? It's not like we have a license for anything. And these are someone else's cars."

Hunter responded, "Let them come and get us. Until then, let's have some fun!" Hunter revved his engine.

Everyone seemed to agree with him, so I motioned for them to follow me. And these things were nice. We had two

Britton Bean

McLaren, me in one and Eli in the other. Rockwell and Ezra were in two Lamborghinis, Hunter was in a Bugatti, and Porter got a Ferrari.

The power in these cars was insane. It felt like I was in a jet. And these things were loud. I arrived at the highway on ramp and looked at a six-lane highway that looked like it had been through a blender. But it was still drivable. Luckily the bomb had wiped out the divider in the middle, so I yelled over the engines, "Everyone line up!" Everyone got in a lane. Hunter had found a CD of 80s Rock and started playing *"Back in Black,"*.

I waited a moment, steeling my nerves, then said, "On your marks…, Get set" I hesitated and realized I could die. But I mean, what's left to live for? Family? Gone. So, if my friends were going to do this, you bet I would be right alongside them dying. So, I said the fateful word, "GO!!!"

All the cars zoomed forward. 0-60 in two seconds. The loud rev of the engines was deafening. Everyone was neck and neck. I was at 100 miles per hour in no time. The two Lambos were in front. I had my foot on the floor going as fast as I could. We were coming up on a hill, and no one was stopping. It was like a game of chicken. Who would stop first?

We were nearing the hill faster than ever. I was at 210 miles per hour. My head was against the seat, and I realized I wouldn't stop even if I slammed the brakes right then. I jumped over the hill going 217 miles per hour. The McLaren's max speed.

Learning to Fly

It felt as if time stopped. Everything stopped. My hair, which was pretty long now since we didn't have scissors in the bunker, was standing up. All of our problems seem to melt away. It seemed for a moment that I was the king of the world. And maybe I was. Maybe my friends and I were the only ones left. And that was fine by me. There was an entire world that needed exploring. And we were the ones to do it. I realized that all was not lost. Maybe our family was dead. But we weren't. We were alive. And so, I would live for my friends. Maybe our lives were worth living. The world is what you make it. So, let's make it ours.

The crash of the car landing brought me out of my thoughts. I slammed on the brakes and saw everyone do the same. Brakes went screeching all over the place. I turned the wheel and spun, ramming into the Ferrari. After a few more spins, I finally came to a stop.

Out of the corner of my eye, I noticed Porter's airbag went off. I hopped out of the car and hurried over to Porter. I pushed down the airbag and saw his nose was bleeding, and he had a gash on his eyelid. Everyone else started running over. And that's when Porter said, with a smile on his face, "That was AWESOME!!"

I chuckled, and Rockwell pushed me out of the way to take a look at Porter. I have to admit, this was pretty fun. Rockwell checked Porter's nose and made sure he was okay. Everyone else was discussing who won.

"I won by a long shot; how is this even a conversation?" Boasted Ezra.

"I came first!" Hunter argued. "You did come second, though, Ezra."

"Hunter, you had a Bugatti; of course, you came first," I stated.

"Well, what about me?" Rockwell followed by Porter, who had his hand on his nose, "I was right beside Ezra."

"He's not wrong," I confirmed. "But that's beside the point. So, what are we going to do with cars and Porter? It's not like Porter is in driving shape. Rockwell, what are you thinking."

"Well, it's definitely broken, but I'm most worried about the cut on the orbital socket above his eye."

"English, please," I commented.

"Basically, I need an antibiotic. And we ran out when we used it on your leg. So, we need more." Rockwell explained.

"C'mon Britton." Hunter muttered jokingly.

"Shut it." I muttered to him. "Alright, but we also need to find a home base for now. Eli, how are the cars looking?"

Eli, who had been examining the cars, turned and said, "The Ferrari has looked better and might not run, and Rockwell's Lambo has a big dent in the right-side wheel well, rubbing up against the tire. And then there's Hunter's car." We all looked at it. The entire front of the car looked like it had seen the wrong end of a machete. "So, yea, other than that, all the other cars look good."

I took command, "Alright, why don't we have Rockwell and Porter ride in Ezra's Lambo. Hunter can ride with me. I don't think Hunter's car is worth saving."

"Ahh man! I liked that car." Hunter muttered.

I continued, "Yea, whatever. How about we leave the other two broken cars here and come back for them. As for a home base, let's camp at the house where we got the cars. Eli and Rockwell will gather supplies while Hunter and I try to find a place to live for the foreseeable future."

"Wait, we are living here?" Ezra cut in.

"Do you have a better idea?" I retorted, harsher than I meant.

"Well, I mean....um–"

"Good." I said firmly, "Now, back to business. Hunter and I will also look for survivors. Though I doubt we will find any, we will still look. Ezra, we need you to take care of Porter at the house. Are you good with that?"

"Yup, I can do that," Ezra said, annoyed. I don't think he liked being put on the sidelines. I think he wanted to explore.

I turned to him and said encouragingly, "You got this." Then I turned back to everyone else. "Perfect, and remember, guys, have some fun. Does that sound like a plan to everyone?"

Everyone nodded.

"Alright, Hunter and I will meet you guys back at the house at dark. Ohh, and I almost forgot, Rockwell and Eli, when you guys are done gathering supplies, try to get the damaged cars back to the house. Just leave all the other ones on the street. And find some scissors; I need a haircut." Everyone chuckled. "Alright, see you guys at the house."

Chapter 5

Finding Harry

Hunter and I sat in the nice leather chairs of the McLaren. It really was a nice car. Whoever owned the house before the nuke must have had quite a bit of disposable income. I raced down one of the main roads heading towards St. George. Driving really was exhilarating. I had driven my dad's car in some parking lots before, but nothing like this. I felt like a NASCAR driver, zooming around corners and going 90 miles per hour. This was like a dream.

    I finally slowed down when I started to reach the edge of the blast zone. I had to sit back and think for a while. I stopped the car at the edge of a cliff, overlooking the blast zone. I let out my breath. I hadn't realized I'd been holding it.

"So much for looking for people," Hunter said. "You were going so fast; I can't believe you even made some of those turns."

"Yeah, well, I'm pretty sure no one's here." I looked over the destroyed landscape.

"What? How do you know?" Hunter asked.

"Hunter." I looked at him, "Do the math. Think clearly. We would have seen someone by now. What would you have done if you had just watched a nuclear blast happen? You'd start looking for someplace else to stay. Someplace where there is plenty of food, water, and people. Safety is in numbers Hunter."

"That can't be. At least one person would stay, right?"

"I just don't know Hunter. But I think someone would notice a plane crash. They would also notice six cars going 200 miles an hour over a jump."

"I guess. Yeah."

We went silent for a minute. Then I got out of the car and walked to the hood of the car. I leaned back against it. Hunter came out and joined me. "It's kinda beautiful in a way." I looked over the decimated land. "A barren wasteland, with nothing but the sun. Back to the way nature made it. You know?"

"Not gonna lie, Britton, that sounded kinda stupid," Hunter said, also looking over the wasteland.

"What? No. That's prophetic." I argued, looking back at Hunter.

"What does that even mean?" Hunter asked, still looking over the area.

"It means cool or wise," I explained.

"Ahh." Hunter shook his head, "Those words weren't that."

"Oh my gosh." I rolled my eyes. "What would be prophetic, Hunter?"

"Hmmm. Let me think." Hunter held up his finger. "Oh! I got it." Hunter extended his hand towards the wasteland and said in a deeper voice, "Everything the light touches is our kingdom."

"Ha!" I laughed. "That's actually kinda true!"

"See!" Hunter said, looking at me for the first time in the entire conversation, "Sometimes I know what I'm talking about."

"Ahh, 'sometimes' is a little generous," I slid off the hood and walked towards the car door. Hunter headed towards the car. "I think 'every once in a lifetime' is a better phrase." I opened the door and got into the car. As I sat down, Hunter slugged me in the arm. "Hey!! I'm just speaking the truth." I defended.

"Let me drive," Hunter stated.

"How do we ask?" I said, looking at Hunter.

"Let me drive NOW!" Hunter said as he lunged for the keys in the cup holder. But I was too fast and snatched the keys. "Ah, ah, ah. No, Hunter." I said, bringing the keys out of his reach. "How do we ask?"

"Fine!" Hunter said as he slumped back into his seat and said, defeated, "Can I please drive the car?"

"No." I put the keys into the ignition.

"What?! But I said 'please'!!" Hunter complained.

"That doesn't mean you always get what you want." I knew when I said it, I'd made a mistake. Hunter turned his head and got that look in his eyes. "Hunter…" I put my hands in the air, ready to defend myself.

Hunter lunged for the keys in the ignition. I tried to grab them, but he got there first. He pushed me hard into the door of the car. Then Hunter brought the keys up to my face and dangled them. "'How do we ask?'" He mocked.

I scoffed and said, "Alright, Hunter, you win. This time. But one day, you won't."

Hunter drove to Washington, which was where we lived. Washington was another sub-city of St. George. But when you say you live in Washington, Utah, people think you live in some rural town. So, everyone just says, St. George.

Washington had been spared the bulk of the blast, which basically meant that there were still some ruins still standing. Nothing like the peace in Santa Clara, though. Washington still looked like a wasteland.

Hunter didn't tell me where we were going. But after about five minutes in Washington, I recognized the area. Home.

Hunter pulled up to where our houses should have been. We did live right across the street from each other. As I mentioned earlier, this area hadn't been hit as bad. But the

Britton Bean

nuke still had done its damage. Hunter's house had one of the garages still standing. My house had a single support beam standing but nothing else. One pole, stripped of its paint, standing strong. It looked kinda funny that way. I almost laughed.

Hunter put the car in park and stepped out. I followed. We were curious, after all. Was there even anything left? He walked to his house, and I walked to mine. I walked carefully through the rubble. It was hard to believe I had once lived in this place. Now all it looked like was a bunch of trash. A junkyard. It almost made me tear up. Lots of memories here. I started pulling rocks, looking for nothing in particular. And then I saw him. Harry.

Harry was not a person. I thought I should clarify that. He was a hat. And I know that sounds stupid, but he was my lucky hat. And he had a good right to be. I got him for my birthday when I was ten. He was a baseball cap with simple blue material in front and white netting in the back.

I loved Harry. I took him on all my family's trips. He had survived three moves and gone on vacations to Hawaii, Mexico, Honduras, Belize, Jamaica, Haiti, and all over the USA. I can't believe he survived. He was in pretty good condition too. That's why I called him my lucky hat.

I looked for about ten more minutes and didn't find anything else. Just plaster, wood, and broken metal. I walked across the street to see Hunter. Hunter was looking through the remains of his garage. His dad was a handyman, so he had a lot of tools in that garage. There wasn't much of anything left in

Learning to Fly

the house. It was really destroyed. I did see some metal screwdrivers and screws and nails littered the ground.

Hunter was rummaging through the rubble like I was. You look for anything when you have nothing left. Hunter looked up as I approached.

"Guess who I found." I tapped the top of my hat.

Hunter looked at my head. "You have got to be kidding me."

"I found Harry. Told you he was lucky." I said with a smug grin on my face.

"How does that survive? And yet nothing in my house survived but screws and nails." Hunter motioned to my head and walked past me towards the car.

"I'm telling you," I said as I followed him toward the car. "He's lucky!" I opened the car door and slid in.

Hunter was already in the car. He started the car, looked at me, smiled, and said, "Still, don't buy it."

I laughed, "You will, but, like all things, it takes time."

"Nope, I'm pretty sure I'll never think that thing is lucky."

"Hey!" I said, offended, "He's not an it. He's a boy."

"You're mental."

"Who said that was a bad thing?"

"The dictionary."

"Good luck finding one."

Hunter scoffed.

We decided to drive by what was left of our school. There really wasn't much. Just like our houses, the entire school was destroyed. You could see where the original bomb had exploded.

A sudden memory hit me like the bomb itself. The explosions. The people running. Kai's hand. Hunter pulling me back. I shut my eyes and gritted my teeth, trying to think of something else.

I realized Hunter was talking, "You good Britton?"

I got my breathing under control. "Yeah. I'm fine."

"Alright." Hunter shrugged, "You want to go explore?"

I looked at the school again. The memory came back again. I looked out the opposite window, hiding my face from Hunter. "No, I'm good. I…umm…need to think some things over."

"Ok." Hunter shrugged as he stopped the car roughly and hopped out. Out of the corner of my eye, I saw him jog toward the rubble.

I looked out the other window and took several deep breaths. My heart was still racing. I tried to think of something else. Anything. *Calm down, Bean.* I thought. *Calm down. You're okay. You got this. Calm down. Breathe Bean. Breathe.*

I bit my lip. I looked out where the tennis courts had been. As I looked up, something caught my eye. Only for a second. Just out of the corner of my vision. Behind the car. I jumped over to the driver's seat. I turned the key and turned the car around.

Sure enough, there it was. Two houses on the hill. Both of them sat sturdy and golden under the sun. I was about to smile when the passenger door suddenly opened.

Learning to Fly

I jerked, surprised, as I saw Hunter sit down. "Calm down, man. It's just me." Hunter said. "Before you ask, I didn't find anything."

"Man, you scared me!" I breathed out a sigh. "I want to show you something." I pointed towards the buildings. "What do you think?"

"Nice buildings. Why did you show me them?" Hunter asked, confused.

"What do you think about living there?" I asked.

"For how long?" Hunter asked.

I smiled as I thought about it. A future with my friends. Growing old and just having fun. Living a carefree life. Just living life. I could handle that. So, I said, with a smile on my face, "As long as we live."

Britton Bean

Chapter 6

The Wii

We arrived back at the home base just after the sun had set. I pulled the car to the curb and saw that Rockwell and Eli had pulled the Ferrari and Lambo into the garage. I also noticed that there were lights on in the house. Hunter and I walked in through the front door.

"Something smells good!" Hunter walked into the kitchen.

"What is it?" I asked.

"Chow Mein," Porter responded. As he turned to me, I saw his nose was patched up with tape. He had an eye patch over his right eye. Rockwell had done a good job.

"Looking good, Porter," Hunter commented sarcastically. "How'd you get the electricity?"

Learning to Fly

Porter responded, "Ezra found a generator and some gasoline. He got it working, and it produces enough energy for what we need."

"What about the cars? How are they looking?" I asked.

"I don't know about that. You can ask Rockwell or Eli, they're upstairs."

"What are they doing?" I asked.

Porter shrugged.

"When is dinner going to be ready?" Hunter licked his lips expectantly. I shook my head and chuckled. Leave it to Hunter to always want food. I started to head up the stairs to my right.

"Five minutes at the most. Help me set up Hunter. There are plates in the cupboard right there." Porter said as I climbed up the carpeted stairs. First time I had seen carpet in a while.

I made my way up the stairs. Rockwell and Ezra sat on a couch. Eli was standing up. A TV was across them. I was really confused for a second, and then I saw it. And you won't believe this, but they were playing Wii Sports Golf. I covered my mouth with my hand and laughed. I couldn't believe it. They were playing video games in a post-apocalyptic world.

"Bean!" Ezra said as I walked upstairs. Eli swung his wrist, and the ball on the screen flew into the water.

"Ezra! You messed me up!" Eli said as he turned around. "Oh, hi, Bean. We got the electricity running, and these guys just happened to have a Wii. And it works!"

"I can't believe it!" I stared at the TV. "You're terrible at golf!" Rockwell and Ezra laughed.

"I'm not that bad!" Eli defended. Everyone laughed.

"Porter said there's food ready. I bet you can smell it." I spoke.

"Ohh, I'm hungry!" Ezra quickly got up and headed downstairs. I followed him down the stairs. Eli and Rockwell followed.

***

"So, did you guys find a place to live?" Eli asked from across the table.

"We did." I responded through bites of noodles, "It's about ten miles from here. It's close to the airport and between what I think is Hurricane or Washington. I can't tell. It's also on a hill, which is good. And it's big. Two buildings. I'm pretty sure it's a house."

"So, when are we moving in?" Asked Rockwell.

"Tomorrow. So, after we get in, we can get settled and get supplies set up."

"Smart. Have you checked inside yet?" asked Ezra.

"No, it was getting dark, and I wanted to return before pitch black."

"What'd you name it?" Porter joked.

I used to always name my pencils. It helped me keep them. It started in sixth grade when I kept losing my pencils, so I named them to grow more attached to them. Some people call it mental, but I call it a tactic. And that tactic just grew into several other items like Harry.

I said the first thing that came to mind, "Narnia."

Hunter choked on his water. Rockwell had put his hand over his mouth, trying to swallow his food without choking. Eli burst out laughing.

"No way you named it that!" Ezra challenged.

"That was supposed to be a joke, Bean," Porter added.

"That's just the first thing that came to my mind!" I defended myself.

"That's what you're thinking of?!" Rockwell asked incredulously.

I rolled my eyes while everyone else just laughed and laughed.

After the laughter died, Hunter said, "Speaking of supplies, what do we need to get?"

"What? We weren't saying anything about supplies." Porter said, confused. "Were you?" He pointed at me. I shook my head.

"It's called a transition," Hunter said, extremely proud of himself.

I said in a baby voice, "Ahh, good job Hunter. 'Transition' is a big-boy word. I can't believe you know that."

"I just learned it," Hunter said, beaming with pride, not getting the joke.

Everyone laughed.

We talked about making a list, but we aren't that organized. We decided to just go with the flow, do what we wanted, and have some fun. This would be a very different summer than I was used to.

Chapter 7

Living Large

We woke up and got straight to work. It was actually the first time we had slept on such nice beds. The bunk beds in the bunker were really cheap. The owner of this house did not skimp out on bedding.

Anyways we had breakfast and delegated jobs. I would examine the cars and see if I could fix them. I probably couldn't, but it was worth a shot.

Hunter would head up to the house with everyone. We also had to check if the place even had furniture in it. Once we had that information, we would start taking stuff from the house to the new base. We had decided that the owner wasn't returning, so taking the property was okay.

Learning to Fly

We would also have to find a pickup or a trailer. While the supercars were cool, they weren't convenient. We would start taking trips to the house and see how much stuff we could grab. Eli and I were delegated to transfer the supercars' new home. I could get behind that idea. Then we would reevaluate the situation.

So, I said goodbye to the others, and they headed towards Narnia. Everyone had started calling the house that. I checked out the cars and realized I didn't know where to start with them. I just looked at all the parts and chuckled and thought to myself. *You may be good at some things, Bean, but this is not one of them.*

After that, it was like a day at Ikea. I just went through the house and looked at everything. Every cupboard, every drawer, every room. Everything. I was looking for anything that I like and that we should take. There were some nice desks, and of course, I took the Wii. I also found a really nice gaming PC. I decided to take that too.

I felt so powerful, just taking what I wanted. It felt awesome. I felt like a rich man. "I want that." I said to myself, "Oooh, that looks cool. I'll take your entire stock." I laughed at my own joke.

I placed all the stuff outside. I made a mental note of the things I couldn't carry. Eventually, everyone showed up. They had found two trucks, a Ford and a Chevy. I wondered why they took two.

I walked over to the Ford. It had a tiny cabin: only two seats. It was very customized with huge shocks and gigantic tires. It was almost a monster truck. Hunter was driving it. He rolled down his window. I saw Eli in the passenger seat. I pulled myself up and looked in.

The inside was squeaky clean, like it was brand new. "Wow," I said. And then, to indulge Hunter, I said, "Why'd you get the Chevy?"

"That's what I said!" Hunter exclaimed. "I told them, 'A F-150 is all we need.' But noooo. Mr. Chevy over there..." Hunter hooked his thumb out the passenger window towards the other truck, "said we needed another. And, of course, it was a Chevy."

I snickered. Hunter believed that Fords were the best. Mr. Chevy was really Ezra. Yet another rivalry between the two. I just stayed out of it. I really didn't see the difference. But I never said that. Because if there was one thing that Hunter and Ezra agreed on, it was that there was a difference.

We got to work loading everything into the trucks. Surprisingly we got everything into them. Eli found a clipboard and a piece of paper. He used it to keep track of what we had. Eli stood between the trucks, watching everything we brought out. He looked like a manager, noting down everything.

We finished putting everything in the trucks and decided to eat. It was really nice outside, so we ate in the Chevy bed, which had less stuff. We had some soup again. It really was one of the only things we had. We also had to discuss our next plan.

"Well..." I said expectantly. I wanted them to fill me in. Everyone looked at me, waiting for me to continue. "What did

Learning to Fly

you guys find?" Everyone started talking excitedly at once. "Guys, one at a time!"

"I got it," Rockwell said louder than everyone else. Everyone quieted. "We went to the new house-"

"Narnia." Eli corrected.

"Yeah, Narnia, whatever." Rockwell said, annoyed, "We found out it was empty. Both houses. One of the buildings was bigger than the other. The smaller one did have a basement, though, so that's cool. But anyways, we do need to get some more furniture."

"And also, better food!" Hunter exclaimed. "Like, what is this stuff?" Hunter held up his spoon as soup dripped from his spoon into the bowl.

"Hey! I cooked that for you." Porter exclaimed. Hunter shrugged.

"I think I'm with Hunter here, Porter." I agreed. "We could head to Walmart or something."

"Ohh, Bean, you're thinking too low," Ezra said. "Technically, we're rich now. So, let's go somewhere rich."

"Like..." I waited for Ezra to respond.

Ezra got that smug look on his face, and he leaned in like he was telling a secret. We all leaned in as well. "The Dollar Store."

Everyone groaned and leaned back against the truck. Rockwell shook his head, "You almost had us, Ezy. Almost."

Ezra smiled, "What can I say? I like to mess with you guys."

"You're stupid, Ezra," I said.

Britton Bean

"I know." Ezra smirked.

We finished our lunch and drove the trucks to Narnia. Rockwell was right. The house was brand new and completely white with a black outline. It was one of those modern houses. We decided on everything we needed. A fridge, couches, beds, stuff like that. We drove the truck to the nearest convenience store, a locally owned Lins. It smelled bad from all the rotten food. I tried to breathe through my mouth.

We pushed through the smell and raided the store of everything that wasn't bad. We got some apples, potatoes, and a lot of other things that hadn't gone bad yet. By the time we were done, we had both trucks filled to the brim with sacks.

We headed back to Narnia again and dropped off the sacks. We decided to start moving in. I got the generator from the old house working. We had to go "borrow" another fridge to store all the food we got.

We did have some issues getting the furniture through the door. We had to take the door off, and even then, we had to take one of the desks apart and then put it back together. That was a pain.

After a while, Eli sent me to start working on the plumbing. I really don't know how, but by some Harry luck, I got the water working. I just turned some knobs, and somehow the faucet shoots out water. I really didn't know what I was doing. But now that's it working, I just don't touch anything related to the water system. I'm afraid something will break.

After hours of working, we finally got everything moved in. We were all exhausted and decided it was time to eat. Porter actually made French fries. Now they didn't look like traditional French fries. They were just some potatoes cut into strips. But man, those things were awesome. Porter was really happy to have new ingredients to make food with.

That night we slept in sleeping bags on the floor. We still didn't have any beds. It was late, and the sun was setting. Hunter and I were tired and decided to head to bed. Back home, Hunter and I had early bedtimes. We weren't used to staying up late.

Back home. I realized that "back home" didn't exist anymore. My home was reduced to ashes and rubble. I turned my head to Hunter, "You know, Hunter, this is not where I thought I would be a month ago."

"I still can't believe it has only been a month," Hunter said, looking up at the tall ceiling of the living room. "It feels like two years ago."

"Yeah, it does," I said wistfully. I just wanted to go home. I'd had enough excitement for my life. I just wanted to wake up from my dream and go to school. But it wasn't a dream. It was real. It was still hard to believe. "I just want to go home." I sighed.

"Me too, man." Hunter said quietly, "Me too."

Chapter 8

Teaching People How to Fly a Plane

"Alright, guys, this is a Cessna 182, alright?" I explained to the group. I was on the runway of St George Regional Airport. It was early morning, and the sun had just risen.

We decided to do something fun today, and Hunter and I convinced the others to start our own makeshift pilot training. I know it sounds crazy, but hey, we were bored.

Hunter and I had filled the potholes with quick-drying cement early that morning. We found a cement truck and just drove up to the airport. We hope it worked; it's not like we had poured cement before. I continued explaining to the others.

Learning to Fly

"This is the plane that we will all be practicing on." I placed my hand on the Cessna 182 fuselage. "We have the most of these with seven Cessna 182s at this airport."

"Is that number including or excluding the one you crashed?" Eli asked sarcastically.

"Excluding. Now flying a plane is the easy part; landing is the hard part. Now I will admit, I have never landed a plane before, so we will all learn together."

"Aww, yes, because that makes us feel much better," Eli said.

I continued, ignoring the comment, "Anyways, to take off, you have to be going 60 knots…"

***

After what seemed like forever, we each got in a plane. Everyone started their engines and taxied to the runway.

"This is Lion One, taking off. Over." I said over the radio.

"Wow, Britton. So cool." Hunter said sarcastically.

"I have wanted to do that my whole life." I pushed my throttle up, and my plane started moving. It wasn't long before I pulled up and away. I looked out and watched everyone take off. Hunter pulled up too quickly and almost stalled. Luckily, Cessna's are hard to stall.

"That was close, Hunter. Almost stalled." I said over the radio.

Britton Bean

"Key word: 'almost.'" Hunter retorted.

"That man's going to die," I mumbled to myself.

We flew around for about two hours till everyone got comfortable with their planes. Everyone remained mostly quiet the whole time, extremely focused. Then I began the hardest part of flying, which is, ironically, landing.

"Alright, people, take out your landing checklist, which is in a cupboard in front of the co-pilot seat," I said over the radio. I pulled the checklist out, and I had no idea what any of the words meant. And Ezra confirmed the same thing.

"Umm, Bean, do you know what this stuff means?"

"Nope!" I threw the checklist away. "Looks like we are doing this ourselves."

"We are going to die." Rockwell said resignedly, "We are going to die."

"We will if you talk like that." I retorted. "I'll go first and show you, unbelievers, that you can, in fact, land an airplane," I said with much more confidence than I felt.

I looked at my airspeed, which was at 160 knots. I lined up with the runway and put flaps to 15 degrees. This tips my nose up, making me lose speed. I used the Instrument Landing System on board to help me get to the right altitude. This system basically tells you where to be to land safely.

I positioned myself according to the system and then put my flaps to 30 degrees, slowing me down even more. I was 800 ft from the ground and gliding down faster than I thought. I was falling at 750 feet per minute. The regular landing descent

Learning to Fly

rate is 500 feet per minute. I set my flaps to 45 degrees, the highest it could be.

And then I did the stupidest thing I have ever done: I pulled my throttle to idle. I now had no thrust, and my nose was pointed up. I started gliding slower and slower, and then, at 300 feet from the ground, the stall warning went off.

My joystick started shaking, and my eyes widened as I looked at my speed. 45 knots. I pushed my nose down and returned the flaps to zero. I pushed the throttle to half. My nose was now pointed down, and the ground was only 200 feet away. I pulled up with all my might. My nose lifted up, and then my back wheels contacted the ground. I brought my throttle to idle, braked hard, and my front wheel touched the ground. I came to a stop after what seemed like forever. I gasped and coughed. I had been holding my breath the entire landing.

"YEAH BEAN!!" I heard Eli say over the radio. Everyone else followed and cheered.

Then I heard Hunter say, "You almost stalled there, Britton."

I laughed, "Keyword: 'almost'"

***

After everyone landed, roughly, I should add, we decided to take the rest of the day off. Which really means playing board games and the Wii at Narnia. For the next few weeks, we kept practicing landings. We started doing touch and go's, which is basically where you touch the ground and then take off.

We kept doing that until I came up with the "Flight Test." It was basically doing some set maneuvers in the air while doing three successful touch-and-goes in a row. Everyone passed, but Eli was by far the best. Not as good as me, of course. We considered flying out to other cities but figured we should get things set up here first. But that didn't mean we didn't have fun.

Learning to Fly

Chapter 9

I Drift a Plane

It all started when we were bored one day and were tossing around ideas of things to do.

"We could play Wii sports," Eli suggested while lying on the couch facing the ceiling. He threw a ball into the air and caught it.

"No!" Everyone replied. We all had gotten tired of Wii sports. It was one of the only good games we had, and we'd played it too much.

"We should do something outside," Rockwell said, looking out the window.

"It's 11 am in St. George, in the summer; it's 110 degrees outside," I said. "We ain't going outside."

"Do you have any other ideas?" Rockwell asked.

"I got it!" Hunter exclaimed from the couch next to me. "You know those things where they fly the planes?"

"Wow, Hunter, that narrowed it down a lot," Eli said. "'The things where they fly the planes.' Really helped us."

"Are you talking about a plane race Hunter?" I said dully, knowing the way Hunter thinks.

"Yes!" Hunter said excitedly, "We could just do that with our planes. We're good enough to do it."

"Alright, what's the route?" Ezra asked.

"We could start at the airport, obviously, then to Narnia, then to the D, and then back to the airport," Hunter explained. The "D" was a huge letter 'D' painted on a mountain to the west that stood for Dixie. Everyone in St. George just called it the "D."

"I'm starting to like this idea." I smiled. "This could be fun."

"See?!" Hunter's eyes light up. He was clearly happy with himself. "I'm so smart," Hunter said to no one in particular.

"I'm down," Eli said.

"I'll do it," Porter agreed.

We all looked at Ezra and Rockwell, who were sitting next to each other. They both looked at each other, nodded, and Rockwell said, "Let's do this."

***

Learning to Fly

We all lined up next to each other in the air, going as slow as possible. Our wings almost touching each other, I turned on my radio. "Alright, on my count."

"How come you always get to count?" Eli interrupted.

"Yeah!" Hunter agreed. "Let us do it."

"Alright." I relented. This was a battle I didn't want to fight. "Who wants to count?"

"I want to!" Hunter said quickly. "Three, two, one, go!" Hunter's plane suddenly accelerated.

"What the…" Porter said, surprised. No one was ready.

I didn't wait for anyone to say anything else. I punched my throttle to max and accelerated. "This is why we don't let Hunter count, guys!" I said, pulling my nose up to gain altitude.

I had a plan for this race. It involved a slow and steady approach. The idea was to gain altitude and then dive down, gaining lots of speed. While my speed would be slow at the start of the race and the end, I'd be going way faster than everyone.

Now we had discussed the route a bit more and decided that you had to go around the northside of Narnia, above the hill that the D was on, then be the first one to land on the runway. Whoever came to a stop first won.

I gained altitude to 10,000 feet. We had agreed on radio silence for the entire race. The other planes were already at Narnia. Hunter was in front, but Porter was close behind. I continued gaining altitude. Then at 13,000 feet, I dove. My speedometer dial started moving faster and faster. 200 knots. Already way past max speed. I was approaching 250 knots when I pulled up. I heard my wings shuddering from the speed of the aircraft. I flew past Narnia at breakneck speed. I was at 5,000 feet elevation and still had room to dive.

I saw the rest of the group flying just above the D. Hunter hadn't judged his altitude just right and had to point his nose up to avoid hitting the rock, slowing him down. Porter and Ezra flew past him, and Hunter went into third place. Hunter was barely above the ground. Porter and Ezra were also pretty low.

I flew above them all. I was still behind them but quickly closing in on them. I was still at 180 knots. I decided to dive a little more, bringing me to 200 knots and 2,500 feet. I flew over the D and watched everyone taking wide turns towards the airport. They wanted to get lined up with the runway.

I glanced at them and then looked at the more direct route to the edge of the runway. Weighing the odds, I turned tightly, leaving the other planes. I mumbled to myself, "Here goes nothing."

I quickly passed over the head of Rockwell, who was in last. He wasn't our best pilot. In fact, I'm pretty sure he was the worst. I looked down and saw his eyes gaping up at me. I chuckled at that.

I pressed forward and quickly overtook Eli and Hunter. I was now gaining on Porter and Ezra. I couldn't believe it. I had a chance of winning this thing. Sure, I'd thought I could do it, but I didn't think I would actually be right.

Learning to Fly

I pulled down my hat as I flew past Ezra. Now it was only Porter. He was further to my right now, getting lined up with the runway. I knew I'd have to slow down too much to start my approach. I would lose if I followed Porter's route.

I bit my tongue as I looked back at the runway. I was basically horizontal to the runway. I was heading northeast while the runway was pointing northwest. I just had to hope I was good enough.

I lowered my altitude to 1,000 feet. I would lose a lot of height in this maneuver. And I really didn't want to crash into the ground. Then again, I did have to land the plane. That was when I realized what I was doing. And how crazy I was.

I was going to drift into the landing. I was going to drift an airplane like a car. It was crazy, but it could work. If I timed it just right, I could get lined up on the runway just in time. And then I'd be in front of Porter.

I could feel my heart beating in my chest. You know that queasy feeling you get when you're about to jump off the high dive? That was it, except a million times worse. I glanced behind me, looking for Porter. He was coming around the turn and was lined up with the runway. I saw his plane wings move up and down, telling me not to do it.

I shook my head and looked down. The runway was right where I wanted it. It was now or never. If I failed this maneuver, I'd be a dead man. There was no pulling out of this move. I would crash right into the mountain. I would die because I wanted to win. But sometimes you need to take some risks for the simplest things.

Britton Bean

    Before I could chicken out, I pushed hard on my right rudder and pulled the yoke up to lose speed. Time seemed to slow down. I felt the weightlessness of the zero G's. The plane jerked up and to the left. I kept my foot pressed on the rudder. I felt the plane start to stall. I pushed my nose down and saw the runway right below me. I let my foot off the rudder and pushed full flaps and airbrake. The nose pointed up, and the back tires hit the ground. Smooth as butter.
    I slammed on the brakes. I saw Porter fly over my head. I smiled as I came to a stop in the middle of the runway. I said to myself, "Good going, Bean."

Learning to Fly

Chapter 10

We Finally Get Meat

After that adventure, the guys wanted to chill for the rest of the day. Not Hunter and I, though. We decided that we wanted to go and search for animals. We wanted some good ol' steak. We had a garden, but I didn't want to be a vegetarian for the rest of my life.

So, we got in the Ford and went out and searched every farm that we knew of. It was devastating and gross. Everywhere we went, farm animals were dead. Chickens had no food. Sheep had grown heavy coats and had died of heat exhaustion. And man, they stank!

We searched and searched and found nothing. Finally, we decided to take a walk. Hunter pulled the Ford to the base of a mountain and hopped out.

We wanted to climb that mountain. That's the fun thing about being by yourself. You can just say, "Let's climb that mountain." No trail needed. Just hike up. We just needed a break from life. So, we stepped out of the Ford and started walking.

An hour later, we reached the top. We could see Narnia from up here. It wasn't hard to spot. It was the only house with bright green grass. It looked funny that way.

Hunter sat down, legs hanging over the edge of a cliff, and leaned back. I sat next to Hunter. We didn't say anything for a long time. The sun was setting over the land that I cherished. The land that had once been full of life. I thought of my family, the friends that I had lost. The things that that bomb had destroyed. But I loved this place. We sat together for a while and watched the sunset. I think we were up there for at least an hour.

We would have stayed up there longer, but it was getting dark, and we decided to pack it up and go home. About halfway down, I saw something move. I stuck my hand out to stop Hunter. That's when I saw it: five chickens pecking at the ground. I didn't think to bring the net. I motioned to Hunter to flank them.

We crept around them, being as quiet as possible. We just needed two. We started closing in. I spotted a male and a female beside each other and motioned for Hunter to go for

Learning to Fly

those two. I quietly crept up next to the three others. I glanced at Hunter. He was tense, ready to jump. I held up three fingers. I slowly counted down.

When I had one finger left, we both jumped and grabbed a chicken. All the others scattered. But as luck would have it, we each grabbed one more. We had done it. Only one of them had gotten away.

Hunter and I cheered and laughed as we held the squawking chickens. We were covered in dirt, but we didn't care. I held onto the small, scrawny chickens for dear life. I felt like crying; I was so happy. I couldn't believe it. I'd caught a chicken with my bare hands.

We returned to the Ford, ensuring not to drop the chickens, no matter how hard their talons dug into our skin. We threw the chickens in the cab with us because we didn't want them to jump out the back. Hunter and I were still laughing by the time we got to Narnia.

We arrived at Narnia and were welcomed with joyous shouts of laughter. We named them after all of our past pets. Storm, Lico, Rouge, Bandit. We made a chicken coop for them. I loved those chickens. They laid eggs and gave us even more chickens. We had to make a whole fence for them in our backyard. But for once, I was glad I had to work.

On Rockwell and Ezra's birthday, we had our first chicken dinner. Rockwell and Ezra were our first birthdays since the nukes, so we had to do something special. Porter cooked the chicken perfectly. Man, that stuff tasted great. We ate all of it in one meal.

Britton Bean

As we approached the end of September, the heat started to become bearable. We decided to go to Santa Clara's Main Street to see if we missed anything. That's when we found the paintball guns.

Hunter and I were walking down a side street off Main, just talking.

"I'm telling you; you should be able to smush two words together to make another word." Hunter tried to explain to me. We were walking together, and Hunter had come up with another one of his crazy theories.

"Hunter, they already do that," I explained, looking around the area.

"They do?"

"Yes, Hunter. They do." I said monotonously. I felt like I was talking to a five-year-old.

"No way! Prove it."

"Football, basketball, snowball," I said quickly, still looking for anything interesting,

"That's only things that end with 'ball,' though." Hunter retorted.

"Bullfrog,"

"It's got to be a real animal, Britton," Hunter said like I was the idiot.

I sighed. "You're hopeless, Hunter."

Hunter started to retort, but I wasn't listening. Something had caught my eye. It was a small shop front, with its open sign still working. Those must have been some good batteries. I started to walk towards it.

"...how does a bull and a frog make a real animal? They are two completely different things. Britton, are you even listening to me?" I was suddenly aware of Hunter. I decided to keep ignoring him.

A bell rang as I opened the door. The store was a shabby, dusty, and broken-down place. A counter was in one corner, and a huge rack took up the rest of the wall space, even behind the counter. There were what looked like 30 guns on the shelves. The window looked like it hadn't been cleaned in years. There were some words on the window. I could only make out *Landon's Pai Sho*. All the other letters had become unrecognizable.

"Pai Sho?" Hunter said, reading the window. Then he nodded like he knew the answer, "Chinese Food. We must have wandered into Chinatown."

"I don't think so, Hunter," I said, walking behind the counter. I opened several drawers, looking for a flashlight. "Do you see any tables?"

"Well, maybe it's one of those standing restaurants." Hunter guessed.

I looked at Hunter confused, "A standing restaurant?!"

"Well, maybe? I don't know."

"Have you ever been to a standing restaurant Hunter?"

"Well..." Hunter thought about it and didn't continue.

"That's what I thought."

I opened a drawer and found a flashlight. I clicked the flashlight on and shined the light on the wall. There I saw guns lining the wall. But they weren't any normal ammunition guns. They were paintball guns.

And the idea started forming right then. I smiled as I thought about it. I looked back and had just begun to count the guns when Hunter said, "Wow. That's a lot of paintball guns."

"Yes, it is."

"Where's the ammo?" Hunter asked, looking around in the dark space.

I looked around a little more and found five giant jugs of blue, yellow, and red paintballs. I opened one up and squeezed on one of the balls. That was a mistake. Yellow paint spread over my hands.

"Ugg. What is this stuff?"

"Gelatin," Hunter answered simply.

I looked at Hunter as I wiped my hand on the counter, "So you know what paintballs are made of, but not what a bullfrog is?"

"Hey! I know guns." Hunter defended.

I scoffed and turned my flashlight back towards the rack. I counted 30 guns. There were snipers, miniguns, Gatling guns, and rifles. On another shelf were several sets of full paintball body armor. Ten sets to be exact.

Hunter was thinking what I was and said, "We should do a paintball fight! We can do it all over the city. We could go to abandoned buildings and stuff. It would be a real-life battle royal!"

Learning to Fly

I smiled and said, "Just what I was thinking." I grabbed my radio from my back pocket and spoke into it, "Everyone meet at the old home base. We found something."

Chapter 11

Bluffing on Bluff Street

"Took you long enough," Eli said as he stood up from under the shade of a tree, walking towards me. The rest of the guys were under there with him. Hunter and I had just pulled the truck up with all the ammo, paintball guns, and body armor.

"We had to load some stuff up," I said as I closed the door. I walked to the back and jumped into the bed of the truck. Eli followed.

"Woah..." Eli said, looking at our collection of guns.

"I know, right?" Hunter said as he climbed into the bed of the truck. By this time, the other guys had joined us.

"Holy cow," Porter said, peering over the edge.

"That's a lot of guns." Ezra gawked at the guns.

"Those are paintball guns." Rockwell pointed out.

"Yes, they are," I confirmed. "And we're going to play cops and robbers with them. Everyone cheered. I continued, "So, who wants to be the cops?"

Ezra, Rockwell, and Porter raised their hands. I nodded, "Alright, so that means it will be me, Hunter, and Eli as robbers."

"What are boundaries?" Eli asked.

"Well, doing it here's kinda boring," Rockwell said. "How about Bluff Street." Bluff Street was the street that ran right under the D and was just outside of Santa Clara.

"Yea, Bluff Street would be fun." Eli agreed. Everyone else nodded.

"Alright then, Bluff Street it is." I proclaimed.

"Anywhere on Bluff?" Hunter asked.

"The entire street." I clarified. "Don't go anywhere past it."

"Alright, so what are the rules for cops and robbers?" Ezra asked.

"Cops have three shots, then they're dead. Robbers have one. The robbers have to get from one end of Bluff to the other. Any questions?" I explained.

"So, it's like fugitive?" Ezra asked.

"Exactly." I said.

"Well, Bean, how do we know if we get hit?" Porter challenged.

"There're paintballs, Porter," Rockwell said obviously.

"Precisely." I pointed at Rockwell.

Britton Bean

"Alright, let's go!" Hunter said, excited.

We drove the truck to the end of Bluff Street. I got out with Hunter and Eli and put on full-body gear. The cops (Ezra, Rockwell, and Porter) went to the end of Bluff and then had to drive back. They were allowed a car, while we robbers had to use our good old legs.

We loaded our guns and put the remaining ammo in Hunter's backpack. That backpack also had flashlights, extra guns, and other spare items. We had divided the guns evenly among the cops and robbers. Each side had 15 guns, although we robbers couldn't carry all of them, so we left some at the end of Bluff Street.

I motioned for Hunter and Eli, and we huddled up to make a game plan.

"Alright, Bean, what you got," Eli said.

"Me?! I don't have a plan. I thought you had one." I defended.

"You motioned us over here!" Hunter challenged.

"Yeah, because I thought Eli had a plan!"

"Why would I have a plan?"

I was about to retort when Hunter broke in. "Guys, guys!" Hunter sighed. "I have a plan." Eli and I just looked at him in disbelief. Hunter continued, "Stay on the west side of the street."

"That's your plan?" I argued. "Just stay on one side of the road? I hate to break it to you, Hunter, but we were looking for a little more detail."

"Hear me out." Hunter started. "All the big four-story buildings are on the west side. If we get inside, then we can see where everyone's going. We just have everyone stationed along the route, telling each other where the cops are. And we might even be able to fire down on them."

I was astonished. Hunter had actually thought up a good plan. Not just "Run and gun 'em." I turned to Eli, "That's actually pretty genius."

"Surprisingly, yes, it is," Eli said, surprised.

I turned to Hunter, "Good job Hunter. Now we got to go. They'll be here any minute."

We ran across the street to the west side. We ran for half a mile, hiding behind buildings the whole way. Hunter was right. These buildings were big. They were all at least three stories high. One was even seven. At the half-mile mark, we rested behind a four-story office building.

Out of breath, Hunter said, "Why don't you go into the building and take a look around."

"Okay, one sec." I held up my finger, exhausted. I did not like running. I took a deep breath and then ran into the back door of the building. It was the emergency exit and had direct access to the stairs.

I stopped at the foot of the stairs and looked up. I groaned and started climbing up the stairs, two at a time. I reached the top, out of breath. I was on the roof and crouched to prevent anyone from seeing me. I crept to the edge of the roof and looked over.

I immediately hit the deck. A white Chevy was driving slowly down Bluff Street. Apparently, they had decided to change cars. Rockwell and Porter were in the back, looking for any signs of us. I grabbed my radio and whispered harshly, "Get in the building! They're right in front."

"On it," Hunter responded, a little too loud. I heard him from the roof.

"Quiet!" I said into the radio. But it was too late. The truck stopped, and Rockwell and Porter were jogging towards the building. "Gosh dang it, Hunter," I muttered to myself.

I shot up and fired a volley of shots at them. They immediately jumped for cover behind a long-abandoned car. But Porter was too slow, and I hit him twice. Then paintballs flew right over my head.

I ducked and saw that Ezra had exited the truck and was now moving toward the building. I knew if I jumped up again, I'd be a dead man. I could hear shuffling below me; the cops were moving into the building.

I crept back to the doorway that led to the stairs. I hurried into it and rushed down one floor. I ran smack into Eli. I remembered the first time I'd done that.

"Woah!!" Eli stopped, almost touching noses with me. "That was close."

"We've got incoming." I cautioned, "They're in the building."

"Crap," Eli muttered.

Learning to Fly

"Hey, if you guys are done having your chat up there, I'd like to get in a more comfortable position," Hunter yelled from behind Eli.

In response to Hunter's yelling, I opened the third-story door. I walked into a kind of lobby. There was a reception desk and several chairs and couches off to the side. It was a small space and wasn't the best place to hide. I was about to turn around and tell Hunter to leave when I heard rushing footsteps on the stairs. This place would have to do.

Eli and Hunter heard them too and rushed into the room. Hunter closed the door and looked at it. His eyes widened. "There's no lock!"

I looked around frantically. There weren't many places to hide. Hunter and Eli heaved a couch over to the door to block it, just in time too. The door shuttered as someone ran into it. I motioned for Eli and Hunter to get behind the reception desk. We leveled our guns at the door.

The door shuttered repeatedly, straining under the pressure of the hits, but the couch held strong. Hunter lowered his gun and opened his backpack. "Anything good in there?" I whispered; my eyes still glued to the door.

"I got nothing but ammo and guns," Hunter responded quietly, shuffling through the bag. "Oh, and some trail mix." He pulled out a Ziplock full of trail mix.

"Oooh, pass me some." Eli held out his hand. Hunter threw him the Ziplock.

"Hunter, I'm talking about something actually useful," I said, keeping my eyes on the door. "And Eli, would you stop eating all that food!"

"Sorry," Eli said with his mouth full.

"That plane didn't work so well, Hunter?"

"Man, I know!" Hunter frantically searched the backpack.

"Why can't I have the trail mix?" Eli complained.

"Because I said so."

Hunter kept searching his backpack. Finally, he gave up and groaned, "Ahh!" He slammed his hand against the wall.

And then the craziest thing happened. The wall fell down. It was like it wasn't nailed in at all. The entire wall just slowly glided to the ground. Behind it was a bunch of construction equipment and a huge room. Plaster was scattered around the area. It looked like they were doing renovations.

Eli and I looked at Hunter, shocked. Hunter looked at the wall, then at his hand, and then back at the wall and said, "Woooah!"

"I think I underestimated your strength, Hunter." I gaped into the open room. Eli walked over to the fallen wall. And then I picked it up with his hand. "Wait…" I walked over to the wall. I grabbed it and easily lifted it up. It was a fake wall that people used during renovations. The wall was made of PVC and fabric. "Ohhh!" I sighed, "That's why Hunter seemed so strong."

"Hey! I'm pretty strong, alright." Hunter protested, "I'm stronger than you!"

Learning to Fly

I was about to protest when Eli cut in, "Guys! We could hide behind this, and the cops won't even notice."

I thought about it briefly and then said, "Good thinking." I grabbed Hunter's backpack and threw it at him. He caught it, and then we stepped behind the wall while Eli pushed it back up.

We waited silently behind the wall, waiting for the door to open. But our couch was just too strong. "Suffering from success," I mumbled. Hunter chuckled. We finally decided to try and find another way out.

We checked the windows, but we were three stories up. Jumping wasn't a viable option. We searched for a fire escape or another door. We didn't find anything. Just some electric drills and other construction equipment.

We sat there stumped. We couldn't do anything. Then our radio cracked, "Alright, Bean, give it up." It was Ezra. "There's only one exit in that room, and that's through us."

That's when I had an idea. I put my finger to my mouth and mouthed, *Play along.* I started panting and then said into my radio, "Wait...what do you mean?"

"Ohh, Bean, you know what I'm talking about," Ezra said. "We know you're in there."

I continued fake panting, "Wait, you think we are still over there?" I acted like I was talking to Hunter, "Bro, we can stop running. They're all the way back at the office building. We can walk the rest of the way."

"Bean, we know you're bluffing."

"You're right. I'm bluffing." Hunter and Eli threw up their hands in aggravation, "We totally can't see the end of Bluff Street. Totally…"

There was a long silence followed by Ezra: "If you're not in there, then shoot a paintball in the air."

Eli and Hunter looked at me, concerned. I put my hand out to calm them. "Alright." I knew that paintballs were too fast to spot. Not to mention the fact that it would be way too far away. No way they would see it. I waited a few seconds and then said, "We did it."

"Well, we didn't see it!" Ezra said, mad.

I smiled. I had him now. "Well, where are you?" I asked.

"On the roof!" He screamed.

I stood up and motioned to Hunter and Eli to move. They crept towards the fake wall. I continued to distract him, "Are you sure you didn't see it? Maybe *you* just can't see it. We'll shoot again. Make sure *everyone's* looking."

"Alright." Ezra groaned.

Hunter moved the fake wall out of the way. Then he motioned towards the door. Eli and Hunter quietly moved the couch away from the door. Then Eli opened the door. "Clear!" He whispered harshly.

"Alright, we shot five this time," I said, following Hunter out the door. "Did you see them?"

"You're bluffing, Bean. We know you're down there." Ezra said as we ran down the stairs.

"Oh yeah, I forgot to tell you," I said as we burst out the door and sprinted towards the Chevy. "Always lock the car."

Learning to Fly

Hunter opened the truck door and looked for the keys. They were already in the ignition. Eli and I quickly crammed into the passenger seat while Hunter started the car and stepped on the gas. The vehicle roared forward. I heard paintball hitting the car as they shot at us. I ducked down instinctively but soon realized that paintballs can't break glass. I looked out the window and waved at them.

There was one little issue with our escape plan: we were going the wrong way. Hunter slammed on the brakes and turned hard. Smoke erupted from the tires, and I smelled burning rubber. A loud screeching sounded in my ears. I flew into the window, and Eli crashed into me. Luckily, my paintball armor lessened the blow.

Hunter straightened the car and accelerated. We were now headed toward the end of Bluff Street. I saw Rockwell sprinting towards the road from out of the building. But he slowed to a stop as he saw us flying past him. He watched us zoom past him, and we all just laughed. I couldn't believe that bluff of mine had worked. I guess it had something to do with the location. I bluffed on Bluff Street.

We would have many more games and adventures like that, but that's not what this story is about. Over the years, we would develop new ideas and competitions. We did many activities like that. We grew up in that town. But in the end, none of them really mattered.

Chapter 12

The ISS

I needed a new project. It had been years since I had had my own project. And, of course, I was bored. There are only so many games of capture the flag or real-life battle royal you can play till you get bored.

So, I started reading up on how satellites work. I wanted to connect with any satellite that was still up there. Rockwell, Eli, and I started working on a research lab. We commandeered the house next to us. I had to get the water running, along with electricity. That was easy enough.

Learning to Fly

After that house was up and running, we started getting all the technology we could get. We found some pretty good computers and even hit the motherlode with an entire server system in a school that had survived the blast. While I figured it out, it was really annoying. I'm pretty sure I might have died if it hadn't been for the food that Porter always brought me when I was frustrated.

After about five months of working, the place looked like a real research station. State of the art, I might add. And that brought us to today when, after a long time of researching satellites, we turned on the transmitter.

It was pretty basic. Just a repurposed transmitter I found at a radio station. I did the same with a receiver. I hoped it worked. By all my calculations, it should. But then again, I only had an 8th-grade education, so….

***

"This is Lion One. How are we looking in there, Rockwell? Over." I asked over the radio.

"Bean, you don't need to say Lion One. It's not like anyone is listening. And saying my name over the radio defeats the whole purpose of using code names." Rockwell retorted.

"Rockwell, it's not about the security. It's about coolness. Anyways, that doesn't even matter right now. I just need you to tell me how our power supply is looking?"

"Power level 100%. We've got three gas generators running right now, as you said we would need. Are you sure we should do this at night?"

"Yes, maximum coolness needs to be achieved. Start energizing the transmitter."

"Got it." After a few seconds, Rockwell returned, "Alright, all you need to do now is hit the button out there when I say."

I hovered my hand over the button on the outside transmitter. "Copy that."

"Hit it!"

I heard a surge of power rush into the transmitter.

"I got all greens out here," I looked at the control panel on the transmitter screen.

"Same here. Do you want to head over to the receiver?"

"On my way." I ran over to the transmitter on the other side of the house. We hadn't thought about making them close. That's just where Hunter dumped the receiver. He doesn't think that far ahead.

"Alright, I'm at the receiver," I said breathlessly.

"Energizing receiver. Hit the button when ready."

"Hitting the button." I pushed the button and heard a surge of energy course through the receiver. "Alright, input the coordinates, Rockwell."

"Way ahead of you."

"Are we sure this will work?" Asked Hunter, running up behind me.

"Well, there are two possibilities, one, the system works perfectly, or two, the system doesn't connect with the other

Learning to Fly

satellites in space, and Narnia's power supply goes boom." I made an explosion with my hands.

"Wait, Narnia can go boom?"

"I don't know if that really happens; I just wanted to sound cool," I said smugly. "Why didn't you put the receiver next to the transmitter?" I asked.

"Because that would be too easy." Hunter nodded.

"But that's how it's supposed to be. Easy. This isn't a movie, Hunter." I challenged.

"I thought you wanted, what did you call it, 'maximum coolness?'" Hunter retorted

I was about to respond when the radio cracked, and Rockwell said, "Alright, final checks complete. Here goes nothing." We waited in silence and anticipation for several seconds.

"Umm, Rockwell, you there?" I asked into the radio.

Silence. We waited a few more seconds till the anticipation was too much, Hunter.

"That's it; I'm going down there." Hunter turned and sprinted towards the research base.

"Hunter, wait!" I said, running after him into the house. He ran downstairs into the basement where the research lab was and opened the door. I saw Rockwell frantically typing into the computer.

"What's wrong?!" I asked, alarmed.

"It's not what's wrong. It's what's right. I've got huge amounts of signals coming!" Rockwell exclaimed.

Britton Bean

I scrambled over to the computer and saw it: NAVSTAR 6 <ERROR_CODE 707-LOCATION_FILE_NOT_FOUND>.

I gasped. The satellites were falling back to Earth. Without people in NASA's command, the satellites couldn't adjust. "Get out of my chair right now, Rockwell!!"

Rockwell, surprised, jumped out. "What's wrong?"

"No time; start deciphering that code," I said urgently

I started sending signals to try to re-engage the boosters. One problem: I'm not a rocket scientist. I focused on the GPS and other necessary satellites. The error code kept flashing on another monitor. I finally got the boosters of NAVSTAR 6 to engage and reposition into steady orbit.

After a while of finicking, I got into a rhythm of re-engaging boosters and positioning them in orbit. But I didn't save all of them. Some satellites came crashing to Earth. Namely, NAVSTAR 23, NAVSTAR 15, NAVSTAR 14, and NAVSTAR 3. I did manage to save LANDSAT, the main satellite that takes pictures of the Earth from space. I also saved some other random satellites and the James Webb telescope. But I saw something that shocked me to the core. ISS<ERROR_CODE 707-LOCATION_FILE_NOT_FOUND>.

I looked down in defeat. Rockwell and Hunter, who had been hovering over my shoulder and had figured out what was happening by now, looked at me with knowing in their eyes. "You saved all you could, Britton." Hunter patted my shoulder.

"It's not that, Hunter. I can't save that one."

"Well, they are just machines; we lived without them before."

"Not this one, Hunter. This one had people on board."

"So, wait, is that the 'ISS Error Code….'" I looked at him and knew that he knew. "How long could they have survived? There's got to be some kind of escape pod."

"There should be, but since Ukraine, the USA made Russia send the escape pod down so they could send up their own. They didn't trust Russia with their astronauts' lives. They never got one up there in time. Let's go outside. See if we can see the fire in the sky."

We walked outside. Hunter ran over and woke everyone else up. Everyone else joined us on the roof of the research house. We all sat there, just looking at the stars.

"So why are we here? Did you find anything?" Asked Porter through a yawn.

"We found out the actual date: April 3, 2028," Rockwell whispered to Porter. "But that's not important. Just look in the sky."

"What are we looking for?" Asked Eli.

"You'll know when you see it," I said somberly.

We sat there a few more minutes when we saw it. The fiery, bright light the size of a building lit up the sky. Everyone gasped. I watched as it came farther down the horizon. I felt a tear slip down my eye. I bowed my head.

I remembered what Hunter had said. *You can't save them all.* He was right, of course, and I really wish he wasn't.

Britton Bean

A couple days later, when everyone was asleep, I walked into Hunter's room. I had been thinking of Russia ever since the ISS. I thought of everything they had destroyed. All the happiness they prevented. Everything they ruined. Ideas that never got thought of. I thought of how they had destroyed my country. The country that lived and breathed on freedom and liberty. Life could have been better. I began to feel hate I hadn't felt for a long time. "You know what, Hunter?" I started.

"What?" Hunter groaned

"I really hate Russia."

"Don't we all?" Hunter closed his eyes, trying to sleep.

"No, I really hate them. If I had the chance, I would destroy that country."

"Violent, much," Hunter said, impersonating Yoda. "Control your feelings; you must."

"Hunter, I'm serious. I want to get back at them in some way."

"What are you going to do? Drop a bomb on them?"

"Precisely," I said as an idea began to form. "We're going to nuke them."

That got Hunter's attention, "Say, what?!"

"We are going to nuke Russia," I repeated confidently.

"Britton." Hunter began, confused, "How- Wha- Wait, did you say *we?*"

"Hunter, it's simple." I began showing him with my hands, "We have access to all we need. We could get a B-2 bomber

Learning to Fly

from a military base, load it with a nuke, fly over Russia, drop the nuke, and fly away."

Hunter, still dumbfounded, said, "You think the United States Air Force is just going to have a two billion, billion with a 'b,' two-billion-dollar aircraft just sitting around. Not to mention a freaking nuke, just chilling in a hanger. I don't think so, Britton."

"If they don't, we will figure something else out. I just want to get rid of them."

And then Hunter said something I thought I would never hear him say, "Everything has a cost, Britton, nothing is free, and sometimes you don't know how much it will cost you."

I was taken aback. Hunter never said such profound things. He knew that if I wanted to, I could devote my ideas, skills, and life to this, but it wouldn't be easy. It would provide several unforeseen problems. But one can only try.

I wondered if my best friend would support me in this, "Will you help me?"

Hunter turned to me and said with a smug grin that only Hunter could have, "Britton, do you know me? Do you think I would say no to something involving explosions? Of course, I'm going to help you. I wouldn't want to die without you dying next to me." That was the Hunter I knew.

In the morning, I called a meeting. Everyone gathered around me in the living room. Hunter, my best friend; Eli, my wingman; Rockwell, our doctor; Porter, the cook; and Ezra, strong outside but soft inside.

Britton Bean

    I thought of the things that came from one stupid war. One person pushed a button. One person flipped a switch. One person did one thing that destroyed the world. And why? Because they didn't like someone else. Because one person said or did something that someone else didn't like. And so, Russia got mad and decided to kill America. But when all seems lost, a hero always rises from the ashes. Where there is evil, there is good. When the mighty fall, the weak rise. I stood up and looked at my friends, family, and team. The forgotten. And so, with power in my voice, I began my speech.

    "I'm done being peaceful. I'm done being nice. Russia nuked St. George. What was their purpose? To destroy America. We are no longer kids. We're 19. We can fight for what we believe in. So, let's do it. So, let's attack Russia. How? With our skills, our talents, our beliefs. And through us, we will succeed."

    I looked over at Hunter, and he looked at me, smiled, and gave me the "good one" look, then said, "When do we start?"

Chapter 13

We Get Some Upgrades

"Nellis Airfield, this is Lion squadron. Please respond, over," I said into the radio. The boys and I were in three Cessnas, flying to Nellis Airfield in Las Vegas, Nevada. You see, after we agreed to stand up against Russia, we decided that we needed to get better supplies. You can't fight an entire nation in Cessnas. We also thought that we could find some survivors. So, we decided that Nellis was the best place to go.

"I don't think they are going to answer," Hunter told me from the seat next to me.

"Way to be optimistic, Hunter," I said sarcastically. But Hunter was right. No one was home.

"Do you want to land first, Bean?" Eli said over the radio.

"Yeah, I will," I responded.

When everyone was on the ground, Hunter gave us our guns. M-4's You could never be too safe.

"Alright, people pair up and split up," I said confidently. "Hunter and I will check the hangers. Eli and Porter hit the south side of the main building. Ezra and Rockwell hit the north side. Got it?"

"Sounds good." Said Porter examined his gun.

"Good." I tossed everyone a radio. "Channel three. Move out."

Hunter and I checked the hangers starting from the south side of the compound and worked our way down. And boy, did this place have a lot of airplanes.

We found F-16s, F-35s, F-22s, B-1 Lancers, and all kinds of aircraft. We even found a C-5 cargo plane. And you don't realize how big those cargo planes are until you stand next to their engines. Those things were ginormous.

"Alright, everyone, what did y'all find?" I said into my radio.

"We found a bunch of ammo," Ezra said back.

"Airplane or gun ammo?" I asked

"Both."

"How much?"

"An entire warehouse full."

"Alright, cool." I said, "How about Eli. What'd you guys find?"

Learning to Fly

"We found a lot of electrical equipment if you want it," Eli responded.

"Alright, good, we'll take a lot of that stuff home."

"Only one issue, Bean." Ezra started, "We got no way to carry it."

"Ohh, we do." I looked at the C-5. "We do."

It took us almost four hours of lifting ammo and electronics until we decided we had enough. And the C-5 was only a quarter full, probably less.

"I'm going to die." Rockwell groaned as he laid down on the ground.

"I agree." Porter stretched his arms.

"Ahh, you guys will be fine." I waved them off.

"Man, shut up." Porter said, "Let us vent."

"Alright, everyone, let's get to our planes. And can we have Porter fly the C-5? I'll fly a F-35, and Eli can take the F-22. Everyone else gets a Cessna." I said.

"So, we have to fly in slow Cessna's, and you guys get to fly in planes that can break the sound barrier?" Hunter complained, "That hardly seems fair."

"You can fly the planes when we get home Hunter," Eli said to Hunter like a child. "And not to mention the fact that you've never flown an F-22. Bean and I are the best pilots out of all of us."

"Fine." Hunter resigned. "Way to be humble, Eli." But he knew it was true.

"Wait, Bean," Porter started, "I don't know how to fly a C-5. I mean, those things are huge. Are we sure that we have enough runway to even land the C-5 on the St. George runway?"

"Ohh, we have plenty of runway." I responded, "The only issue is landing that plane. But I know you can do it."

"And how do you expect me to do that?" Porter shot back.

"Learn quickly." That stunned everyone.

"Kill me now," Rockwell said, looking up. "Heaven, take me away."

"That's wishful thinking," Hunter told him sarcastically. "You think you're going to heaven?"

Rockwell glared at Hunter like he was going to kill him.

"Alright, people, let's go," I said before Rockwell could make his move. I started walking to the F-35.

"No, no, no," Porter ran after me, "You don't get to just run away. I don't know how to fly a C-5!"

"Then learn quickly; read the manual." I started. "I think I know your problem. You're thinking about the future. You want to know my motto: Focus on the present."

"But that's illogical, Bean," Porter responded.

"Have I ever struck you as a logical person?"

"Well…"

"Didn't think so. Good luck. And have fun." I said as I shut the glass cockpit of the F-35 cockpit. I started up the engine and revved the engine. I loved that power. I winked at Porter as I taxied to the runway. Then I said into my mic, "Hey Eli," I laughed, "Race ya home."

Then I pushed my engine to the max and took off, reaching takeoff speed in a little under ten seconds. The power

Learning to Fly

felt amazing. Who needs to worry about the little things? Only worry about what you need. Food, water, and of course, your friends. So that's what I did, pointing the nose of the aircraft straight up. It didn't take long to stall, but I didn't care. I dived down and pulled a seven G turn. I loved the feeling of high G turns. The pressure of the turn and then the relief you feel when you pull out. And so, I turned and pointed my nose home. To the world that I loved.

***

"I won," Eli said as I met him on the runway.

"HA! Good one." I laughed.

"I'm serious. I beat you to the valley."

"Ohh," I started somberly, "You must have found some beer in there, didn't you? Man, I thought you were better than drinking while driving. And not to mention underage drinking. I thought better than you, Eli."

"Nonoo, I didn't drink. There wasn't even beer there."

"Must have been drugs then."

"Oh my gosh. What are you thinking, Bean?" Eli rolled his eyes.

"Well, you must be high if you think you won."

Eli slugged me in the arm.

I just laughed and said, "So you admit I won. And believe me, you want to leave it at that. I can go farther."

Eli just shook his head. "That wasn't your best one, Bean."

"Yeah, I know." I agreed, "It took too long to get to the punch line."

"Yeah, you gotta make it snappy and quick." Eli snapped.

I chuckled. Then I realized something, "Hey, Porter should be coming in soon."

"Should I get the casket? Or are we going to wait for the flames to die down?"

"Good question. If we wait, the body might not be there. And, trust me here, ashes are really hard to get back in the urn."

We had a good laugh out of that one.

"But seriously here," Eli started, "Do you think he can land that C-5?"

"I know Porter can." I said, "That's why I chose him to do it."

I saw the C-5 come around a hill from the west and start the approach. I watched as he dropped the gear and glided down to the runway. Smoke came rushing off the tires as the plane landed. The whole plane seemed to bounce. Like when an ATV makes a jump and lands, the ATV sinks and then pops back up. But eventually, the aircraft came to a stop. The C-5 taxied to our biggest hanger, where Porter shut off the engines and opened the cargo bay door. I smiled as Porter walked out and said, "You learned quickly, didn't you?"

Porter just shook his head and sighed, "Shut up. That was the most stressful landing of my life."

Learning to Fly

"I can't believe you landed that thing." Hunter said, entering the conversation after he had landed and taxied, "Those Cessnas are so slow compared to those fighters you got there. You guys could have been home by the time I took off."

"Where's everyone else?" I asked.

"Right there." Hunter pointed to the runway where Ezra and Rockwell were taxiing to where we were. "Hey, can I take that F-22 out for a spin before we start unloading?"

"Fine Hunter. We'll refill the planes and put them in the hangers while you fly around in that F-22." I said.

Hunter motioned for me to come closer. He whispered into my ear. I smiled and then nodded. "Five 'o clock, not a minute later."

"Yes!!" Hunter exclaimed. Hunter ran over to the F-22 and started the engines. He looked like a kid who just got ice cream. I guess Hunter was 19, yet it felt like he was 30. I looked around and it was hard to believe *everyone* here was 19 because it felt like we were all so much older because of everything we had experienced. We should be going to college, not waging a war. But you work with what you got. My brother used to say, "If you're not enjoying, what are you doing?"

We finished refueling the planes and making sure they were put away. Since we didn't have a hanger big enough for the C-5, we put the tail of the C-5 under our biggest hanger and covered the rest of it in tarps.

That's when I told the gang to follow me.

"Where are we going?" Ezra asked.

123

Britton Bean

"That's on a need-to-know basis, and you don't need to know." I hopped into the white Chevy. "Hop in. We got a bit of a drive ahead of us."

Learning to Fly

Chapter 14

Hunter Flips a Switch

We drove to the place Hunter had given us instructions for. I knew the area. It was an opening in the forest about the size of a runway. Hunter had once bet me I couldn't land there. I would have tried had it not been for the power lines that stretched over the trees. There was also a giant wooden pole in the middle of the field. So, I decided that my life wasn't worth proving a point.

We had to hike for a long time, and Eli was *very* tired when we arrived. "I'm exhausted." He collapsed onto the ground.

Porter had brought some food for dinner when I told him we wouldn't be back till eight. Ezra placed the backpack and our picnic box on the ground beside him.

I turned to Eli and said, "You might want to see this." He didn't move. I looked at my watch. 5:00 PM. I looked towards the sky.

"What are we looking for?" Rockwell asked as he started walking forward to investigate.

I didn't get a chance to respond.

An F-22 with newly painted pink wingtips and green engine nozzles flew right in front of us. The engines roared as the F-22 did a barrel roll only 30 feet from the ground.

Time slowed down. I saw Hunter through the cockpit glass. He grinned at me, and I smiled back. That was my Hunter right there: daring and dangerous.

The F-22 started spinning, doing barrel rolls while pointing up. Then the plane dove down and left our vision. I smiled. Hunter sure did have an interesting color choice.

"Pink and green?" Ezra critiqued.

"Not my first choice," Porter added.

"He does have stupid color choices, doesn't he?" I agreed.

"So, wait, that's it?!" Eli complained, sitting up. "We came all this way for that?!"

I laughed, "We got some food, but yeah, that's it."

"You have got to be kidding me." Porter groaned. "I thought this was supposed to be fun. We climbed a freaking mountain!!" Porter motioned to the ground. I smiled and nodded. Porter shook his head, "I'm going to at least eat some food!"

***

In the morning, we unloaded the C-5 and shuttled the supplies in trucks to Narnia. We then unloaded the trucks and moved all the supplies into the research base. Then we talked about our next plans.

"I think we should keep gathering supplies from bases and see what we find." Eli looked at his clipboard.

That clipboard seemed to be his life. That clipboard kept track of everything we had, have, and need. I'm pretty sure that clipboard was the only thing that kept Eli sane in the bunker. And it drove us insane. Every time we used something, we had to report it to Eli. Now Eli had asked me to make a program on the computer that we could just enter in what we used, and Eli would just enter that data into his clipboard. That was going to be my next project.

"Well, if we do that, where are we going to look?" Ezra asked.

"I'll take it from here, Eli." I said, "We would go to the following locations." I turned on a projector we had found in a school. A map of the US appeared that had several red dots.

"Wow, this man was prepared." Hunter jeered.

Everyone laughed. I chuckled forcefully and said, "Yeah, anyways, these are the locations I think we should target." I pointed to the red dots with a meter stick. "We start at Area 51; let's see if there are aliens." Hunter grinned and nodded. "Next up: Cape Canaveral. Then we got Houston. The NASA command center in Houston, of course. And lastly, we got Hickam."

"Where the heck is that?" Rockwell asked.

"Hawaii," I answered.

"Isn't that under Russian control?"

"Yup."

You could have heard a pin drop with that silence. "Well, let's get started, shall we."

***

"This is the Lion Squadron from St. George, Utah. Please respond. Area 51, over," I said into my radio.

"I don't think anyone's home Britton," Hunter commented as he pulled up next to me in his green and pink F-22.

"I don't think so either," I said back from an F-16. I'd convinced the others to stop in Nellis so I could try out the F-16. "Alright, everyone, prepare to land. I'll go first. Wait about two minutes after someone has landed before you start your approach."

I heard several voices agree.

Learning to Fly

I waited for everyone to taxi from the runway next to me. We had brought three planes. I was in an F-16. Porter, Rockwell, and Ezra were in a C-5. And finally, a pink and green F-22 was flown by Hunter.

"Let's see if there are aliens in there!" Ezra said.

"This is like my dream." Hunter smiled.

"I thought flying an F-22 was your dream." I teased.

"Well, that is part of it."

"Alright, Hunter, get the guns and radios," I said. Hunter ran into the C-5 and pulled out six M-4s and six radios, and gave them to me.

"Channel two." I passed out the radios. "Pair up and explore."

I paired up with Hunter. The twins, Rockwell and Ezra, paired up and Porter and Eli. Same as last time.

"Alright, everyone got their wingman?" I looked around the group to be sure. "Great, Hunter and I will take the hangers; you guys take the base. Same as last time. Got it?" Everyone nodded. "Perfect, stay in touch, and good luck."

Everyone split up, and I looked at the hangers and said, "Which one first?"

"Let's just go down the line," Hunter responded.

"Alright."

We started with the first one. As we walked in, it was pitch black. I saw shapes in the dark. I tried the light switch, but nothing happened.

"Do you have an…" I started as Hunter handed me a flashlight? "Thanks."

"No problem."

I turned on the flashlight. It was pretty disturbing. It looked like someone had been eating. Food was prepared on a table, or what was left of food, and a TV remote was on the couch. I wrinkled my nose at the smell. A TV hung on the front wall. Chairs had been tossed over. It looked like whoever had left, had left in a hurry.

"See anything of value?" I asked.

"Maybe the TV," Hunter said, looking at it.

"Nah, we've got plenty at Narnia."

"Yeah. I don't see anything of value other than that."

"Alright, let's head into the aircraft portion."

I opened the door to the aircraft portion and caught my breath.

"What the heck is that?" Hunter stared. "Do you know what that is?"

"I have never seen anything like it." I was stunned.

What stood in front of me was the craziest aircraft I'd ever seen. I'm not even sure if you could call it an aircraft. It was a black triangle with a glowing blue orb in the middle. There were several other green and red lights on it too. And this thing was massive. It was the size of a B-2. I walked up to it and looked at the marking on it.

"'TR3b - Black Manta,'" I read.

"That's sick!"

"I wonder what's so special about it." I rubbed my hand across the fuselage.

"Let's try it!"

Learning to Fly

I hesitated, remembered my philosophy of "do now, think later" and said, "Sure, why not."

We set our guns on a table. Hunter started opening the hangar doors while I brought the ladder over. I climbed in and looked at the controls. They were like a regular F-22. I started what I thought was the engine. Nothing happened.

"Pull the pins, Hunter!" I screamed, thinking that was the problem. Maybe some safety feature.

I saw Hunter run around the entire aircraft pulling all the red pins. Then he pulled the ladder out, climbed onto the wing, got into the cockpit, and closed the hatch.

"Hey, do you see an engine start button on this console?"

"Uhh… is it that one?" Hunter pointed to the button I already had pushed.

"I tried that one."

"Maybe it needs gas."

"That's the issue; I don't see a fuel gauge."

"Hmm… Maybe give it some throttle."

I pushed the throttle a little bit and tried what I thought was the start button. Nothing happened.

"Man, how do you start this thing?" I slammed my fist against the console.

"Hey, what's that button?"

"'Reactor.'" I read, "What do you think it does?"

"Only one way to find out."

"Hunter wai-"

Hunter flipped the switch, and I heard a loud humming, and then it leveled out. Then Hunter looked at me with the look that said, "See, I told you I was useful."

"Hunter, in the future, let's NOT flip switches labeled 'Reactor,' ok?" I told him.

"It worked, didn't it? So, I think I will in the future." Hunter said. "Let's try this thing out, shall we?"

"You're stupid." I scoffed. I looked at him, and he grinned that grin. "Let's do this."

I pushed the throttle forward. Then something happened that I did not expect. The aircraft went up instead of forward. We were hovering.

"What the-," I said, confused.

"Woah!" Hunter grabbed the seat tightly.

"That's new."

"I think I figured out why this aircraft is special."

"Yeah, me too."

I pushed the yolk forward and slowly flew out of the hanger. Then I pushed the throttle to its max and pulled the yolk back. My head flew back into the seat. It felt as if I was melting into the chair. I quickly got to Mach 1. Some people measure how fast their cars are by 0-60. I measure it from 0 to Mach 1. And this was fast. 15 seconds fast.

"WOOO" I yelled as we flew straight up and leveled out.

"That was fun!" Hunter yelled.

"Let's see what this bad boy can do."

I started doing barrel rolls, taking 7 G turns, the most G's we could take safely. I even flew straight up to try and stall the plane. I thought it would start to slow down. Nope, it just sped up. I kept going, quickly finding myself 50,000 feet and still climbing.

"This thing isn't slowing down!" I said to no one in particular.

"Space it is, then," Hunter said.

"I wish, but we don't have space suits. Not to mention the heat of the atmosphere would kill us."

"Haven't you figured it out yet? We don't need those. This thing was made for space."

"Yeah, right. Where'd you get that information?"

Hunter pointed at an oxygen gauge that I hadn't noticed before. "See. We'll just go as high as you can till, we can't breathe."

"Ahh yes, that's a good idea, go until you die. It doesn't matter anyways. We would have to make it through the atmosphere, which could burn us."

"We could just abort and turn around. C'mon Britton. This could give us the chance of a lifetime."

I looked down and sighed. Life wouldn't be life without risks.

"If we die, I blame you." I resigned

"I told you, Britton, I wouldn't want to die without you dying next to me," Hunter repeated.

I looked at my altimeter, it read 150,000 feet. In normal planes, oxygen is needed this high, and we were doing just fine. But the heat would be coming right about now, so that was my next concern.

Britton Bean

"Moment of truth," I muttered.
"What do you want your last words to be?" Hunter asked.
"I blame Hunter."
"Mine would be 'See you in heaven.'"

I started to see fire rising up the nose. I held my breath. For what seemed like forever, we broke through to the black. I let out my breath. I looked at the oxygen level gauge. It had 80% left. Then I felt weightlessness set in.

It felt like I was on that part of a roller coaster when you suddenly dropped. Except it felt like that every second. Like I was free falling. I relaxed my body, and my hand started to float. I unclipped my radio, and it floated in the air. I chuckled and smiled. I was in awe. I couldn't believe what I was seeing. It felt fake.

Then I looked out the cockpit. The aircraft had rotated to show the earth. I was speechless. It was beautiful. I looked down at the world. That wonderful marble we called a planet. Everyone that I loved was on that planet. To think that only six years ago, I had been with my family. To think that we had been laughing, loving, and just having fun only six years ago. And now... all I had was five of my friends. Just us six, trying the best we could to survive.

And now the plan was to take on the biggest country in the world. We were crazy and ignorant. There was no way around that. I'd calculated the numbers, and statistically, there was no way we were winning this fight.

But being ignorant isn't always a bad thing. Ignorance is never giving up, even when the numbers, people, and

Learning to Fly

everything else says you're wrong. So, that's exactly what I am going to do. Never, under any circumstances, give up. Because, gosh dang it, I'm ignorant. And what's the worst that can happen? We die? Alright then, but at least we'd all go together.

We flew in space astonished for another 30 minutes until we had 30% oxygen left. We had to leave the wonderful feeling of weightlessness (I also wasn't feeling too well from the prolonged weightlessness) so I guess it wasn't all bad to have to leave. We were about 3,000 feet from the ground when we heard our radios chattering.

"Bean, are you there?" an alarmed Ezra sounded.

I picked up my radio and said, "We're fine. Better than fine. We went on a bit of a joy ride. You won't believe what we found."

"Where did you guys go?" Ezra asked.

I looked at Hunter, and we had a mutual understanding: we wouldn't tell them where we went. I don't know why, but it felt like something that should stay between us.

"We found a pretty cool plane." Hunter ignored the question.

"Yeah, it's sick." I confirmed, "Don't worry; we are coming in for a landing."

"Alright, good because we also found something you will want to see,"

Britton Bean

Chapter 15

SAM

"What is that?" Was everyone's reaction. We all gathered on the ground around the Manta. I was still stunned. I don't know how they did it. How did the air force do it? That was the question on everyone's minds. It was by far the coolest thing I'd ever seen.

"I bet we got something even cooler." Eli proudly proclaimed.

"The only thing cooler is aliens," Hunter said from under the glowing orb in the middle. He poked the sphere with a stick.

"Hunter, I don't think we should be lying under that thing." I was still a bit wary of the plane.

"Maybe, but we don't know unless we try it."

"What happened to the Hunter who was yelling at me for pushing him out of a plane?" I asked sarcastically.

"He grew up," Hunter said, looking at me. Everyone laughed at that. I grinned.

"Bean, you have got to see this," Eli said adamantly.

"Alright, alright, let's go." I followed Eli inside. "Hunter, do you want to see aliens or not?"

"I'm coming!" Hunter yelled from behind the plane.

I walked into the base to see that they had electricity and asked Porter, "How'd you get the electricity?"

"Ohh, that. Rockwell flipped a switch that said 'Reactor.'" Porter responded.

"See!!" Hunter exclaimed from behind me.

"Oooh, shut up." I wanted to slap Hunter.

We walked down a hallway deeper underground. We came to a key-coded door that had been blown open. I bet they had some fun doing that. We arrived in a testing room. It was an elevated room with several computers and measuring equipment. There was a long plexiglass window at the front of the room. Down past the plexiglass window, there was what looked like an Iron Man suit. Seriously, that was the best way to describe it. A gold suit connected with giant wires from the ceiling in a huge testing room. It had to be at least seven feet tall. Everyone gathered in the room and looked out the window.

"I present to you," Rockwell started in an announcing voice, "Project Suited. The air forces attempt at making an Iron Man suit."

This suit was crazy looking. It was a human-sized, gold-plated suit. The suit was made of overlapping gold plates about six inches wide each. It had slanted-down eyes that made it look angry. There wasn't a mouth or nose. Just plated gold metal. It might have actually been actual gold.

"This is crazy." I gawked at the suit, astounded.

"Definitely cooler than the plane," Hunter commented.

"Is it operational?" I asked Rockwell.

"I can check real quick," Rockwell said, turning on a computer.

"I wonder what all the wires are for." Eli wondered.

"Power," Rockwell said.

"Well, that doesn't make it an Iron Man suit, does it now?" Eli joked.

"That's why they terminated it…" Rockwell whispered to himself.

"What?! They terminated something this cool?! How could they?" Hunter asked, alarmed.

"They terminated the program on January 11th, 2023." Rockwell looked at the computer screen.

"Why?" I asked

"Not a sustainable power source."

"Well, why couldn't they just use a battery?" Hunter asked.

"It wouldn't provide enough energy. According to the notes, 'energy output of SB not sustainable.'"

"What does SB mean?" Eli asked.

"Super Battery" Rockwell said, looking up from the computer like it was obvious.

"Because I was just supposed to know that," Eli said bitterly.

"I want to see this 'super battery.'" I was already contemplating uses.

"It doesn't say where it is," Rockwell said, looking at the screen.

"Alright, but what kind of specs does that suit have?"

I saw Rockwell scroll down the page on the computer screen. "Foldable guns, foldable ammo, flight capable, lasers, radar, sonar, GPS, worldwide radio, custom fitting software, hand movements sensing software, hologram HUD, state of the art targeting system with custom made rockets, and finally, space capable." Rockwell finished out of breath.

"They fit all that in one suit," I asked, looking back at the suit. "No wonder they couldn't find a way to power it all. But it still works right now with the power cables, right?"

Rockwell changed screens and confirmed, "100% online."

"I'm going in," I said. No one tried to stop me. They knew me well enough.

I walked out a door on the side of the observation room into the testing room. I walked over to the suit and looked up at it. The thing looked a lot bigger down here. I'm not sure who the test pilot was or how this thing worked, but it seemed a little big for me. I had grown from my barely 5 feet tall days, but I wasn't a giant. I also wasn't sure how to get in. I walked up to the front, and nothing happened. I moved my hand across the suit's surface, searching for a button or switch to open it. Nothing. I walked around the suit until I got to the back, when the entire suit opened up. I jumped back in surprise.

The gold plates separated, and the suit opened to a dark suit room. I unstrapped my radio and set my gun on the ground. I cautiously stepped in and realized I was way too small for the thing. I could do a full 360 if I wanted to. I saw some painted footprints that indicated where I was supposed to stand. I stood on them, and that's when the whole system turned on.

The platform I was standing on made a weird sound, like it was measuring something, and then the entire platform I was standing on started moving up. Higher and higher toward the head of the suit. That scared me. I thought I was going to get crushed. Then an automated voice said, "Please stand straight up and hold still while measuring."

I followed the voice and didn't move. A grid of lasers came over me and then quickly disappeared. But the platform kept rising. I started to panic, thinking I was too short and the system would crush me. I stood still against my instincts. Then just as my head was about to hit the top, the system stopped. I breathed a sigh of relief.

"Please put arms in arm holes." The automated voice said. I cautiously put my arms in the arm holes. This is the point in the movies where the AI would turn evil and cut my hands off or something. But then again, I wanted to use this thing.

Learning to Fly

When I put my hands in, I immediately realized that my hands were *way* too small for the huge suit. I saw a red light shine in the armholes. Then the automated voice said, "Please hold still while adjusting."

There was a loud hissing sound, and the walls closed in on me slowly. At that point, I had a little more confidence that the system wouldn't crush me. It tightened around my body. I felt the arm holes tighten around my hands and arms. The voice came on again and said, "System setup complete. Please hold still. Initializing flight system. Please hold still."

Then I felt a sensory needle prick in my right wrist and jerked, "Ow!"

The voice said again, "Please hold still while measuring." I sighed and relaxed again. Then I felt multiple micro needles stick into my back, shoulders, legs, and chest. I groaned but still held still. It felt like I was getting a bunch of shots all over my body. Then I felt a headset come over my temples and forehead.

"This is weird," I muttered to myself.

An eyeglass that was attached to the headset came down on my right eye. An earbud was placed in my right ear as well. I felt the earbud adjusting in my ear which was… unsettling. I still couldn't see anything through the pitch black. Then I felt my body move forward meeting the front of the suit.

Suddenly, an entire heads-up display came up where my eyes were. Everything started moving. There was a loud whirring sound and I felt pressure on my head as the suit tightened. Then my entire vision was filled with the testing room. The heads-up display started throwing icons onto it. The icons were overlaid on my vision. Then my right eyeglass came online with its own mini-HUD or Heads up Display. It's basically those things you see in the futurist movies where they have their holograms and stuff. I saw a targeting system come up and get coordinated.

Then the voice said, "Please state your full name."

I hesitated, unsure of what to do. I decided I'd take my chances, "Britton Bean"

"You are Britton Bean of St. George Utah, Age 19." The voice said, almost as a question.

"Ummm, yes," I said, surprised.

"Height and weight are as follows: Height is five foot eight inches; Weight is 157 lbs."

"Wow I'm fat." I laughed.

"Asking for verification to unlock the system." I waited in silence for about 30 seconds. I was *very* confused about what I was supposed to do.

"Yes?" I tried. Nothing happened. I tried navigating the HUD or moving around, but nothing happened. I tried moving one of my legs, to the same result. So, I decided to just wait a bit longer, thinking the system would just work itself out. Suddenly the voice came on again, "Verification complete. Unlocking system."

I heard a buzzing in my ear, and then Rockwell said, "Bean are you alive?!"

"Of course, I am. Do you know me?" I responded with a grin.

Learning to Fly

"Alright well I just clicked 'Verify' so you should have control now."

I looked around and I felt the entire suit move with me. It felt natural. I didn't feel clunky at all. It just felt like I was moving normally. I looked down and saw my legs. I was huge. This was a feeling that I had always wanted, but never felt. Being tall. This was great! It was the greatest feeling I had ever felt, and I'd just gone to space, so the bar was set pretty high. Pun unintended.

I started walking around. I tried to make a gun pop out. Then without doing anything the gun popped out.

"Wow." I gasped. I thought about taking out a missile and the missile popped out alongside the gun.

"Whatever I *think* happens," I said to myself, then into the radio. "Hey Rockwell. Whatever I think happens."

"That's sick!! Does it work with flight?" Hunter answered. I guess he had stolen the radio.

"I can try." I thought about flight and I heard a loud roaring and felt myself lifting up. An altimeter came up on my display along with speed.

"This is so cool!" I shouted. "Man, this thing is the best." Then I wondered something. "Hey Hunter, what was the last thing I said?"

"Said." Hunter thought he was so smart.

I scoffed, "Actually Hunter."

"Umm, 'I can try.'"

No way. I thought. The suit reads my thoughts, and knows if I want to speak over the radio. I was really starting to like this mind reading thing. "Hey guys, this mind reading thing works over the radio. The suit senses if I'm talking over the radio or not. Isn't that cool?"

"So cool, but we want to see some action." It was Eli.

"Ok, Eli," I said to myself. "Ok." I flew up to the window and looked at everyone. "How do you like me now?" I pulled out my machine gun and pointed it at them. Everyone ducked, scared.

"Bean, are you crazy?! PUT THE GUN DOWN!!" Rockwell screamed at me.

"It's not even loaded," I said indifferently.

"HOW DO YOU KNOW THAT!?!" Rockwell screamed from behind a desk.

"Because it says on my HUD. 'No Ammo'. Here I'll show you. I'm pulling the trigger and it's just clicking and there is a red border around the 'No Ammo' display." I thought about putting the gun away, and the weapon collapsed into the suit. Then I did something that everyone does at least once in their life – I tried to break something.

I quickly thought of taking out the gun. I wanted to check the response speed of the gun, and see if I could potentially get it stuck or break it or something. The gun popped out. But, before it was even all the way out, I thought of putting it away. I did that really quickly, seeing how the suit would handle it. It handled it perfectly, with no issues at all. It just kept going out and then in again over and over.

I maneuvered myself around the room seeing how fast I could go. The boys had gotten up by now and were watching me fly around. It was crazy being able to just think and you would go. I started experimenting with the icons on my HUD. Even those worked by thought. I saw they had missiles, guns, and then I saw a button that said, "VA" As my eyes looked at it, it came up with a caption "Virtual Assistant." I clicked on it. When I "clicked" on it, I really just *thought* about clicking it. There was a loud ringing and then a mechanical voice sounded, "Yes sir?"

"Woah, an AI!" I shouted.

"Yes sir."

"Sooooo, what can you do?"

"Anything you need, sir."

"Alright let's test that theory. What is the largest nuke in the world?"

"The Russian Tsar Bomb sir." The voice answered quickly.

"Alright...where am I right now?"

"The Top-Secret Air Force Division of Area 51 sir."

"Alright, one more question. Are aliens real?"

The voice hesitated momentarily, "Depends on your definition of aliens, sir. If you are thinking of little green men, I assure you, they are not real. But if you are talking about plant life from interstellar space, it is in the quarantined section of Area 51. The plant is called "Cyphorian," and according to testing, there are no effects or benefits of the plant. It is like a common dandelion, sir."

"Well, that's underwhelming."

"Yes, it is sir."

"So, how'd they get it?"

"The specimen is from a meteorite that crashed in Afghanistan when the USA had their presence there sir."

"I see." There was an awkward silence where I didn't know what to say. I mean, how do you talk to an AI or Artificial Intelligence? I had used ChatGPT before, but this was eons ahead of that. It spoke like a real person, besides the "sir" part and the weird voice. I finally said, "So do you got a name?"

"If you count 'Virtual Assistant' as a name sir."

"Hah." I laughed, "You're funny, you'll fit right in."

"Thank you, sir." The voice said indifferently.

"So can I give you a name?"

"Yes, sir."

"Hmmm, how about SAM."

"Sam sir? Like 'Sam I am? The human in green eggs and ham?'"

"No, no, no SAM is an acronym. Smart, Artificial, Man."

"Quite the acronym sir."

"Thanks," I said proudly.

"With all due respect sir, that wasn't a compliment."

"Ohhhh, you are awesome, SAM."

"Anytime sir. Now I would like to ask you a question, sir."

"Alright, shoot."

"Which gun, sir?"

"No SAM it's an expression. Like I'm saying, tell me your question."

"That doesn't make sense, sir."

Learning to Fly

"SAM, humans don't make sense."

"I can tell sir."

"So, what was your question, SAM?"

"You keep implying that there is somewhere that I will 'fit in.' Where is this place, sir?"

"It isn't necessarily a place, SAM. It's a who. My friends. You probably have them in your database. Try searching, Eli Stuki, Porter Butterfield, Ezra and Rockwell Dansie, and Hunter Haws."

"All of them are from St. George, Utah, USA sir?" SAM asked.

"Correct."

"Very interesting people sir."

"Yup. So, what can this thing do SAM?" I asked moving my hands to fly in a different direction getting a feel for the suit.

"This suit is relatively untested because of program shutdown on January 11th, 2023. But I can tell you what I know sir."

"Alright, hit me."

"I'm sorry sir, I cannot harm the suit."

I wanted to slap SAM. "SAM, it's an expression."

"Apologies sir."

"Just tell me what you know, SAM," I said, annoyed. It was like I was talking to Hunter. And one Hunter is good enough for me. Ahh, but I still like Hunter.

"The engine output is able to put this suit over Mach 1. This suit has specially designed weapons that use foldable bullets as their ammo. The ammo is always loading in the guns to prevent from having to wait to reload the weapons."

"Wait wait wait." I interrupted, "Why did it say that the weapons were not loaded then?"

"Because you didn't want it to be sir. The weapon is always loaded but without directly thinking about it, the weapon will not fire. The warning is just for human comfort. It's a safety feature sir."

"Oh." I was guilty that I *had* pointed a loaded gun at my friends.

"Would you like me to continue sir?"

"Yes, please continue." I lowered the suit to the ground.

"This suit has a GPS connecting to NAVSTAR satellites." I gulped, thinking about the satellites that we had lost. I decided not to bring it up. SAM continued, "This suit also has different profiles based on fingerprint, facial recognition, and DNA recognition. This suit will also adjust for your height and weight. It also has perfect neurological sensory calibration. That would be the sensory micro-needling you felt, sir."

"Yeah, that didn't feel so good. Not a good first impression."

"Apologies sir, but it must be done for security reasons and the operation of the suit. You can set this suit to only work with certain profiles."

"Not like anyone else would even find this," I said under my breath.

SAM gave me a tutorial on the suit for the next hour and a half. Everything was enabled by my mind. I could also change

Learning to Fly

it to hand movements or verbal commands. The suit could also go into drone mode. Basically, go without a pilot (or SAM was the pilot) and do what we told it to. There were also eight highly advanced cameras all around the suit. These cameras could see a penny from space.

The suit was also made of the strongest material on earth: Gold-infused graphene. That's where the gold coloring came from. This made the suit like a superior bulletproof vest. After the lesson, I decided to go and check on the guys. The suit disengaged and loosened the suit walls. Then the platform lowered me down, and I walked out the back. I stretched and felt where the suit had stuck me. I'd have to find a way to fix that. I jogged over to the door that led into the testing room.

Everyone was asleep. Hunter was lying on the ground under a table, Eli was lying on a table, and so was Ezra. Porter was slumped in a chair, and Rockwell was laying head first on a keyboard. I smiled as I tiptoed to a table, disconnected a computer, and lifted it above my head. I slammed it on the table.

Everyone jerked up. Ezra fell off the table with a thud. Hunter jerked up too fast and hit his head on the table above him. It was all so fast and so funny. There were a bunch of groans, mainly coming from Hunter and Ezra.

"That was loud!" Porter rubbed his eyes, "Ezra, you good?"

"Yeah, I'm fine." Ezra groaned

"Hunter you, ok?" I asked, looking at Hunter on the floor holding his head.

"You suck!" Hunter exclaimed, rubbing his forehead.

"Yeah," Ezra agreed, getting up slowly.

"Why were you out there so long," Eli asked.

"I was learning," I responded.

"Yeah well, while you were having fun, we found that Super Battery." Eli pointed over to the corner of the room. There sat a black cube about the size of an apple. There was a blinking blue light on the top.

"I tested the power output when fully charged and it should be able to power a computer for about 26 hours." Rockwell yawned. "Not bad huh."

"Not good enough to power SAM, though."

"Who's Sam?" Hunter asked, getting up.

"He's a virtual assistant for the suit – Smart, Artificial, Man or SAM."

"Who came up with that acronym?" Eli asked sarcastically.

"I did," I answered proudly.

"Of course, you did." Ezra rolled his eyes.

I explained the basics of the suit and they put their profiles in. After that, we disconnected the suit from the power cables and all six of us lifted the 700-pound suit into the C-5. We also grabbed all the hard drives from the computers. It was getting dark so we decided to head home.

Learning to Fly

Chapter 16

We Get Our First Kills

Hunter took the Manta while I took the F-16 and Eli won the rock, paper, scissors game for the F-22. Everyone else got in the C-5 and we headed home.

We decided to stay together this time instead of racing home. That was a good decision. It was about 4:30 p.m. when I saw them. Four dots, flying in formation on my radar. About six miles away and gaining on us fast. They were F-22's, probably loaded with missiles.

"Guys we got issues!" I tensed as I looked behind me, looking for the fighters.

"What?" asked Hunter from the Manta.

"F-22s. Gaining fast!!" I responded, still looking for the fighters.

"Can't we go faster?!" Eli asked.

"Not unless we want to leave behind the C-5," I said. "Let's just see if they make contact. Eli, you got cannons though, right?"

"Yup," Eli responded.

"Good, so do I. Form up behind the C-5. Maintain speed and watch my eyes." I flipped my helmet visor up.

Then over the radio, came the first voice other than my friends I had heard in years. "This is Delta three from the 271st defense squadron. You have a classified military aircraft in your possession. Land immediately or we will fire. Over."

Two F-22's came behind me and the other two came up behind Eli. I looked at Eli, and tried to convey with my eyes that he had to stay calm and maintain course. I put my hand up to calm him down. *You weren't in theater classes for nothing.* I thought to myself. I turned on my mic, "Ohh you have no idea how good it is to hear someone else's voice. It's great. And who is this again? Over."

"The United States 271st defense squadron. This is not a joke. Stand down and land or we will fire over."

"Well, I think that this is above your paygrade son." I tried to sound older than I was. I honestly didn't know what I was doing. I just had to think on the spot. "We are Lion squadron and our job is to transport classified military equipment. So how about you let us do our job and we can all be on our way. Over."

Learning to Fly

"There is no Lion Squadron, over."

"Well, that's because it's classified," I said like it was obvious. "Again, let us do our job, or one of us is going to be in big trouble. Over."

"What is the National Verification Code? Over."

Crap. I thought. I was not ready for this. "We didn't get one," I said halfheartedly. I said it almost like a question. I knew it was over. "Over." I was just praying as hard as I could.

"Every flight gets one. Over."

I tried my best, but convincing air force pilots of a lie is pretty hard. "We didn't because classified missions are different. Over." Then I heard a loud beeping in my cockpit as one of the F-22's locked onto me with a missile lock. "Hey there's no need for that. We're on the same team here, over." My heart started beating faster and I knew that I couldn't finesse my way out of this one. I looked at Eli and made a motion with my hand and he nodded. I held up three fingers on my hand, ready for the countdown. I looked back, the planes were still behind me, almost on the wingtips.

"Land Now. This is your last warning, over." The voice threatened. My heart was going a million miles an hour. I tried to control my breathing. I started counting down. I lowered the number to two. Then I just shook my head and held up one.

I breathed in and out again and made the shooting hand signal. I engaged the airbrake, brought the throttle to idle, and pulled up; right as the F-22's fired. Then I pushed my nose down, increased my throttle, and then pulled the trigger on my stick.

Britton Bean

The entire tail section of the left F-22 came off and the plane started spiraling out of the air. The one on my right escaped and pulled up again to meet me. Eli had taken out one of the other F-22's.

I banked right, evading bullets getting sprayed at me. I dived down and pushed my throttle to the max. Then pulled up before I hit the ground almost fainting from the G's. The F-22 was on my tail.

"Get out of here guys!!" I screamed as I banked left. I looked to my left and saw a lake. "Eli, head to the lake!" I banked right as the F-22 fired more bullets. I heard my aircraft shudder as bullets ripped through the fuselage. Alarms start popping up on my display. Engine temp high, weapons destroyed. I was hit.

"Eli get as close as you can to the water. The water will mess with their targeting system. We can't beat these guys in a dogfight, but we can outsmart them. Go as fast as you can right for me. Then, when I say, kill power, airbrake, full flaps and bank right."

"Ok." Eli strained. I saw his plane right in front of me, getting closer by the second. I saw his helmet in the cockpit. I heard the rush of bullets passing me and heard them tearing through the fuselage. I was getting closer and closer. Then, going Mach 0.91 I screamed, "NOW!!"

I killed power, pulled the airbrake, set flaps to full and pulled my stick as hard as I could to the right. I quickly passed out from the G forces. A sudden explosion woke me up. The

Learning to Fly

explosion of two airplanes colliding. Two F-22s to be exact. I couldn't believe it. My plan worked.

"That was SICK!!" Hunter screamed over his radio.

"Wait– Why are you still here Hunter?" I said, catching my breath.

"I told you" Hunter started, "I wouldn't want to die without you dying next to me. And so, you better believe that I would never leave you. I mean, miss all the action? Never. That's once in a lifetime stuff right there."

"You're an idiot." I smiled. I was secretly glad that Hunter had stayed.

"Britton, we all are." Eli chuckled.

***

Hunter, Eli, and I all landed at Narnia, where the C-5 had made it home safely. After the happy greetings Hunter explained the whole story, with a little exaggeration of course. I didn't intervene. Everyone decided to head home and relax.

We relaxed for four whole days. After all the adventures we had just been on, we just rested and played games. We drag raced with the cars and set up aircraft races and competitions to see who could do the best tricks in the painted F-22.

We also decided to "borrow" two more F-22's from Nellis and use those for dogfights. Eli and I had the best record with Hunter close behind. We would also do doubles dogfights.

Britton Bean

Hunter would always be my wingman, even though Eli was better. I just trusted Hunter more.

Now don't get me wrong, I trusted all these guys with my life. But Hunter and I had something different. We understood each other more than anyone else. Hunter may not be the best pilot, but he was the guy that I knew would never leave me, even if the odds were 200,000 to one.

Those four days were the most productive days of my life. Everyone found an aircraft they loved. Hunter and Eli loved the F-22s because of the speed, I was a fan of the F-16 because of its maneuverability, and everyone else liked the F-35 except Porter. We all agreed that Porter was crazy because, well, he liked the F-102.

We had taken the jet because Porter said it looked cool. It was literally a museum piece. It was on display at Nellis. And sure, maybe it did look cool, but the thing sucked. It had little to no range, hardly any weapons load, and the thing was ancient. Made in the 50s. It was just disgraceful. And it seemed like I always had to repair something on it.

But we finally decided to devise a new plan for the supplies we needed. We all gathered in the War Room that I had made in the research station.

"Alright people, we need a new game plan. Apparently, the USA isn't totally destroyed, but they are definitely weak. We don't even know if they're organized. It could just be a few bases. But they evidently knew that we had *borrowed* the Manta and they sent fighters after us to stop us. I wish we didn't have to fight them, but if they attack us, we have to defend ourselves. Eli, how are we looking on supplies?"

Eli looked at his clipboard, "Well we have a surplus of everything. The estimated number of computers that we got at Nellis was way underestimated. So was the amount of aviation equipment and fuel we got. And we got a crazy amount of information from Area 51. Overall, we don't need any more supplies."

"Well, that's good." I crossed out Cape Canaveral and Houston on the map.

"Except" Eli started, "We need missiles. Nellis only had 20 for some reason and so we expected Area 51 to have more, but they didn't. Area 51 only had the little ones for SAM."

"So, what type of missiles do we have other than the tiny ones?" I asked.

"15 Air to Ground and five Air to Air," Eli responded, looking up from his clipboard.

"I didn't see any when we were unloading the C-5. Where are they?" I asked

"I deemed them too dangerous to carry so I left them at Nellis," Eli answered, looking at a sticky note on his clipboard.

"Alright then, here's the plan, people. We still need to take Hawaii. Or at least one of the islands. If we can, we'll have a checkpoint into the Pacific Ocean. Now we don't know the status of the base. Hunter and I will take the Manta and check it out while you guys are preparing for the attack. We are all going to be flying fighters."

"I call the F-102!!" Porter yelled.

"You are not flying that thing," I said sternly.

"Ohh yes I am." Porter retorted as he stood up.

"You didn't let me finish Porter. Everyone *except you* will be flying a fighter."

"WHAT?!" Porter screamed.

"We need you to fly an aerial refueling plane. We can't make the trip without it. I mean the F-16 might be able to, but the other fighters can't. I'm only asking you to do this because you are the only one with experience with large planes."

"That's so boring though," Porter complained. Then he muttered, "I always have to do the boring stuff."

"You can return with the Manta and you'll be fine. That thing has unlimited range."

"This is dumb," Porter said under his breath.

I pretended not to hear it and continued, "So tomorrow we are going to practice aerial refueling and landing with live ordinance. Tomorrow morning Porter and I will go and get the missiles and the KC-10. We'll also go over the battle plan after Hunter and I scout the area out. Any questions?"

No one said anything, "Good. Let's rock and roll people"

Chapter 17

The Plan

I eased my way up to the hook coming out of the KC-10. We had started aerial refueling testing and now we were pretty good at it. I did have to get a new nozzle after Rockwell went too fast and smashed it. And the F-35 was pretty banged up too. But we got it eventually. We also went and got another F-35 from Nellis for Ezra.

I slowly raised the aircraft's nose and the hose locked in. Then I waited there until I got the go ahead from Porter, "You're good Bean."

"Alright." I slowed my speed and fell back in formation. Porter was still a bit bitter about not flying a fighter, but I knew he would be fine. Next time I could do it.

After everyone landed, I gathered everyone together. "Alright guys, Hunter and I are going to take the Manta and look around at the base. We should be able to outrun anything they throw at us. If they even do throw anything. You guys meet at Nellis with all the supplies. And get some rest, if there's anything to attack, we're leaving at 1:00 a.m. Got it?"

"When should you be back?" Ezra asked.

"I don't know. Before midnight for sure." I responded. "Any more questions?"

No one said anything. "Alright then, let's get to work."

I walked over to Hunter, put my arm around him, and said, "Let's do this Hunter."

"This is a stupid idea, you know," Hunter said.

"Oh, I'm full of stupid ideas, and so are you," I replied, smiling.

"Yeah, but your ideas are stupid, stupid," Hunter said, laughing. I laughed along with him.

"Says the one who decided to click the 'reactor' button." I grinned.

"Hey that worked, didn't it?" Hunter had that smug grin as he slugged me in the arm.

"You know one day you're going to die by pushing a button." I laughed.

Learning to Fly

"Wouldn't that be an interesting way to go." Hunter said in an announcer voice and framing the words in the air with his hands, "Death by Button."

"Dumb ways to die. So many dumb ways to die" I sang.

We just laughed. I climbed in the cockpit of the Manta while Hunter ran around the aircraft making sure everything looked good. He gave me a thumbs up and I started the reactor. I chuckled as I pushed the button. Hunter moved the ladder and climbed on the wing and hopped in. I closed the cockpit and asked, "Ready for another spin?"

"Of course," Hunter replied excitedly. "But this time, I drive."

"You sure? It's going to be a long flight." I said.

"I'm sure," Hunter said confidently.

"Alright."

Hunter pushed the throttle up pushing the aircraft into the air. Then as Hunter pushed the stick forward, the plane started moving faster. We soon were at 80,000 feet where Hunter leveled the plane and set speed to Mach 7, the cruising speed of the Manta.

"I think I'm going to take a nap," I said to Hunter. "Got a big day tomorrow you know. I'll drive on the way back."

"Alright," Hunter responded.

We were over the ocean when Hunter woke me up. "We're here." He said. I looked out the cockpit and all I saw was darkness and crashing waves.

"Where's here?" I said, still tired.

Britton Bean

"Right there." Hunter pointed to the left. I leaned forward and saw lights down below. I took out the cockpit's binoculars and looked at the lights. There were runway lights. I quickly spotted an aircraft next to a large building. It was a fighter aircraft, fully armed and capable. I kept looking and realized there was no movement. No one in the watchtowers or on the ground. No spotlight or anything. Russia had gotten lazy. And why wouldn't they. They were the strongest power in the world. America was done for. Nuked into submission. The second most powerful country was China and they were Russia's allies. No one could take them down, they thought.

"This will be fun," I said under my breath. "They're not even ready. Let's head home, Hunter. And let's get ready to blow these guys up."

***

I landed at Nellis at about 12:15. I was a bit late, but that was okay. One of the guys had turned the runway lights on for me. I'd have to thank whoever did that. I didn't even think about needing that, which scared me a little bit. If I didn't think of the most basic thing, how could I plan an entire attack? I brushed it off. I wished I hadn't.

I woke Hunter up, and we walked towards a hangar where all of our fighters were lined up. We walked in and saw

Learning to Fly

everyone sleeping. I turned on a flashlight and said, "Alright people, it's time."

Everyone gathered in what had been a war room. The room was lit with several LED lanterns we had found. We didn't have time to get the power going. I used a whiteboard and a marker to show the plan.

"Alright, guys, here's the plan. Russia is lazy, and the base is virtually undefended. We will be flying in formation. We will also be coming from the West, making them think we're Russians. They will only see my radar blip because I'm not a stealth aircraft. I mean, they might see Hunter's aircraft because he ruined his stealth coating with the pink and green color job. There are going to be several possibilities. We will do this plan to account for every possibility." I took a deep breath, hoping I was right.

"First, I will attack the radars and communication systems. This will make the Russians unable to communicate with other Russian bases and call for reinforcements. Then everyone else will attack the runway, preventing planes from taking off. Any planes that do manage it, we take out. There are going to be 5th Gen fighters, so pay attention. I will not lose a single person in this battle." A bad feeling crept into my gut, but I ignored it.

"After that, we will destroy any troops or helicopters on the ground. Remember, we only have 15 air-to-ground between us. Do not waste any." I glanced at Hunter. If anyone was going to waste something, it was him. "Then we will move on to the second phase of the mission, the land assault. Using the vertical land capabilities of the F-35, Rockwell and Ezra will land with M-4s and attack any remaining soldiers. The rest of us are here for air support."

I motioned to Porter, "At this time, Porter will be coming at max speed of Mach 7 right towards us to help with the land attack. When we take this base, we will get all kinds of weapons, missiles, and supplies we will need. We will also be making a statement. A statement that no matter what they try, we have the will. We have the strength and we have the determination. Try all they want; they will never…Break. Our. Stride. This is how we do it. So, let's show 'em who's boss."

Everyone cheered. I felt pride. *This is going to work, Bean.* I thought. It had to.

But I had a nagging feeling in my stomach. Something was wrong. Something. I couldn't place it exactly, but something was off. I just bit my lip, and ignored it.

Chapter 18

Something Went Wrong

We were all in our planes. I pulled my hat, Harry, down and Hunter looked over at me from his pink and green F-22, which stuck out like a sore thumb in the dark. He pulled his mic closer to him and said, "That's a stupid hat Britton."

I responded, "You won't be saying that when it's *him* that helps us win." Hunter and I chuckled together.

There we sat. Six planes sitting, waiting on a runway. All of us. About to start a new war. A war against Russia. A war that was clearly one-sided. If there was a time to vote for the underdog, this was it. Outnumbered 200,000 to one. Six humans, fighting against an entire country. The biggest in the world. The country that had overthrown the former strongest nation in the world. The biggest military in the world. The biggest air force. Everything was the biggest. The odds were against us. But they always were. This was nothing new. I don't know if any other group guys would do this.

I figured out why. We were ignorant. We were determined that no matter what the odds, what the numbers said, or what people said, we didn't care. We *knew* we could do it.

"Alrighty boys," I raised my hand like I was holding a glass, "to the people that died, to the people who survived, to families broken, we give this token."

I pushed my throttle as hard as I could, to the max. I once thought, *you could stay where you are, or go full steam ahead.* It was hard to believe that moment was five years ago. I personally liked full steam ahead more. Sometimes I wonder what would have happened, if I hadn't pushed that throttle forward.

***

We refueled 1,600 miles from the California coast and said goodbye to Porter as he turned around.

"Leave me some bad guys, Bean." Porter piped.

"I'll try," I responded, smiling. "Have fun, Porter."

The missiles were divided evenly between all of us. One air to air each and three air to ground each. We flew for another 1,100 miles when I turned the group away from the island to

Learning to Fly

come in from the west. We got our first radio contact from 30 miles out. It was in Russian, so no one understood it. We kept going until we were almost right over them. I broke the radio silence and yelled, "Get 'em boys."

"You got it," Rockwell muttered.

"My pleasure Bean," Eli growled.

"This'll be fun," Ezra said.

"I got one big gun, and Russia is written all over it." Hunter snarled.

We all broke formation and split up. I fired two air to ground missiles at the radio and the communication towers, blowing up both of them. If they didn't know we were here before, they knew now. I saw a few fighters get off the ground. Hunter swooped down and fired his gun at one of them, making it explode.

"That's one!" Hunter counted.

Rockwell fired all AG or air-to-ground missiles at the runway, putting it out of commission. But some fighters had gotten off the ground. Ezra fired his AG missiles at the base and blew up what looked like a barracks. "I count five bogies, not including the one Hunter got," Ezra confirmed.

"Take 'em out." I acknowledged. I saw AA or Anti-Aircraft bullets flying past me. I banked left and got a lock with my missile and fired at an AA, destroying it. "I got AA's. Three, I think. I got one. No missiles left."

"I got 'em," Hunter said as two air-to-ground missiles flew from his wings. I saw two more explosions on the ground.

Then I had a warning in my cockpit. A Russian missile was locking on my position. I banked right, then dove and banked left. I pulled up just before I hit the water. *That was close.* I thought. *Too close.*

"I got one on my six!!" I yelled.

"I got a lock on him," Rockwell said. "Bank left Bean, NOW!" I banked left and saw the fighter behind me blow up just as he was about to fire his missile.

"Nice one," I commented. I turned around and saw Hunter chasing a fighter. The fighter evaded Hunter's movements and got behind him. I increased my speed. Hunter screamed, "I got one on me!!"

"I'm coming Hunter," I said. Hunter kept trying to evade but the fighter matched his every move.

"He's got a tone!" Hunter screamed.

"I'm coming," I muttered under my breath. I closed in on the fighter and fired. My missile flew into the fighter. The plane blew up into a huge fireball. I avoided it and pulled up next to Hunter, "Aren't you glad I had Harry, Hunter?"

"You suck, you know," Hunter muttered. I chuckled.

I banked left and swooped down. I saw Eli out maneuver a fighter and destroy it. Three down. Two to go.

"Got 'em." Eli hooted, "He wasn't very good."

Then I heard a loud beeping in my cockpit and banked hard left. A missile flew right past me. "HOLY!!" I tried evading him but he stuck to me like a bug. "He's on me tight. I need some help over here."

"Where are you?" Ezra asked

"IN THE SKY EZRA, I don't know," I screamed and strained as I banked right to avoid another missile.

"Britton, listen to me," Hunter said calmly. "Fly straight. You got to trust me, Britton."

"Are you insane, Hunter?!! That gives him a clear shot!"

"I know," Hunter said, still calm. "But it gives me a good shot too. You just have to trust me."

I banked left and right and then, while shaking my head. I leveled off and increased my speed. I heard a beeping sound.

"C'mon Hunter. C'mon." I said under my breath. The beeping got faster and faster until there was hardly a break between the beeps. I closed my eyes and gritted my teeth.

BRRRRT!! Bullets tore through the sky.

I heard the roar of an engine as one roared past right behind me. I opened my eyes and pulled up.

"Ladies and Gentlemen, that is two kills!" Hunter cheered.

"Oh my gosh" I exhaled. "I can't believe that just happened."

"I told you to trust me. You didn't think I would leave you out to dry?" Hunter asked. I could almost see the smug grin on his face.

"Now I don't want to interrupt anything but, that's only four." Ezra stated, "Where's the other one?"

"Everyone check your radars, that plane cannot get back to Russian airspace! If it does, our whole operation is blown. We need to take down that plane." I said urgently. I waited for 30 seconds before I said, "Does anyone have anything?"

"I got nothing," Hunter said.

"Nope," Ezra responded.

"Same here." Rockwell agreed.

"I got nothing, Bean," Eli said lastly.

"Alright Rockwell and Ezra, begin the land assault. Eli, provide air support and watch for Porter. He should be within radio transmission any second now. Hunter and I will scout for the plane. The only place that would get him back into controlled airspace is west to China or southwest to Fiji. I'll head for China, Hunter, you head for Fiji."

"Would he not go back to America?" Hunter asked.

"He'd get attacked by the US," I said as I turned my plane west.

Then I heard Porter say, "Alright boys, did you leave a—" Porter cut out, and then, to the east toward America, there was a huge explosion. It was so close to me that I felt my airplane move sideways, almost sending me into the ocean. The light was blinding. I saw wreckage fall to the ground. Molten metal fell into the sea.

Without thinking, I ejected from my plane. I was flung into the air and my parachute deployed, but I didn't care. I unclipped the parachute cords and plunged into the ocean. The water was cold and my legs hurt from hitting the water, but I didn't care. I swam as fast as I could. Pushing my arms as hard as I could.

I searched the wreckage, diving under the water until I ran out of air. All I wanted was to find my friend. All I wanted was Porter. I'd never wanted anything more in my life. I prayed and

Learning to Fly

prayed, hoping that Porter's head would just pop up out of the waves. But it never happened. Porter was gone.

I didn't cry. I just stared, questioning all that I had ever thought. A piece of metal bumped against my leg. I barely looked at it. But something caught my eye. I grabbed the piece of metal. It was a Russian star. The wreckage was not from one plane, but from two. That's when it hit me.

I was wrong. The plane went back to America. But the Manta was so stealthy that the aircraft ran right into it. And it was my fault. I had just assumed that the plane would go west. But why? Why did this happen? What were the chances? And it was all my fault.

I got tired of treading water eventually and swam back to shore. Rockwell was there to greet me. I tried to keep my face calm.

"What was the explosion?" Rockwell asked, almost not wanting to know the answer.

"Porter." I said face straight, "Porter's gone."

"What?" Rockwell gasped.

"He's gone, Rockwell." I choked on a sob, "Gone." I felt a tear crawl down my face. I just shook my head and rubbed my eye with my sleeve. We kept moving and found Ezra. He had all the Russian groups troops in a cell at the base.

"Hey Bean, what was the explosion?" Ezra asked all too innocently.

"Porter," I responded sadly. "They killed him."

Ezra looked stunned. He just looked around in disbelief. I tried to get my mind off of what had just happened. It was hard. I willed myself not to cry. I stumbled through the words, "We need to repair the runway with iron plates so that Hunter and Eli can land. Keep an eye on them. I'll do it." And I walked away. I just walked away. I walked away from Rockwell and Ezra when they needed me most. But I couldn't stay.

I grabbed iron plates that Russians used to repair runways quickly. I laid them over the potholes. I kept thinking about the explosion. It was like a broken CD, it kept repeating and backtracking. I crouched down as I laid another plate over a pothole. As I tried to get back up, I collapsed instead. My legs couldn't hold the weight. I felt my knees on the cold plate. I hung my head. I tried to hold back the tears. My friends needed me. I couldn't be here sobbing. I've got to be the person to bring order to the chaos. I took a deep, shuddering breath and stood up. I kept placing plates on the potholes. After an hour, I finished and walked back inside.

I walked up the Control Tower staircase to get to a shortwave radio. Surprisingly the runway lights were still working. I radioed to Hunter and Eli, "You guys are cleared to land."

"Bean, is Porter down there?" Eli said, alarmed.

I couldn't tell him like this. It wasn't right. I just said, "Land Eli. Land."

Learning to Fly

Chapter 19

The Spark

I laid my head against the cold cement wall feeling miserable. I had never imagined something would happen like this. Everyone was gathered in the base's war room. Ezra had locked the Russians in the kitchen. We just wanted them out of our hair.

The room was deathly silent. Everyone was at the table in chairs except me. I was on the floor under a TV.

I didn't know what to do with myself. I was ashamed. I had been blunt and stupid. I had been an idiot and told my friends to fight for something impossible. What had I been thinking? I was flying planes that regular pilots trained for

Britton Bean

years on, and I had just tried to figure it out with only an eighth-grade education. I didn't know anything about aerodynamics, let alone the ability to take a whole country down! And now I was here, sitting in a Russian base, with my head against a wall, not knowing what to do with myself. I was 19 and was trying to take on an entire country. All I had was five airplanes. I *used* to have six friends. I couldn't believe it. How had I been so stupid?

Hunter got up from his chair like a man on a mission and walked over to me. He sat down next to me and said quietly, "You said they wouldn't go east."

"I did," I answered quietly.

"You say that the two planes collided."

"They did."

"Why would the Manta collide with the Su-57, if the Su-57 was going to Russia. West, not east. And yet, there the Su-57 was. Going east."

"What's your point Hunter?"

"I asked you if they would go east. You said they wouldn't." Hunter shook his head. I thought I saw a tear creep down his eye, "I'm supposed to be the wrong one, not you."

My heart broke. It was shattered. Crushed. There is no word that describes what I felt. My best friend, the person I respected the most, the person who I trusted the most, had just called me out. I felt as if I was going to die. I wanted to die. But I had a job to do. I stood up to walk away when I felt Hunter's hand on my shoulder. He spoke loud enough for everyone to hear,

Learning to Fly

"You know Bean; ugh that feels weird." I chuckled through tears. Hunter really did not like to call me Bean. "I think that motto of yours needs some changing. I think that we should focus on the present, but I also think that we should learn from the past. Don't focus on it, just learn from it. So have you learned from your experiences today?"

I shrugged.

"I think you have. I think you've learned that you're not always right. You've learned that whatever happens, there will be unforeseen problems. But for every unforeseen problem, there's an unforeseen solution."

Hunter looked at me calmly, "And Britton, we need you. We don't know what to do. We don't know what to think. Focus on the present Britton. Learn from the past. You can do it. You're our leader. So be one." Everyone was looking at Hunter.

Then Eli said with a faint smile, "I didn't know you were one for speeches Hunter."

Hunter shrugged and said, "I learned from the best." He nodded at me.

My broken heart stitched itself together. I was glad to be the leader of this group. I stood up and looked across at my friends.

I walked over to the map on the wall. I looked at it for a while gathering my thoughts. I took a deep breath. I didn't know what to do. Turn around and go back, or push forward?

I heard a powerful, yet small whisper in my head. A still, small, voice. Porter's voice, *"What are you waiting for Bean?*

A cook? You don't need me. All you need is you. I'll be waiting for you on the other side. And when you get here, you better have won."

"Will do man. I owe you that much." I whispered quietly. I nodded to myself. I turned around and pointed at the map on the wall and confidently said, "Y'all ever been to Fiji?"

***

Everyone was in their respective planes. All were fully loaded with all the missiles we could fit on them. Hawaii had a surprising amount of rockets in storage.

I was in Ilyushin Il-78, a Russian refueling plane. We made a trail marker in memory of Porter. We would come back someday and create a proper monument. We decided to leave behind the F-16 and one of the F-22s in favor of the longer-range Su-57s. But Hunter insisted he needed his pink and green plane. The Su-57 could get to Fiji without refueling, which would be helpful. We decided to keep the F-35s for the vertical landing capability.

"Does anyone speak Russian?" Eli asked in the Su-57. "Because that would be really helpful right now. I really don't like flipping switches at random."

"I mean, I like doing that." Hunter chimed in.

"He's not wrong." I agreed. "You'll figure it out, Eli."

"Glad I'm not in there," Rockwell said from the F-35.

"Same." Ezra agreed in the other F-35.

"Alright I'm taking off. Follow me if you want." I pushed my throttle forward and the huge plane thundered down the runway. I lifted up into the air. I saw the sun rising in the distance. To think that one day ago the Russians had control of Hawaii. And only one day ago, Porter was alive. I looked toward the wreckage in the sea. I would remember him. Always.

I looked behind me and saw a pink and green F-22 come up beside me.

"Ready?" Hunter asked.

I gulped. I fought off tears as shivers crept down my spine and said, "Always."

After about two hours of flying the F-35's and the F-22 needed to gas up. I deployed my two fueling nozzles and the F-35's approached. I got a green light on my right nozzle and shortly after on the left one. I initiated fueling.

"After this, I'm going to head back and grab a Su-57 from Hawaii," I said. "Fly slowly at about 700 miles per hour so I can catch up. I'll be flying as fast as I can to meet up. I should be able to catch you guys right when you reach the base. If I'm not there yet, Hunter's in charge. It's the same plan as Hawaii. Blow 'em up, land, and go."

"Sounds good," Hunter replied.

After a few more minutes the two F-35's disconnected and flew back into formation. Hunter came up and refueled after them. After he was done, I retracted my nozzles and banked

Britton Bean

left, heading back to Hawaii. All the while thinking of plans for the future. Oh, how those plans would be ruined.

***

I was flying Mach 2 when I saw the blips on my radar. Except this was way too early. But there they were. Four planes, two F-35s, a Su-57, and an F-22. I lowered my speed and banked left toward them. There was a heavy fog, and I could barely see five feet in front of me. When I finally broke through the mist, I saw an island. The island was not Fiji.

It looked blocky with harsh edges and was made of pure sand. It was obviously manmade. There were no trees, or greenery of any kind. Just sand with a runway, a dock, one hanger and a relatively small base. And there they were four planes that I could see on the ground. Our planes. I slowed my speed and prepared to land.

After circling three times to slow my speed and ensuring this wasn't a trap, I landed. I taxied my Su-57 next to the other Su-57. I opened the cockpit and grabbed my M-4. I clicked off the safety.

I stepped onto the wing and then jumped onto the ground with my gun raised. I walked through a hangar with a huge aircraft in it. I think it was a transport plane. I walked past it and into the main portion of the base. I opened the door slowly with my finger poised on the trigger.

Learning to Fly

There was a long hallway that had doors all along the sides. I tried one of them, but it was locked. I wanted to keep quiet, so I kept walking down the hallway, not daring to try another door, fearing it would make too much noise. I came to a large vault door at the end of the hallway. It was open. I walked forward, looking left and right with my gun raised. I didn't see anyone.

I came into a research room of sorts. Computers everywhere. More computers than at Area 51. It was a square room with one door to the left side of the room. I walked towards it and grabbed the doorknob, putting my gun down. I was about to turn the knob when the door burst open, "-going to see if Britton's here yet." A familiar voice said.

"AHH!" I screamed as I fell to the ground, aiming my gun at the door.

"AHH" Hunter screamed. "DON'T SHOOT!!"

I breathed out a sigh and relaxed at the sight of Hunter, "You about gave me a heart attack." I tried to catch my breath.

"You're the one with the gun pointed at my head." Hunter retorted. By this time, everyone was looking down at me. Hunter held out his hand, and I took it. He pulled me up, "You gotta see this. Maybe you know what it is."

"You know, you say that a lot," I said, strapping my gun to my chest. I walked into a small concrete room about 7x7 feet. A small, floating, blue, spinning orb surrounded by metal bracing was on a pedestal, connected by all types of wires. It was about the size of my hand. Four small, rectangular metal plates were attached to the metal frame and extended towards the orb, almost connecting to the spinning orb.

"Woah." I gazed in amazement. "What is it?"

"I asked some of the Russians, but they didn't tell me anything. I don't think they understood me." Rockwell said.

I turned around and asked, "There are Russians here?"

"Yeah, but no guards. I didn't even see a gun," Ezra responded. "It was pretty easy to take this place over."

"That's why we didn't blow it up," Hunter explained. "Ezra landed first and decided to go in first to check the place out. He sure took a while." Hunter glared at Ezra. Ezra just shrugged.

"Hey, I was getting things ready for you guys, alright." Ezra defended.

"You should have just waited for us," Hunter muttered.

I ignored them, "You get this isn't Fiji, right?" I jested. Everyone looked at Eli.

"Hey!" Eli said defensively, "How was I supposed to know that this wasn't Fiji. I've never been there before."

"You thought Fiji was half a mile wide?" I asked incredulously.

"You know what, I think we should get back on topic." Eli nodded

I scoffed, "So where are the scientists?"

"In a locked room down that hallway you came down," Ezra said, pulling a key out of his pocket.

Learning to Fly

"I'm going to see if any of them speak English." I explained, "Want to come, Ezra? Intimidation is key." I looked at Ezra and held out my hand for the key, "Pun unintended."

"Good one." Ezra threw me the key.

Something about Ezra seemed to have changed. I couldn't quite place it. But something was off. I figured it was because of Porter.

I shook my head to clear my thoughts. "See if you can get anything from those computers," I told Rockwell.

"On it." Rockwell gave me a thumbs up.

I walked out with Ezra and we walked out of the vault door and down the hall. I turned back to look at the vault door and asked, "How'd you get the vault open?"

"It was breakfast when we walked in, and one of the guys had a keycard," Ezra said quickly. "I had to punch him in the face because he wouldn't let us have it."

"So, what you're saying is, I brought the right person." I chuckled, looking up at him.

"Yes sir." Ezra said while rolling his "R's"

We walked to the door and I gave the key to Ezra again. I motioned to him and I held up my gun. Ezra hesitated like he was about to protest but then he unlocked the door and opened it.

Inside there were about 30 people, in what looked like a break room, wearing what looked like pajamas. Some were playing cards; others were laying on the floor taking a nap. Everyone looked up when we walked in. The room went deadly quiet.

"Little bit generous, giving them the nicest room, don't you think?" I muttered to Ezra.

"There're still human beings. We are the same species." Ezra argued.

"I wish it were that simple." I turned to the Russians, "Do any of you speak English?" Dead silence. Then I had an idea. I whispered to Ezra, "Watch the faces on the left, I'll watch the right." Then I continued talking to the Russians, "We have decided to give you some food and water." Then I saw it. A man next to a table with cards glanced up. He understood.

He was one of the only ones wearing a lab coat and had glasses on. He was tall, about six feet, and was a little overweight. He had a demeanor about him that made you think he was a genius. I motioned to Ezra and walked over to him. Ezra closed the door and locked it. I went over and pulled up a chair next to him.

"You speak English." I said more as a statement than a question. He looked at me confused like he didn't understand. I continued, "How about this, you translate for us and I won't kill your buddy here." I pointed my gun at a guy holding cards next to him. The guy immediately dropped the cards and put his hands in the air.

Ezra grabbed the muzzle of my gun and pushed it down, "What my friend means, is that we won't give you, or anyone for that matter, food or water until you help us." Ezra looked at me sternly. I glared back at him. I didn't like it when people undermined my plans.

Learning to Fly

The man looked around, clenching his teeth and then said in a thick Russian accent, "Yes, I help, we get base when you leave."

"Yea no." I shut the idea down. We were the ones holding the guns, so we made the negotiations.

Ezra kicked me under the table, "What my friend means to say is that we will send you to a different base. Maybe Fiji, perhaps." I wanted to punch Ezra in the face. He was undermining my whole plan. If they left the island, they would tell the other Russians and destroy my entire project.

The man thought for a moment and answered, "Yes."

"That's great!" Ezra seemed genuinely excited, "What's your name?"

"Dominik."

"Good to meet you Dominik. If you would please follow us this way." Ezra stood up and led the way out.

I was angry. If we let these guys leave, the whole Russian army, navy, and air force would be targeting us. Those Russians could not leave this island. But they also couldn't stay. They would contact the Russian command and alert them also. I really should have thought this through. We needed to go back and regroup at Narnia. This plan and mission was a mistake. But it still frustrated me that Ezra went off book.

Ezra led Dominik into the vault room and walked into the room with the blue orb. Rockwell was looking at the computers but walked over to us when we walked in.

"It's all in Russian." Rockwell whispered to me, "I can't read any of it."

"It's alright." I motioned to Dominik "He speaks English." Rockwell nodded and we walked into the orb room and shut the door. "So, what is it?" I asked Dominik harshly.

Dominik looked at the orb and thought for a moment. "It's a power source. It releases... I don't know word in English... a lot of energy."

"100 megawatts?" Rockwell suggested.

"No, more," Dominik said, trying to think of the word.

"A gigawatt?" Hunter suggested.

"Hunter, this is no time for joking–" I started.

"That's it!" Dominik interrupted.

"Wait seriously?" I was astonished. "That thing can produce a gigawatt of energy? That's how much a nuclear power plant produces! That can't be possible."

"I show you." Dominik opened the door and rushed over to the computers. I ran after him thinking he was running and almost tackled him. But when I saw him next to the computers I stopped. Everyone ran over and looked at what he was doing.

"I head scientist here. I make the Spark." Dominik proclaimed as he was doing something on the computer.

"The Spark?" Eli questioned.

"That it name," Dominik responded. Then he pulled up a graph. The graph showed a line bounce up and down subtly. I heard a humming in the Spark room. I looked in and the blue light was brighter than usual.

I smiled, thinking of the possibilities. But there was one possibility that I was fixed on. SAM. The perfect power source.

"You got any blueprints on this?" I inquired.

Learning to Fly

Dominik pulled up another screen on the computer and showed blueprints of the Spark and footnotes on the side in Russian. I smiled, "I'll take 'em all."

"All of them?" Dominik sounded distraught. "You cannot do that!"

"It's part of the deal, my friend," I said absently. I wasn't really paying attention.

Dominik looked like he didn't know what to say, then he looked at Ezra. Ezra looked flustered and just shrugged. Dominik sighed and whimpered, "Ok fine."

"Thank you. Now do you have a pilot in this place?" Ezra said before I could say anything else.

"Yes." Dominik looked down.

"Alright let's get you to Fiji."

***

We had gathered the hard drives in my plane and were just waiting for Hunter to land after he had escorted the An-124 out of the island's airspace. I was in my plane waiting on the runway for Hunter to get back.

We had done the math and decided that the F-35's could make it to Hawaii with one tank. I waited in my plane, thinking of the possibilities and my new plans for the future. We had given Rockwell the Spark. Dominik had told us it wasn't radioactive, but we weren't sure we believed it, so we put the

Britton Bean

Spark in a radioactive container. It barely fit in the small F-35. But I have a make-it-fit-function.

I heard a knock on the left side of my plane. I looked out and saw Ezra climbing up the side of the aircraft. I opened the cockpit.

"Mind if I join you?" Ezra said.

"I mean, there are two seats for a reason," I grunted, still bitter that Ezra went off book. *Maybe he came to apologize.* I thought optimistically. Ezra climbed in behind me and closed the cockpit.

"Alright Bean, calm down."

"I am calm," I replied defensively and confused. That was a weird way to start off a conversation.

"You stuck a gun in an innocent Russian's face just to get what you want. Doesn't that sound like we're the bad guys?" Ezra questioned.

"It's not that simple Ezra!" I boomed, "Sometimes you need to do hard things to fight hard wars. You don't get it. You're the one that went off book and ruined my whole plan."

"I do get it, Bean. I get that you're mad that the Russians killed Porter. But remember, we attacked them first."

"No no no!" I said quickly. "They deserve this when they nuked the USA!"

"Did the people in that research station pull the trigger Bean? Did they press the button? Bean, fighting is the last resort. That's something that the world needs to understand. Call me soft, call me weak, but Bean, talk first, fight last."

"Yeah, well then what are we fighting for Ezra, huh?"

Learning to Fly

"We're fighting for freedom and liberty. The same thing that our forefathers fought for 300 years ago. We're in almost the exact same situation. Fighting against a force that outnumbers us a 200,000 to one. And yet, they came out on top. They tried to talk it out beforehand. Then, when they knew there was no other way, they fought for what was right. We saw that Russia would not relent. The USA tried to conduct peace talks with Russia back in 2022. They didn't respond. Bean, we are fighting for what is right. But I will not kill anyone who doesn't have to die. And I won't let you either."

I sat there fuming mad. "What about Porter?"

"Britton," Ezra started, using my real name, "Don't make me answer that."

I almost turned around and punched him. Here was Ezra telling me what to do. Telling the man who had led this mission to success what to do. Ezra was the one who had just ruined my plans by sending back the Russians. He just didn't understand. "Get out." Ezra was lucky I didn't turn around and give him a black eye.

Ezra obliged and didn't say a word as he opened the cockpit and climbed out. I started my engines before Ezra was even off the wing. He quickly jumped off and ran to his plane. I pulled down my radio and said indifferently, "Meet at Hawaii."

Then I increased my throttle to the max and took off. I didn't lower my speed until I was ten miles from Hawaii. I liked speed. Speed was comforting. Going Mach 2.5 without a

Britton Bean

care in the world. This was life. I knew where I belonged. The sky.

Learning to Fly

Chapter 20

I Get a New Project

We all stood there in the bunker where we had lived five years ago. The bunker hadn't changed much. It was dustier, I guess. That was about it. There were still bunks unmade, cards laid out on the table, books strewn about on couches. We really weren't the most organized people back then. But we weren't there for that today.

On the ground next to a cairn was a frying pan. A well stained, worn, frying pan. A cook's frying pan. Porter's frying pan. Everyone had brought a flower to lay beside it. I placed my black tulip next to the monument. I felt a tear fall down my face as I stood up while everyone else put down their own flower. But my tears weren't ones of sadness. They were ones of anger. The Russians would regret what they did. They would regret ever launching the invasion of Ukraine which started this whole thing.

After everyone was done, I turned around and walked toward the stairs. I left the staircase and clicked a button on my key. The falcon wing doors of my McLaren rose open. I climbed into the car and turned it on. I turned onto the road and started accelerating fast. I had a job to do. And it wasn't going to do itself.

I drove up to the airport and walked over to Rockwell's F-35. I opened the cockpit and lifted out the radioactive container. I brought the container to the McLaren and threw it into the passenger side of the car.

I drove as fast as I could to Narnia. I pulled into the driveway and shut the car off. I grabbed the container more determined than ever. I walked into the research facility and down into the basement.

There he was. SAM.. We hooked him up to some generators but when we tried to turn him on, the power required overloaded the generators. The cords were still hooked up to him though. I put the container on the table and I took off my sweatshirt. I put Harry on backwards. Time to get to work.

Learning to Fly

Chapter 21

The Spark Actually Works

"Solder," I said from under the suit. I looked at the clock on the wall. It was three in the morning. Rockwell and I had been working on putting the Spark in the suit for months. And Rockwell was exhausted.

At first, we were making great progress. We started researching the Spark and learned it was in fact, not radioactive. We also confirmed that it did produce a huge amount of energy. We hooked it up to the main power line and it powered the house no problem. Then we hooked it up to all of Narnia. It handled that as well. After studying the blueprints

Britton Bean

(with a little help of a Russian dictionary), we learned how it was producing electricity.

There were four insanely powerful magnets all repelling each other. They were connected by brackets made of the strongest material in the known universe. Graphene.

In doing this it pushed all the energy into a spinning, spherical orb. We did calculations and the magnets would run out of their power in 2190. But that's what didn't make sense. Energy had to go somewhere.

But the Spark didn't have any fancy storage components. It just continuously released energy. So, our main question was where is all that energy going. After two weeks of experiments, we learned of what we called the Rockwell Particle.

This particle basically absorbed radiation. Earth naturally has radiation on the ground, in the air, and in the sea. We decided to test the limits of this particle. We conducted what we call, The Nuke Experiment.

Rockwell and I walked out to the blast zone of the nuke. We had radioactive suits on along with Geiger Counters. We walked out to the middle of the blast zone and then set down the radioactive container. I pointed my Geiger Counter at the ground. The counter read 150 CPM. Extremely high radiation. Regular levels were 15 CPM.

"Ready?" I asked Rockwell.

"Ready," Rockwell answered, holding onto a stopwatch. The stopwatch would be left here. We couldn't take anything back. We only would take back the Spark because of its Rockwell Particles.

Learning to Fly

    I took the lid off the container and picked up the Spark. Rockwell started the stopwatch. I set the Spark on the ground and held my Geiger Counter up. The number steadily decreased. 140…120…80. It started going faster and faster. Absorbing radiation faster and faster. Then the Counter read 0. I motioned to Rockwell. I heard the stopwatch beep.

    "30 seconds." Rockwell gawked at the Spark, amazed. "That's amazing!"

    "That's insane!" I pointed the Geiger Counter around the area. I pointed it at Rockwell. He read 0. I pointed it at myself. Same result. "This'll be fun."

    After the experiment we started to try to import the Spark into the suit. I took the back of the suit off looking for where that super battery would have gone. I found it quickly. It was a large indentation into the back of the suit. There were wire holes where the super battery would have been connected. I chained the suit to a gurney and lifted it so I was laying down under the back side.

    Rockwell did a deep dive analysis and drew up some plans for where the Spark would go. I thought that it should go in the front where it would be visible and intimidating, but Rockwell said that was just stupid. He said that would be the worst spot to put it because it was most vulnerable there. I still thought it would be cooler in the front. Rockwell decided just to put it where the super battery was supposed to be.

    I started working on it. It took two weeks of working nonstop until I finally got all the wires hooked up. I had to rewire almost the entire motherboard along with sensors and multiple systems. I finally finished and I started by testing power output.

We had wires connected to the suit measuring the output of the system. I was outside the suit watching for issues. Rockwell and the others were in a side room with a panel of glass watching over the procedure.

I checked the suit over again and then I gave the go ahead to switch on the system. Rockwell gave a thumbs up and the suit started booting up. There was a loud humming and it kept getting louder and louder. Then the entire suit started shaking violently. I backed up as there was a loud crash as Rockwell killed the power. The suit stopped moving and quieted down. There was smoke coming out of the back. That was never a good thing.

I moved the gurney and laid down on a rolling cart. I grabbed my drill and undrilled the back and took it off. Smoke enveloped me. After a big coughing fit, I saw the damage. Luckily, the Spark looked fine. That was the only good thing. All the wires connecting to it were destroyed. I about swore. I stood up and threw my drill on the ground. A month of work, gone in an instant.

I was thinking about that as an exhausted Rockwell knocked a hammer onto the ground where I was. "Wrong one," I said.

I heard Rockwell grunt and he knocked off the soldering iron and I caught it. I moved it into position and soldered another wire. It was a painstaking task. Every wire had to be repaired. I had to import a device so the power wouldn't blow

Learning to Fly

up the suit again. You don't really find many things that are *too* powerful.

  I must have fallen asleep because when I opened my eyes, I forgot where I was and jerked up, hitting my head on the suit. "Ow!!" I exclaimed.

  I laid my head back on the cart and looked at a clock on the wall. 9:33 a.m. I grunted as I pulled myself out from under the suit. I stood up holding my head. I could already feel a bump forming. I kicked the cart back under the suit. Rockwell must have gone to bed, because he wasn't there now.

  I walked up stairs and grabbed an ice pack from the freezer. I pushed it against the bump forming on my head. I heard a helicopter chopping outside. Hunter, Eli, and Ezra were already up, probably doing mock fights again.

  While Rockwell and I were working on the suit, the rest of the guys were learning how to fly helicopters. They would do mock landings and takeoffs. They would even do invasions of buildings. They even played a prank on Rockwell and I one time when they "stormed" our research station. That gave me a run for my money.

  They had got the helicopters from up north at Hill Air Force Base. They were Black Hawks. Eli was the first person to figure out how it worked. They stayed up North for a few weeks. They never found anyone there.

  And let me tell you, it was great. Sometimes a person needs a break from their friends. Some alone time. But they came back right before we did the first power test on SAM.

Britton Bean

I had flown with them once. They reminded me of Marines. They were so efficient and quick. They cleared an entire apartment complex in under five minutes. They would throw ropes down to the ground, then whoever wasn't flying, would repel down the ropes.

Usually, this was Hunter and Ezra, but sometimes it was Eli and Hunter. Hunter knew how to fly the Black Hawks but never wanted to. After they landed, they would waste no time and run into the building, guns raised.

Whoever was flying would land the helicopter or provide air support. Eli said they wouldn't want to land first because there might be people on the ground. That's why Hunter and Ezra would go down first. To clear the way, I suppose. After the helicopter landed, the pilot would shut off everything and follow them. It was insane. I was thoroughly impressed.

I walked outside and looked up and saw a helicopter move towards the blast zone. Except this wasn't a Black Hawk. It was an Apache attack helicopter that had several air-to-ground missiles connected to the hardpoints. It took me a minute to realize that they were real missiles. *Don't do it.* I thought.

Eli must have read my mind because I saw his helicopter point its nose down and fire two missiles. There was a huge explosion as the helicopter pulled up. I watched as the hotel Eli had shot at came crumbling down. I shook my head and sighed. Eli sure knew how to cause some damage. I turned and walked toward the main house.

Learning to Fly

It was April. The end of winter in St. George. It was pretty chilly outside that day. It had been half a year since Porter had passed. But the feeling was still just as raw. I sighed thinking about Porter. I missed him. That good ol' smiling face. I wished he was here.

I walked in and went upstairs to Rockwell's room. I walked in. Rockwell had decorated his room unlike a lot of us. The room was one of the smallest but was still decently big compared to regular house bedrooms. After all this was a mansion.

His room was filled with shelves. All full to the brim with books. It was like its own mini library. There was a bed in the far-left corner and a dresser at the foot of it. I turned the lights on and off. "Today's test day Rockwell. You can't sleep through it." Rockwell just grunted and rolled over. He pulled the blanket over his eyes. I left the room with the lights on and walked down stairs to make some breakfast.

***

"Drill." I reached my hand out from under the suit. Rockwell handed me the drill. One of my hands held the back of the suit while the other screwed on the back. Then I grabbed the screw covers. I placed one over each screw until I heard a click. This made the suit look seamless. I pushed myself from under the suit. "Ready?" I asked Rockwell.

Britton Bean

Rockwell smiled, "I'll get the others." Rockwell came back a few minutes later with Ezra, Hunter, and Eli.

"You sure this will work this time Bean?" Eli said sarcastically.

"I will punch someone if it doesn't," I grunted.

Ezra put his hand on my shoulder, "It'll work, buddy, don't worry."

"I really hope so, Ezy." I looked at the suit longingly.

Rockwell motioned for everyone to enter the observation room. Everyone filed into the room except me. I took a deep breath and gave Rockwell a thumbs up. Rockwell returned it, and I heard a loud humming as the Spark went online.

This was it. If the humming got louder and didn't die down, my plan would have failed. If it died down and kept a steady humming, the suit was online and ready.

The humming grew louder. My heart was thumping in my chest. Butterflies in my stomach were battering at their cage. And then came the wonderful sound. The sound of steady humming. I looked at the observation room, and Rockwell smiled and gave me a double thumbs up. I saw him say *He did it*, and everyone went crazy.

They were clapping and cheering. Of course, I couldn't hear them because of the soundproof room, but it still filled me with joy. Joy, I hadn't felt in a long time. And then they burst out of the room, cheering and screaming. I smiled the biggest smile one could, and I cheered along with them.

I had done it. I had done something that the US government couldn't. I had finished what they had started. All I

Learning to Fly

needed to do now was finish a much bigger project that the US had started. War.

Britton Bean

Chapter 22

SAM Flies

I took the suit out for a test drive after Rockwell completed the diagnostics. I stepped into the suit and the platform rose up. I put my hands in the arm holes and the suit made a clicking sound. Then I heard SAM, "Welcome back sir."

"How do you like the new power source SAM?" I grinned.

"Very nice, sir," SAM said in his monotone voice.

"Let's take this bad boy out for a spin, shall we?"

"Gathering GPS systems. Please wait for the system to boot up."

I saw the eyepiece slide into position along with the headset. The suit tightened around me, along with the tiny micro needle sticks. I really hated those.

"System on. Suit flight capable." SAM said.

Learning to Fly

"Perfect." I chuckled. I was looking forward to this. I walked up the stairs. It was a little awkward, but still worked. I had to duck to prevent hitting the roof of the stairs. They weren't designed for a seven-foot robot. I stepped outside. I looked up and took a deep breath. *Here goes nothing.* I thought.

"SAM, engage thrusters."

"Yes, sir," SAM responded. I felt power pushing against the ground. Then I was in the air. Speeding higher and higher. A flight stabilizer system came on my HUD. I moved my arms to lay flat. I was flying at 764 miles per hour. I felt like a rocket. It was way more fun than the F-16. I felt like I was the airplane. Like I could do anything.

The suit had insane maneuverability and could take tight turns with ease. The only limitation was the pilot. I could only take so many G's. Other than that, the suit had infinite maneuverability.

I flew around for another hour until I finally came down. I landed SAM next to the research base. I walked out and it felt weird. I wasn't as tall now. I wished I was back in there, but I had a mission to attend to. I now had our most powerful weapon. It was time to use it.

***

Britton Bean

I stood in the war room with a map of the world pulled up behind me. I was facing everyone sitting in their own seats. One seat was empty. It was Porter's. I nodded to it solemnly. I wished he was here. I wanted him to see what we had accomplished. Who we were now. We were like a military unit. I took a deep breath and began my plan.

"Here's the plan. We can't hold bases. There is just no way. We don't have enough manpower. But we can prevent them from being utilized." I turned on the projector and a map came on. I pointed at the map with a meter stick.

"First we attack mainland Russia." I pointed to Russia. "We have to capitalize on every advantage we have. We are mobile. We can move faster than the entire Russian military. So, this is what we do."

I took a deep breath. I looked around the room. Everyone was watching intently. I continued with confidence. "First, we attack Nagurskoye and then, when the Russians at Nagurskoye call in support, we'll blow the place to smithereens. I call it 'Go, Reload, and Blow.' We go into the base, reload our aircraft and weapons, then blow it up. If we can't hold it, no one can. This will also demoralize the people. Russia will have to move their troops to other bases and reorganize."

I pointed at what had been Ukraine with my meter stick, "That's when we move over to the Eastern Front. We'll make Russia think that the USA and Europe are fighting them. They'll think that they're being attacked on two fronts. This will divide their forces."

I saw Hunter nod his head with approval, "Then we lead a bombing raid, taking out industries along with Moscow. We'll destroy their way of making new forces then we'll take out the forces in the surrounding areas. They will never know how many people they are actually fighting."

With confidence building, I continued, "Then we lead a bombing raid on remaining forces, and when there is no way to defend their nation, we bomb every square inch. Everything will be destroyed. They will have to surrender." I ended, out of breath.

"You sure this will work?" Ezra asked.

"It will." I nodded confidently.

"That sounds a bit crazy to me, Bean," Ezra argued. "I mean how are we even supposed to take an entire base?"

Hunter answered before I could say anything, "What do you think we've been practicing? You think that was for fun? We were training for this exact mission."

"I guess," Ezra responded, still not so sure. "What I mean is: we are fragile. One bullet kills us."

"That's where SAM comes in," I explained. "SAM can go down there, with or without someone in him, and clear the way for us."

"It should work," Rockwell confirmed, definitely calculating something in his head.

"Are we sure we even have all the supplies we need for the bombing of an entire nation?" Ezra asked.

"He's got you there Bean." Eli looked at his clipboard. "We don't have enough bombs to blow even five bases to bits."

"How about C-4?" I asked, knowing I had him.

"Well…" Eli started, then looked at his clipboard, surprised and then continued, "So we have enough C-4, but we would still need bombs to drop on Russia. I mean we could barely succeed in the first bombing raid of the industrial factories. We just don't have enough."

Rockwell came in, almost like a whisper, like he was sharing a big secret "There is this theory." Everyone turned to him and he continued, "On the hard drives we received, there was a theory that if two Spark's energy collided it would release a huge amount of energy. An amount estimated to be five times the Tsar Bomba."

"The Nuke?" Hunter asked.

"The biggest one in the world," I answered in awe.

"We don't even know how to make a Spark." Ezra broke in. "Let alone blow two of them up."

"Actually, we do." Rockwell corrected. "And we have the supplies. It's all laid out in the blueprints we stole. It's actually relatively easy."

"What supplies are we thinking?" Eli asked.

"All of it's at Area 51. The USA was actually looking into the same technology with the super battery. They just didn't have the Rockwell Particle." Rockwell responded. "So, all the supplies are at Area 51. It's just Graphene and high-power magnets, along with some Rockwell Particles. We can get those from the existing Spark. Although that will make the original Spark a little less powerful, but not by much."

"Are you sure this will work?" Ezra repeated.

Learning to Fly

I smiled and looked at Rockwell, "Positive."

Chapter 23

We Blow Stuff Up

"Careful. Careful." Rockwell whispered harshly.

And he had a right to be. I held a very hard to extract Rockwell Particles in an enclosed iron clamp. I walked carefully to the new Spark frame. And then with a twist of my hand, I opened the clamp as a light blue combination of half liquid, half gas rushed into the frame. The magnets seemed to grab hold of the substance and it formed into a spinning, spherical shape.

Then a bright light emitted from the center. Rockwell rushed over to the computer and smiled.

"It worked!" He exclaimed.

"Let's go!" I cheered.

"Alright, time to make more." Rockwell smiled. He was definitely enjoying this. I think he'd gotten bored of being the doctor.

After three more days of working on making more Sparks we had 203. This was the target goal that we were aiming for. Rockwell then started to make a plan on how he would test the destructiveness of the bombs. Or how he would even make them into bombs.

I, on the other hand, started working with SAM and getting to know more about him. This is when Hunter, Ezra, and Eli, who were now calling themselves Lion Team Six, approached me on the landing procedure.

"Britton, we need you." Hunter had told me when I was eating lunch. He was in full body armor along with a M-4 slung over his shoulder. I almost didn't recognize him.

"Nice uniform. Why do you need me?" I asked.

"Training exercises. We need you for the landing operation. We also need SAM."

"Alright," I said, tossing my plate into the sink. "Give me a second." I walked to my room to change into the new clothing I had made. It was a meshy, stretchy, bodysuit. It made it so that the suit could read my movements better. It also meant I didn't need to endure those nasty micro needles. Did I mention I hated those? They were restrictive and they hurt. Now all I had to do was just put the meshy suit under my normal clothes. But due to the holes created in my clothing when I "suited up" I added a feature that would automatically stitch the clothes back together after I walked out of the suit. It simply kept that material on the needles, and then pulled it back into place when I walked out.

I walked back downstairs and clicked the back of my watch twice. This was yet another system I had created which sent a signal to SAM to start up and come directly to me. Within ten seconds, I saw the suit flying around the corner and it landed right in front of me. The back opened up and I climbed in. I rose up on the platform. Everything tightened up around me in a matter of seconds. Soon I was in the air and flying to the airport where the Apache was. Or as we called it – Big Kitty.

I saw all of Lion Team 6 sitting next to it waiting for me. I came in for landing and landed in front of them. The headset and eyepiece came off me. Then I said, "AR Hand."

As I stepped out, a foldable M-4 rifle made its way into my hand. A leather jacket also folded out over me. I had programmed that as well. Sure, the jacket may have been a bit much, but it felt really cool. Everyone stood up as I walked out. Ezra and Eli were also in full body armor with M-4's.

"So, what are we doing today?" I asked.

"Live Landings," Eli said.

"Everything is going to be live Britton," Hunter added. "We're going to blow a building up too. And we've got real ammo in these weapons."

"I suspected that." I nodded unfaced. "So, what do you want me to do?"

"What you'll do when we land for real," Ezra said.

Learning to Fly

"Alright," I responded. "Let's do this then."

I stepped back into the suit. The suit automatically took my gun and jacket. I walked with the suit into the helicopter. Everyone else filled in. Eli looked back to make sure everyone was in and started the engine. The blades above me began to move. I reached my hand up and grabbed the bar.

The helicopter soon took off. Everyone put on headsets. The suit automatically dimmed the sound of the rotors. That's what was so great about the suit. It had so many quality-of-life upgrades.

We were soon over the ruins of St. George. It was the edge of the blast radius, so the damage wasn't as bad. Hunter pointed out the building we were aiming for.

It was a relatively big strip mall. I counted 15 stores. There was a highway bridge to the north that had collapsed. The mall had a big parking lot with several abandoned cars littered around that had seen better days.

"You drop down and clear the way," Hunter shouted over the chopping of the blades.

"Do you want me to actually fire?" I asked loudly as I checked my suit for missiles and made sure everything was working.

"Sure. We'll wait 20 seconds before we rope down. Just imagine there are bad guys there. Eli will come in and blow up surrounding 'troops' and buildings," Hunter explained.

"Alrighty," I responded, readying myself.

"Sir, would you like to try the catching ability now?" SAM cut in.

Britton Bean

The what? I thought.

"The catching ability sir." SAM said, "You can jump out and I'll catch you. All you have to do is spread your arms and I'll align myself to catch you sir. Springs will cushion your fall sir."

Not going to lie, it was still creepy for SAM to be able to read my thoughts. I sighed, "Let's try it. You better catch me SAM."

"Will do, sir," SAM replied.

The back of the suit opened up and I stepped out. "No jacket." I wasn't taking chances. I didn't want the suit to have to work too hard. I wanted SAM to catch me. This would not be how I died.

When I was out of the suit, I plugged my ears. Hunter handed me a headset. I mouthed thanks to him. SAM soon jumped out of the helicopter and flew next to us. After about three more minutes of flying, we arrived in the drop zone.

"Alright Bean. Your turn." Eli glanced back.

I walked up to the edge and looked over. That was a mistake.

"Any last words Britton?" Hunter asked, a little too happy. It took me a second to realize what was happening.

I turned around but it was too late, "Hunter no-" And then, with a huge smile on his face, he pushed me out of the helicopter. Now I know how Hunter felt. And I realized that I deserved more than just a slap.

I started falling backwards and doing flips. I started panicking, which really didn't help my cause. I kept falling

Learning to Fly

faster and faster. My heart was in my throat. I couldn't breathe. I forced air out of my lungs and started quickly inhaling and exhaling. I began to think clearly. I realized my only hope of survival was SAM.

I spread my arms like a bird, doing exactly what SAM had told me. I also straighten my legs. This stopped me from spinning. I looked straight up at the helicopter. I saw Hunter looking over the edge. I swear I saw him smiling. I also could hear Eli yelling at Hunter. But I knew Hunter didn't care.

I flipped myself over into a belly facing down position. And just in time too. I was closing in on SAM fast. I saw the suit making tiny adjustments. Then the back opened up. I clenched my teeth and closed my eyes waiting for the pain of hitting the suit at terminal velocity. But I didn't feel that pain. Instead, it felt like jumping into a foam pit.

I opened my eyes to see the familiar blueish heads-up display. Soon I felt everything tighten around me and the headset fall on my head. The eyepiece followed quickly after.

I laughed. Laughing that I was still alive. And that Hunter had pushed me out of a helicopter. I quickly heard myself saying, "Oh my gosh. Oh my gosh. Oh my gosh." I took a deep breath, "I'm still alive, oh, I'm still alive." But I wasn't out of the woods yet.

A big red warning came up on my display. *Pull Up! Ground Contact!* I felt my eyes go wide, "Shoot!" I hadn't realized I was still falling. I engaged my boosters and started pulling up when I felt my left foot hit the ground. A big red warning came up on my display *Contact! Contact!* Luckily, I was able to pull out.

I slowed down and leveled out. I looked back up at the helicopter. Big Kitty was hovering over the drop zone. I was at least a mile from the intended drop zone. I hadn't realized the suit was going that fast. I turned and flew over to the initial drop zone.

I landed and thought of an AR. There was a quick shuffling sound as the weapon appeared in my hand. All the suit really did was quickly move the folded AR from under the suit into my hand and unfold it. It just did it all in a quarter of a second. I started firing like a madman at imaginary troops all around me.

Soon I saw ropes hit the ground right next to me. Ezra and Hunter zoomed down. They landed and were like completely different people. They wore faces of pure determination. They knew exactly what to do and how to do it. They each shot five times at the windows of cars and both split up into buildings to plant C-4. I decided that I could look cool too.

I flew into a Chinese restaurant feet first, destroying the front of the shop. I thought of C-4 and it popped out in my left hand. I planted one under a table and another in the kitchen.

I heard explosions outside as Eli went ham on the parking lot and a side gas station. There was a deafening explosion as the gas station blew. Not Eli's best move.

I repeated the same thing I had done at the restaurant for the next three buildings, minus smashing through the front windows. I thought I was going really fast, but apparently, I

Learning to Fly

was slow because Hunter and Ezra both did six stores in the time, I did three. This all happened in a matter of minutes.

Soon Eli landed the helicopter and Ezra and Hunter jumped in. I engaged thrusters and flew into the air. After flying up for a while I lowered my power so that I was hovering to wait for the helicopter. The helicopter slowly raised into the air towards me.

As the helicopter rose, an explosion rocked the area. The entire strip mall erupted into a fireball. Hunter had pushed the button. The aircraft started turning toward home. I flew down to meet them. I passed on the helicopter's right, lowering my speed to match the helicopter.

Once I was at their level, I tried something. I hadn't done anything risky in a while and I had to keep the people on their toes.

I banked left. Hard. I flew right through the open sliding door. I flattened myself like a board. I flew right in between Ezra and Hunter, then through the other side of the helicopter. And I did something I hadn't done for a long time. I laughed. A real laugh. I hadn't laughed like that since before Porter died. And I smiled.

I activated my airbrake to decelerate and go back to the helicopter. I looked over at the helicopter and saw Ezra and Hunter against the walls of the helicopter, still stunned. I laughed again, then said over the radio, "Gotta keep you guys on your toes."

Then Eli came on laughing harder than I'd ever heard, "Ahh Bean you got them good." He laughed harder, "You just came in like *NEERRROOO*. And then they just jumped back against the wall. Ahh, that was a good one Bean."

I smiled and threatened, "You're next Eli."

"Wait, what?"

I just laughed and didn't say anything else.

"Bean, whatever you're going to do, you don't need to do it. I'll give you 20 dollars." Eli negotiated.

"You're going to give me a worthless piece of paper?" I shook my head, "What a deal!"

"Man, shut up," Eli said.

I smiled and accelerated, leaving the helicopter behind. And I felt happy. Truly happy.

Chapter 24

A Big Bomb

"Are you sure we are far enough away?" Ezra asked.

"We are," Rockwell assured him.

Everyone was 110 miles from Area 51 on a hill looking over it. You couldn't even see Area 51 from where we were. Rockwell had a box with a button connected to a cord. We'd run a cable all the way to Area 51 using the Black Hawk.

The cord ran inside, down to a bulletproof, 30 inch thick, steel room. The wire ran into an electric drill that hovered over a button. When a signal was sent through the cord, it activated the drill which pushed the button. That would trigger the Sparks. The Spark bombs. This was it. We were about to test that theory of Rockwell's. We were only going to be doing this once, so we wanted the activation device to be creative.

The Sparks were in a nuke proof room. A room that could hold the USA's strongest bomb. Twenty feet of pure steel surrounding the bombs. But we took extra precautions and moved everything of value off the base. And we decided that we should go 110 miles away, just to be sure.

"The question we should be asking:" Hunter said, "How big will the explosion be?"

"Big." I turned to him. "You won't be disappointed." I liked playing with Hunter. There wouldn't be an explosion. The blast would be contained. We just wanted to see if the Rockwell Particles would be contained as well.

"Yeah…" Hunter trailed off excited.

I looked back at Rockwell who was doing his final preparations. He held a Geiger Counter taking the radiation levels. He took notes in a notebook and then put the device away.

"Why are you taking the levels here?" I inquired.

"I took the levels every ten miles. I just figured I should do it here." Rockwell answered sitting down on the rocks.

"Wouldn't they just be normal?" Eli asked.

"Yeah, but it's still good to check," Rockwell explained.

"Are we going to go or just sit here?" Hunter asked impatiently.

"I agree with Hunter on that one." I nodded.

"Alright, alright," Rockwell said as he picked up the remote. "Ready?"

Learning to Fly

"Can I click it?" Hunter asked, almost like a child, "Pleeeeease?"

"Fine." Rockwell relented.

Hunter ran over, excited. He took the remote and smiled eagerly, almost evilly. And then he started to bring his pointer finger down when Rockwell yelled, "WAIT!"

Hunter groaned, "What?!"

"Do you want to burst your eardrums? And do you want to have eyes after this?" Rockwell reached into a backpack, taking out protective headphones and glasses. We all grabbed them and put them on. I heard Hunter faintly ask, "Can I go now?" Rockwell nodded and Hunter turned so that he was looking at the base. Then he clicked the button.

Nothing happened. We waited a few seconds and Hunter clicked it again. We waited another few seconds. I laughed and grinned. Ahh, it was fun to play with Hunter. Hunter looked like he groaned and brought his head back looking towards the sky. I looked back at the building, still grinning. That's when it happened.

The biggest fireball I have ever seen in my life exploded from the base. Even in movies. Never in my imagination had I thought of this. The fireball flew upward growing into the good old mushroom cloud that we all know. Physics at its finest.

And the blast was blinding, even with the protective glasses on. I looked away and closed my eyes. Even then, it was crazy bright. The mushroom cloud looked like it was in space. And it might have been. The thing was huge. The base was gone. I couldn't see the top of the mushroom cloud anymore. All I could see was fire in the sky. It looked like the world was ending.

Holy! I thought, *this is quite the sight to behold! Wait, how did it escape the nuke-proof room?*

Suddenly a loud sound ripped through the air, tearing me out of my thoughts. Luckily the headphones that Rockwell had given us held strong. But it felt like my body was a bean in a shaking can. The sound made the ground shake like an earthquake. It felt like you were on a balance beam on a boat in a hurricane. I got on my hands and knees. That's when I saw the shockwave.

There was what looked like a wave of air destroying everything in sight. Bushes, small trees, nothing was safe from it. And it wasn't slowing down. It was coming right for us. Everyone else saw it too.

I saw Eli point to an outcropping, and we all ran to it. We hid behind it just in time as the shockwave flew past us. Rocks and debris, I saw an entire tree fly past us.

Then everything quieted down. Rockwell peeked out and then looked up. He took his headphones off and then stood up all the way. Everyone else followed. The fireball was still in the air, getting even bigger. Everyone kinda just looked up and stared, speechless. I took off the glasses cautiously and just stared. I still couldn't believe it. The fireball was huge. There are no words that describe how big the fireball was.

We stood there for a minute until Ezra thought leaving might be a good idea. We all agreed and turned around to head back to where the helicopter was. I realized that the helicopter might not be there. I ran to where Eli had landed it. By some stroke of luck, Eli had landed the helicopter on the bottom of the cliff, shielding it from much damage.

The helicopter was covered in shrubs and bushes, but there didn't seem to be any major damage to the Big Kitty. I breathed out a sigh of relief. It would have been a long walk home.

"C'mon guys, I need to get above that cloud to see how high it goes," Rockwell said, running past me down the hill. I followed right after him. I hopped in the pilot's seat.

"You know how to fly a helicopter?" Eli asked as he jumped into the co-pilot's seat.

"I mean, it's just like an airplane, right." I turned on the rotors. The bushes and debris started flying off.

"No, it is nothing like a plane Bean," Eli yelled over the roar of the engines. Hunter and Ezra arrived as well and jumped in.

"Well, there's only one way to learn," I shouted. The helicopter started lifting up in the air. I pushed the joystick forward, pushing the helicopter forward. I almost hit the ground and pulled back. I felt my tail hit the ground. "Too much. Too much" I strained to keep the aircraft under control.

I let the helicopter rise more. I moved the joystick to the left and swerved to get out from under the cliff face. Then I moved the joystick forward and headed home, luckily away from the fireball.

I sighed, "First try!"

"Yeah, right." Eli scoffed, "You haven't even landed yet."

Britton Bean

"Maybe I'll have you do that then," I said.

"What?" Hunter said, astonished, "Britton's not doing something risky? Who are you, and what have you done with Britton?"

"Ahh, I'm just joking. Of course, I'm landing this thing." I grinned at Hunter.

"Good." Hunter sighed, "We might have had to torture you to get the information on where you hid the *real* Britton."

"You? Torture me? Nahhh." I smiled, looking back.

"Eyes ahead, Bean!" Eli yelled at me.

I turned around and smiled. We flew for half an hour until we reached home.

I approached the airfield and looked for the best place to land. I decided on a place in between two of the main hangers. I lowered the power and started to descend. Eli came up next to the co-pilot's seat.

"Nice and easy, Bean," Eli muttered.

"I got it," I said, concentrating.

"Where are you landing?"

"Over there."

"Wow, that helps,"

"In between the hangers."

"Alright," Eli said, skeptical.

I slowly lowered the power of the helicopter. I kept circling the area. Then I finally touched down. It was a skid at first, just one of the gears, then all the gears landed and came to a stop. I let out my breath that I hadn't realized I was holding.

"I did it," I said to Eli.

Learning to Fly

"Somehow." Eli scoffed.

As I turned off the engine, I chucked, "You can have it next time."

Eli didn't say anything, but I think he was a little jealous that I landed it on the first try. I could tell he was mad that I was so good on my first. I would be too.

I climbed out and saw Rockwell looking impatient. The fireball was still in the sky. You could see the flames from here. Pretty clearly, too.

"We need to get up there," Rockwell muttered as I walked out. Ezra and Hunter were already working on refueling the helicopter.

I bit my lip and said, "We could take an F-22. It'll be fast, and it *might* reach above the cloud. I just don't know how high the F-22 can go. That information was classified."

"Could it work?" Rockwell asked.

I thought for a while. Thinking of all the possibilities. My only problem was how high the F-22 could go. I just didn't know. All I knew was that it was higher than 50,000 feet. And that cloud could be 100,000 feet up. Man, I wish we had the Manta. Then I remembered something. My favorite plane of all time. The SR-71. One of the fastest planes ever. It could fly 85,000 feet up.

The SR-71 Blackbird was a USA spy plane made during the Cold War. America needed a new way to spy on Russia after one of their U-2's got shot down. Something fast and something that could fly higher than anything. This was the

Britton Bean

SR-71. With a top speed of Mach 3.4, the jet was only declassified in the 1990s.

"We can't take the F-22, but we can take the SR-71," I told Rockwell.

"Where are we going to find a working one?" Rockwell challenged.

I grinned, "Good old Hill Aerospace Museum."

Learning to Fly

Chapter 25

I Make a Dream Come True

We flew an F-22 to Salt Lake City, Utah as fast as possible. I also checked the service ceiling of the aircraft as well. The engines started to sputter at about 65,000 feet. So, we weren't using the F-22 to get to the cloud. We landed at the runway next to the museum. We brought the C-4 just in case. We had to bust a plane out of the museum after all. We walked into the hangar inside the museum.

It was a big building that held all kinds of airplanes. There were F-16s, F-18s, and even some helicopters. But we weren't here for that. We were here for the main attraction. In the middle stood the SR-71. I climbed up onto the wing and helped

Rockwell up. I walked towards the cockpit and lifted the canopy up.

To my surprise, everything was still there. Good old 60's tech. There were so many switches and levers. There were two back-to-back seats, the front one having a control stick. Now time to bust this plane out of here.

I jumped back down to the ground and searched for restraining cables. There were three. One at the nose and two at the wing tips. And these things were pure steal. Not something that you just cut through with a switchblade. I followed the cables to the ceiling. We would have to disconnect the cable.

I walked over to where the cables reached the plane. They were connected by a welded loop. I couldn't break the loop without damaging the plane itself.

I had an idea. I looked at the cables and then back the loop. Then at the ceiling. It was a risk, but it might just work. And it might be the only way.

I returned to Rockwell, "I need a tape measure and some C-4." I told him.

"Why?" Rockwell asked.

"You'll see," I explained. "I need you too. You'll also need a tape measure."

"Alright." Rockwell shrugged, willing to do anything if it meant getting in the air ASAP.

After finding some tape measures in a toolbox, I took some C-4 and went outside.

"Where are you going?" Rockwell asked.

Learning to Fly

"The roof." I unclipped my radio from my vest. "Channel two." I switched my radio channel.

"Okay," Rockwell said, changing his.

I walked outside and found the roof access ladder. I climbed up the ladder to the roof. I stood up there for a second, looking to the south. The cloud was still there. This was surprising because we were nearly 500 miles away from it. I wondered if Russia had seen the flash.

I turned on my radio, "Go to the edge of the building and measure how far it is away from the first wire."

"On it," Rockwell responded. After a minute, he came back on, "85 feet and seven inches."

"How far in?" I asked, measuring the same thing on the roof.

"78 feet exactly."

I measured it out again and came to the point. I held the end with my finger and retracted the tape measure. I set the C-4 on the point and connected it to my detonator. I ran away from the C-4 and towards the roof's edge. I crouched down, turning my back to the C-4.

I said into my radio, "Stay away from the hooks." Then I plugged my ears with my hands and hit the button with my knee.

There was an explosion and a ringing in my ears. I turned around to see smoke billowing into the air. Then I saw the hole in the roof. I ran over and looked over the edge. The cable was lying on the ground with Rockwell in the far-left corner next to an F-18. He was not expecting the explosion. I grinned. This was fun.

But I had work to do. I identified the other two cables and estimated where they were to plant more C-4 at their locations.

After two more explosions, the Blackbird was free. But some of the roof had collapsed onto the plane. I just shrugged it off. I climbed back down the ladder and into the museum. Rockwell met me as I walked in. "You just dropped the roof on the plane!!" Rockwell gestured to the plaster covering the plane.

"Don't worry. It'll be fine. It's made of titanium; plus, it wasn't even that much." I explained, brushing off his worry. "And anyway, I need you to go grab a fuel truck. I need JP-7 jet fuel. It's made for supersonic jets. They should have some stored for the Ravens if they ever landed here."

Rockwell exhaled heavily, "Fine." Rockwell then turned around and jogged out of the museum towards the main base.

I walked over to the SR-71. It sure was a beast. I just hoped the thing would turn on. I surveyed the aircraft, looking for any problems. There were some scratches on the top from the roof falling, but other than that, it looked good. I climbed onto the wing and went into the cockpit. I slid myself in and looked around.

The aircraft sure had that 60's look. It had dials and switches on almost every available surface. I had no idea what any of them did. I found the start engine, the gear, the flaps, and the airbrake. There must have been 200 switches, at least.

Learning to Fly

In planes today, almost all of this was done with onboard computers. And this stuff was *advanced* for the '60s.

After a few minutes of looking over the controls, I saw Rockwell walk in. I saw him and nodded, climbing out. "Did you find it?" I asked him.

"Yup." Rockwell said, "Only one issue: how are we going to get this guy out of the building? It's not like we can just squeeze it through the door."

"Oh c'mon, Rockwell." I started with a smirk, "That should be an easy one. C-4, of course." I jumped off the plane and grabbed the C-4 on the ground. I then walked towards the door. I stuck the C-4 to the door on my way out, "You coming, Rocky?"

"Yeah, yeah." Rockwell groaned as he ran after me. I could see him rolling his eyes.

After we were at a safe distance, I plugged my ears and clicked the button. After the explosion, I stood up and looked at the building. Only there wasn't one. Just a lot of dust. My eyes went wide, and I said, almost in a whisper, "Whoops."

But as the dust cleared, there sat the SR-71. Completely fine. I guess the roof falling earlier saved it from most of the damage. "Oh look, it's just fine." I motioned to the plane cheerfully.

I looked at Rockwell. He just stood there, gawking at the remains of the building. Then he turned to me and said, "You know, Bean, one day, that luck of yours is going to run out."

I laughed, "I'm telling you," I pulled my hat down, "It's Harry." I turned back to the museum, "C'mon, we're losing daylight." I started jogging to the aircraft. Rockwell ran toward the gas truck.

I climbed through the rubble and to the Blackbird. I started to clear the way for the Blackbird to get through. Rockwell drove the truck over and helped me push aside some debris. Finally, we created a path for the plane. Rockwell drove the truck over and fueled up the tanks. I ran around the aircraft pulling the pins and releasing blockers below the wheels. Rockwell finished fueling the airplane and drove the truck out of the way. I hopped in the cockpit and looked at the controls again.

There seemed to be hundreds of switches. In the F-22, there were like 15. I was glad I wasn't a pilot in the '60s. I think I'll stick to my computers. In the '60s, computers were only in Star Trek. I took a deep breath and started booting up the aircraft.

Rockwell climbed in behind me, closed the cockpit, and threw me an oxygen mask from the F-22. "Ouch!" I shouted, unprepared as it hit me in the face. "What do we need these for?"

"You can't breathe at 85,000 feet, Bean," Rockwell said, matter of fact.

"Oh yeah," I muttered. "I forgot about that."

"Umm, Bean." Looking over the cockpit's edge, Rockwell said, "Is there supposed to be fuel leaking out of the plane?"

"I'm sure it's fine." I looked over to check. Black liquid dripped out from the fuselage. "Eh, it's fine." I waved my hand

Learning to Fly

to dismiss it. I was too occupied with turning on this piece of junk.

I flipped the start engine switch. I heard it coughing, and then it died. I tried again. The engine coughed and died. I tried again, but this time I gave it a little gas. This time it coughed, stuttered, and coughed again, then died.

"Bean, I don't think this is going to work," Rockwell said from behind me.

"Yeah, I know." I groaned as I flipped the switch a fourth time. This time I pushed the throttle to the max. The engine surged to life. I quickly grabbed the throttle and brought it back to idle. The engine leveled off.

"Wow, it worked." Rockwell gaped, surprised.

"I knew it would," I assured him.

"You did not."

"Sure, I did, I was just–" I thought for a second, "Matching the mood of pessimism you had." I knew Rockwell was rolling his eyes behind me.

But I didn't care. I was living my dream. My dream that one day, I would fly an SR-71. I looked forward with butterflies in my stomach. I increased the throttle, and the plane started moving. I tested my rudder and my other mechanics. Everything looked good. I turned the aircraft past the rubble and headed to the runway. I turned on the runway and stopped.

The butterflies in my stomach were trying to escape. Some people say everything seems to slow down when something exciting happens. That didn't happen to me. It felt like everything sped up. It seemed like my arm was working by some other force. It was like my brain had imagined this so many times it had no problem doing it now. Suddenly my hand moved forward. There was a loud humming as the engines accelerated. I clicked the oxygen mask on. Then, without thinking about it, my hand naturally pulled back on the stick. And with that, a dream came true.

A dream that I thought wasn't possible. A dream that never should have happened. A dream that wouldn't have happened if not for the world I chose. If I didn't choose to walk out of the bunker. If I didn't choose to jump out of that plane. If I didn't choose to make a satellite. If I didn't choose to fight back. If I didn't choose to go to Area 51. If I didn't choose to keep going after Porter died. If I didn't choose to make that suit functional. If I didn't choose to make more Sparks.

What would have been? Where would I be? Where would I be if there wasn't a war? Would I be an expert pilot? All of these things came to pass because of one person's choice. Five years ago, I would have stopped the nuke if I could. But now? I'm not sure. You could say it was inevitable. The tensions weren't lessening. And if the Russians had the Spark, it could have been way worse. More people killed. More treasures lost. So maybe it wasn't so bad.

Little did I know how quickly that opinion would change.

***

Learning to Fly

After 30 minutes of flying, we arrived above the cloud. It was 72,000 feet up. It had been three hours since we first exploded it. It was quite the sight. If you looked down, all you could see was gray smoke and ash. It looked like the ground.

"So, why'd we come up here?" I said through the radio in my mask.

"For..." Rockwell hesitated. "Science."

"Really?" I was skeptical. Why would Rockwell have to come all the way up here? It didn't make sense. He could have had all the measurements he needed from the ground.

Rockwell sighed, "I really didn't have to come up here. This was for you."

"What?" I asked, annoyed. I didn't like being lied to.

"Let me explain." Rockwell started. "Ezra told me that you needed something fun but wouldn't do it unless someone needed something. I knew your dream of flying the Blackbird. So, I thought if I lied that I had to go up here, you would have some fun for once."

"I am a fun person!" I said defensively.

"Bean–"

I cut him off, "You guys are trying to make me sound like someone I am not!" I screamed. I was mad. I felt used. I wanted to punch something. Instead, I pulled on the stick. Hard.

The entire aircraft went sideways. I felt 10 G's pushing against me. That amount was the most I had ever pulled. Above the limit a human should be able to endure.

Britton Bean

I leveled out and punched the throttle up. I felt the aircraft accelerate forward. I flew past the cloud and pushed my stick forward, putting the plane into a nosedive. My altimeter needle started spinning. My speedometer reached Mach 3.3. I heard the entire aircraft shaking, threatening to implode from the G's. I kept it like that until I was at 25,000 feet. I was breathing hard and pulled my oxygen mask off. I turned off my radio. And I looked out.

And I cried. I was mad. I was angry. I was annoyed. I felt used. I felt sad. I felt misunderstood. I felt as if no one cared about our mission. No one understood. Then I was mad at myself. Mad that I was crying. And that made me cry harder. I was mad that I made Porter fly the KC-10. I was mad that I was selfish. I was mad that I only did things that made me happy. And then the walls started to come down.

This was the first time I'd allowed myself to think about it. Really think about it. I missed my brother. The man that was my example. I missed my mom. The person that kept me alive. The person that taught me everything I knew. I missed my sister. The sister that would always want to play a game. I hardly ever said yes. Oh, how I wanted to say yes now. And I missed my dad. The one who would comfort me when I was sad. And I missed them. I said it. I missed my family. My friends. I thought of the moment the building collapsed on Kai. That haunting moment. His hand reaching out. I felt chills race down my spine. The moment kept replaying in my head over and over again.

Learning to Fly

Eventually, I turned the plane east toward home. I forced my breath to slow and my tears to subside. I felt drained. I felt exhausted. Like I had just run five miles. I just wanted to go home. I landed at St. George and taxied the SR-71 into a hanger. I was still mad at Rockwell and didn't say anything as I opened the cockpit and jumped out. Rockwell had the sense to not say anything, either. I walked over to one of the many extra cars at the airport.

It was an Aston Martin DB11, convertible style. I jumped over the door and started the car. I put the car into gear and sped out of the airport parking lot. I turned the car onto the paved road that took me to the city, leaving the airport behind. I wanted to blow something up. I pounded my fist on the dash. I sighed and rested my head back on the headrest.

I had so many thoughts. They all seemed to be jumbled together. I thought of my plan to take out Russia while getting mad at Porter for not seeing that plane. Nothing made sense.

That's when it happened. I heard a plane. A propeller, not a jet. Not one of ours. I looked up and saw it. A huge silver aircraft. About the size of a C-5 cargo plane. Except this one had propellers instead of jet engines.

I slammed on the brakes and put the car in park. I stood up on the seats. I looked up through the sun. I pulled my hat down to shield the sun. That's when I saw the guns. And a Russian Star on its fuselage. It was a Russian gunship. Heading straight for us.

Chapter 26

Russia Strikes Back

I jumped back into the driver's seat and slammed the car in reverse. I quickly drifted around and put the car in drive. I floored it, and the car shot forward. I quickly rushed into the airport and slammed the brakes next to the F-16. I jumped over the door and ran toward the F-16. I made sure the fighter had Air to Air missiles on it.

I pulled the pins on all the missiles, and soon I was in the cockpit turning on the aircraft. I accelerated the plane forward. I taxied to the runway faster than I had ever done. I was in the air in a matter of seconds.

Learning to Fly

I flew to intercept the gunship. I was flying right for it. I was at eye level with the plane in minutes. I turned on my radio, "This is Lion Squadron of St. George, Utah. Turn around, or I will fir-" I never got the chance to finish the sentence.

The gunship fired a round of shots right at me. I banked right, but it was too late. The rounds shredded through my left wing. I started to spiral. Alarms were blaring all around me. I struggled to get the F-16 under control. I felt a tug as the left wing came away from the plane. I couldn't save it. I ejected.

I turned around to see the gunship still heading toward the airport. If it got there, it would destroy all of our planes and supplies. I was helpless. I couldn't do anything. I couldn't warn anyone. I wouldn't even reach the ground before the airport was blown to bits. I struggled to find something to do. That's when I remembered SAM.

I tapped twice on the bottom of my watch. I unclipped from the parachute. I started to freefall. I saw the suit come around Narnia at max speed.

The suit reached me at what must have been 2,000 feet. (When you're in planes long enough, you begin to know how high you are). I spread my arms, and the suit caught me. Before I was fully in the suit, I put my hand at my sides and shot up.

"Give me the headset SAM," I said urgently. The headset and eyepiece fell down as my targeting system went live.

"Notify Narnia. We got problems. Russia is attacking." I said quickly. I wasn't even sure if SAM would pick that up.

"On it, sir." SAM's voice said to me.

"Give me a lock on that plane." I closed my left eye to look through the eyepiece. The crosshairs hovered over the plane as I got closer. Then the crosshairs turned red, and a loud tone came on.

"Fire!" I yelled. Two missiles flew out of my shoulders. Flares shot out of the plane, destroying one of the missiles. But the other one hit true. The back fuselage exploded. But that stubborn plane would not go down.

I saw the guns on the bottom turn to face me. They knew I was here now. They started shooting round after round at me. I flew to evade the bullets, turning this way and that. I came up on the plane's right side and landed on the wing. I ran over to the body of the aircraft.

I thought of machine guns, which appeared in both hands. I fired them at the joints where the right wing met the aircraft's body. But the armor was too strong. So, I fired a rocket at the edge of the wing. The end of the right-wing exploded as the entire aircraft started to spiral.

I put my guns away. I punched hard into the metal. The metal dented. I punched again. This time my right hand broke through. The plane started spinning. I was about to be horizontal when I made a gun appear in my right hand. The aircraft was now upside down. Luckily the weapon kept me from falling. I hung there, suspended in the air. I took a deep breath and readied myself. This would not feel good. I engaged my thrusters and drove my head through the metal.

I crashed into the interior of the plane. I grabbed a pipe to keep from getting pulled out. The aircraft kept spinning,

Learning to Fly

making me feel sick. I soon found myself walking on the ceiling, then I was on the floor again seconds later. I slowly made my way through the aircraft's hull to the cockpit.

I finally reached the door and pulled it off its hinges. Three men were in the cockpit, struggling to keep the aircraft alive. They all looked at me when I walked in.

One of them had the smarts to pull a gun on me. He pulled out a sidearm and shot twice. I felt my shoulder rock back at the force. I grabbed his arm and the weapon. I crushed the muzzle of the gun as he pulled the trigger. The gun and the man's arm shook violently. The man screamed in pain and dropped the weapon. I punched him in the face, knocking him out.

The other pilots had turned around now, too, abandoning the plane. They pulled their sidearms too. I was about to reach for them when a giant explosion hit the plane's left. I flew against the right wall of the cockpit. I could hear the blaring warnings. I could make out one of them. The missile locking alarm. Through the cockpit glass, I saw an Apache helicopter cross my vision. It was getting into position to fire another rocket at the plane.

The two men got up from the blast and shot at me. One of the bullets flew right past my ear. That's when I knew it was time to go. I ducked the oncoming bullets and pulled out my own gun. A Desert Eagle .50 cal. I shot twice at the cockpit glass behind the men, breaking it.

The men ducked the oncoming bullets. I jumped towards the window as the men came up. I hit them both in the face with my legs as I powered through the glass. As I did, I saw bullets come flying through. The Apache's cannon bullets. I heard the *BRRRRRT* that came along with it. I engaged my thrusters and shot up.

The entire cockpit blew up as I did. Then the rest of the plane. The blast knocked me off balance, and I struggled to adjust. I fired thrusters, and the onboard computer was also trying to correct itself. I pushed my thrusters to the max and heard a hum inside the suit. I powered up, dodging the falling remains of the plane. I finally got out and into the open. I let out a huge breath of relief.

"That was quite the fight, sir," SAM said.

"Yes." I said in between breaths, "It was."

I stayed up for a while, catching my breath and slowing my heart rate. We had issues. We had waited too long. We hadn't done anything, so Russia did it first. I just didn't get how they got the plane past the coastline. And how did they find us? And why was it only one plane? Why weren't there escorts? Nothing they did made sense. I took a deep breath and sighed.

"Why would they send only one plane, SAM?" I asked, frustrated.

"Maybe they wanted to test your abilities, sir." The monotone voice sounded.

I shook my head. "Maybe. But that doesn't explain how they got past the California coastline. From my understanding, what's left of the US military is on that coastline. We were American aircraft which meant they didn't attack us. But why

Learning to Fly

wouldn't they attack the Russian plane, especially if it was the only one?"

"You were transmitting an American code, right?"

I didn't know what SAM was getting at. I decided to indulge him, "Yeah. So?"

"Well, sir, is it possible that-"

A message started beeping on my screen. It was from Narnia. "Hold that thought, SAM." I read the message. They wanted me back at Narnia. I sighed. "I think it's time we attack again, SAM."

I knew we were running out of time. Russia would attack again, no doubt about that. I just didn't want them to attack Narnia.

"I think that is a great idea, sir," SAM said. I almost thought I could hear a proud tone in the voice. But it was probably just my imagination. I turned on my thrusters and headed toward Narnia. I completely forgot what SAM was about to say on how the Russians got past the coastline.

Chapter 27

Our New Plan

I found everyone in the main house at Narnia. I walked out of the suit, massaging my skin from the micro-needling I had endured. I hadn't been wearing the mesh underlayer at the time, so the experience had not felt good. If I haven't said it enough, I really hate those. I walked in the back door and was greeted with cheers.

I was surprised, "Huh?"

"We thought we killed you." Hunter put his arm around me. Then quieter, Hunter whispered, "It was Ezra's fault if you ask me."

"I heard that!" Ezra shouted while drinking a glass of water at the dinner table.

"Well, it was!" Hunter retorted.

"While this argument is great and all," I interrupted. "We've got a lot of work to do. Russia attacked us, so we have got to get going with our campaign. Everyone, War Room. Now."

Everyone shuffled outside to get to the research building. On the way out, Ezra stopped me. "Are you sure you know what you're doing, Bean?"

"I do." I said harshly, "I don't need you telling me what to do. So don't try and send up your twin to do the dirty work for you." I turned and continued walking towards the research building.

"Bean, you know–" Ezra started angrily.

"Don't even try Ezra!" I turned around angrily, "Just go to the War Room."

At the time, I thought I was being completely fair. But my relationship with Ezra was never the same.

***

"Alright, peeps. Here's the deal. They attacked us. That means they know where we live, and that means they will attack again." I started. I was at the front of the room, again describing what we wanted to do.

Hunter raised his hand, "I have a question: why would they attack us with only one plane?"

"My current theory is that they were searching for where we were. The gunship found us. And it probably would have kept going if we didn't send up a plane." I said. "You can blame me for that one."

"So where are we going first? And when?" Eli asked eagerly.

"I've got images from the satellites we have up there. The best base to go to right now: Nagurskoye. The Russian Arctic base. So, get some Parkas; it's going to be cold." I pulled satellite images of the base up on the screen. "We leave for it tomorrow morning. Get some sleep."

Learning to Fly

Chapter 28

I Get Rick-Rolled by a Robot

"Why is it so cold?" Hunter complained, rubbing his hands together in an F-35.

We were at an abandoned airfield in Alaska. Luckily you could basically land anywhere in Alaska. There was a lot of hard snow on the ground. We were refueling our jets and the helicopter we brought with us. The helicopter was annoying. The Apache had little range, and we had to refuel it several times along the route.

"Oh, don't complain, Hunter." Rockwell groaned from below him. "You're not the one fueling up the jets." Rockwell took the tube out of Hunter's jet and turned to me, "Good to go, Bean."

Britton Bean

I didn't say anything. I was still mad at him. I was outside the suit with the wind and snow blowing hard and biting my face. I looked west toward Nagurskoye. I took a deep breath and held it. I bit my tongue inside my mouth. I just wanted this battle to go better than the last one. I just wanted it to work. I would not lose another friend. Not today. Never again.

I was broken out of my thoughts by Hunter, "Britton! Let's go!" He said, shivering in his seat. "I'm freezing!"

I turned to him and yelled over the wind, "Alright! Rockwell is in the F-35, and everyone else is in the helicopter. Remember the plan, Rockwell!" I said the last part a little harsher than intended.

"Finally!" Hunter muttered as he jumped out of the plane. He ran over to the helicopter in his big winter combat uniform. I walked over to the helicopter, SAM followed behind me. I grabbed a bar and swung myself into the helicopter.

"Wingman mode," I said to SAM.

"Yes, sir," SAM answered.

"Who's such a Big Kitty? You are. Yes. You are." Eli whispered from the pilot seat of the helicopter.

"Eli, are you talking to a helicopter?" Ezra asked.

"Bean does it with his hat. Why can't I do it?" Eli responded defensively.

"I don't talk to it like that," I murmured. I pulled Harry down.

"I'll admit, Britton, it's hard to deny the luck you have. Maybe that hat does have something to do with it." Hunter said, with his hands in his pockets.

Learning to Fly

"I'm telling you, it's the hat." I turned to him. "It's not even that cold, Hunter."

"Yes, it is!" Hunter responded defensively. "I've lived in a hot place my whole life. I am not conditioned for this type of cold."

"Oh my gosh." I rolled my eyes. Then I thought, *Conditioned. I didn't know Hunter knew that word.*

Eli turned on the engines, and I put on the headset and sat on the cold bench. Hunter came and sat down next to me. We started hovering and moving west. SAM engaged his thrusters and started to follow us. Eli saluted to Rockwell, and he saluted back. We started heading west. I could feel Hunter start shivering harder as we started moving faster.

Hunter turned to me, "You know, I think I like St. George better." I snickered.

We waited in silence for another 30 minutes until Eli yelled back, "Ten miles, Bean!"

"Got it," I responded. I tapped twice on the bottom of my watch and stood up. The suit landed on the helicopter and opened up. I stepped in. The suit took off my coat. The suit locked around me and tightened. I tested my fingers, as heaters started to warm me. Then I heard the music. *Surfin' U.S.A* by The Beach Boys.

"What the?" I said, surprised.

"I thought you would like it, sir."

"Not the greatest song choice SAM," I murmured.

The song skipped, and *More Than a Feeling* by Boston came on. "Nope, SAM. I don't need love songs."

Britton Bean

The song skipped again, and then came *Never Gonna Give You Up* by Rick Astley.

"SAM!"

The song quickly skipped. Then came on *(I Just) Died in Your Arms* by Cutting Crew.

"You know what, SAM, next song you play, we're keeping, alright? Please play something good." The song skipped.

Finally, *Crazy Train* by Ozzy Osbourne came on. SAM really did like his 80's. It made me think of the last time I'd heard an 80s song. When I was 14, lined up on a freeway, about to do a drag race in crazy sports cars. Times had definitely changed since then.

"You know what, SAM. This ain't too bad. At least you have some good songs downloaded."

"Yes, sir, I do," SAM said as he switched the sound to external speakers.

"What are you doing, Bean?" Eli asked as he looked back.

"Bro, what is this garbage?" Ezra muttered.

"Don't blame me." I started, "Blame SAM." I jumped out of the helicopter and accelerated towards Nagurskoye with the song blasting. When Nagurskoye came into view, I readied my targeting system. Within minutes I saw an Anti-Aircraft gun swerve to meet me. They knew I was coming. I fired a missile at the AA gun as I did a flyby at Mach 1. The AA gun exploded.

I saw soldiers on the ground raising their guns to point at me. Perfect. Then I saw a Ground to Air missile system start to activate. It turned in my direction and fired one missile. The missile powered towards me.

Right before it got to me, I engaged my right thrusters in a quick burst and evaded the missile. As it flew by, I grabbed the rocket and redirected it back to the ground-to-air missiles. The entire machine exploded. I popped out my missiles and fired them at the ground around me.

Then a helicopter came in, guns blazing. I stole a glimpse at Eli. He was screaming as bullets flew out of guns under his helicopter. Two air-to-ground missiles flew out from the helicopter's hard points. Soldiers on the ground flew all over the place. Eli started hovering around the center area of the base. I flew over to where Eli wanted to land.

I landed, pulled out two machine guns, and squeezed the triggers. I spun around in a circle to clear the area. I felt bullets hit me, rattling the armor, and I could feel bruises forming. I switched to M-4 and shot at anyone shooting at me. Which was basically everyone. I saw ropes land next to me. Shortly after came Ezra and Hunter. They came down on either side of me, shooting their guns beside me. I covered them as they ran towards the base. Eli retracted the ropes and helped with air support. Hunter ran toward the base door and kicked it down.

"Clear!" He yelled as he looked around with his gun. Ezra and Hunter had done this many times, but the only difference this time: it was for real. I placed a charge on the door frame as we entered. The charges were already connected to a detonator.

We entered a circular room with tables set up in rows. It was a mess hall/living room. There were couches in one area, along with a foosball table. There was even a poker table with cards neatly lined up. To the west, there was a rectangular serving counter. That wall was the only non-curved wall that I could see. You could see a kitchen with stoves, burners, and freezers through the hole. It reminded me of my school cafeteria.

Hunter motioned with his hand, and Ezra and I split up. SAM shut the music off as I headed down a hallway to the north with my M-4 raised. I crept down the hallway, placing a charge at the entrance. I reached a door on my left and kicked it open, gun raised.

Inside, it looked like a motel room. Two bunk beds were in one corner, each able to sleep three, with drawers under the bunks. Beside the beds, there was a small table with some paper and a pen, and a small space heater under the table. There was a closet on the other side of the room.

I bent down to open one of the drawers under the bunks. Just clothes. I checked the desk drawer. Just some paper and some pens. I walked over to the closet. I opened it and saw an AK-47 hanging up on the wall. There were more slots, but they were all empty except for one. There were grenades and even a utility belt with a flashlight, a bludgeon, and a knife. Some of the grenades and one of the utility belts were taken. On the ground were three boxes of rifle ammo—1,000 apiece. Only one of them was opened.

"That's a lot of ammo," I mumbled, gawking at the boxes. I grabbed a grenade. I tried to see if they would fit into the suit. A red box showed up on my display. *Storing Bay Full.* I sighed. Guess I would have to carry it by hand. I stepped out of the room when I got blasted by a spray of bullets.

I fell to the ground and rolled back into the room. A warning flashed on my display, *Armor Damaged,* with a diagram of my right leg. I could feel the bruises forming there too. I clenched my teeth through the pain. Then I grabbed the grenade and pulled the pin. I threw the grenade out the door. I turned my head away from the door as the grenade exploded. I leveled my M-4 and took a deep breath, preparing myself for the hits of the bullets.

I quickly stepped out of the room, keeping low. Smoke in the air from the grenade made it hard to see. I switched my visuals to thermals, trying to find the bodies. I saw several pairs of hands and heads poking out the doors farther down the hallway. I counted one on the right side and two on the left. There could be more.

I was about to raise my gun when I heard a rattling as a grenade rolled by my feet. I stared at it for less than a second before I moved. I lunged down to grab it. As I did, bullets started flying at me. I slid to the ground, ducking under the shells. I grabbed the grenade with my left hand, tossed it to my right hand, and threw it hard down the hallway towards the shots. The grenade exploded as soon as it left my right hand, knocking me back hard.

I flew across the hallway, hitting the right wall. I groaned in pain. Alarms started appearing on my display. I sighed and got back up. Ignoring the pain and harnessing the adrenaline rush, I shot down the hallway using my thermal to see where they were. The Russians ducked back into the room. I took out a missile and fired it at the left door. Then I flattened myself against the floor, putting my M-4 away while coming down.

There was a huge explosion on the left door. The rocket had completely destroyed the hallway along with the left room. There was fire and debris all over the ground. Snow started falling through the huge gap in the building. A 20-foot section of the roof had been blown open. I didn't waste time looking at the damage.

I ran full speed with my Desert Eagle pistol drawn. I slowed down and looked into the left room, or what should have been the left room. There was just open air with snow pouring in.

I switched off the thermal vision and turned around. As I did, I felt two powerful shots fired at my belly area. The force knocked the wind out of me. I doubled over on the ground. Alarms started going off like crazy on my display. I looked up to see a man in full black gear.

There wasn't a single piece of skin showing. He was holding a huge black pistol. It was way bigger than a .50 cal. He looked like a hitman. He held the gun to my head. Then he said in a strong Russian accent, "You move, you die."

I scoffed with the little air I had. Then I said between breaths, "No...You."

A shot rang out as Hunter shot a single bullet down the hallway, hitting the man square in his right shoulder. The man pulled the trigger on his gun but was knocked off balance. A bullet whizzed inches from my right ear. Before the man could

Learning to Fly

regain his balance, I grabbed his pistol and crushed the muzzle. I pulled myself up while pulling the gun down, slamming his head into my knee. The man crumpled to the ground. Hunter ran over to catch up with me.

"You could've shot sooner, you know." I sat up, still trying to regain my breath.

"Ahh, I wanted to see if he really would shoot you," Hunter said sarcastically.

"Dude, my body hurts so much all over." I groaned, stretching. "So how are we looking C-4 wise?"

"Once again, I have to pick up your slack." Hunter rolled his eyes. "Mannn, you had one job." Hunter jogged down the hallway.

"Oh, shut it. You didn't have to deal with all this." I shouted after him.

"I can't hear you!" Hunter yelled back. "But those sound-like excuses. And you know what I say about excuses. There're like buttholes: No one likes them, No one wants to talk about them, and…" Hunter said, waiting for me to finish.

"They all stink," I grumbled.

"Precisely. Now are you going to help me or not?"

"I'm coming," I mumbled as I jogged the hallway to catch up with Hunter. I started to wonder where that man had come from. He sure didn't look like any regular Russian soldier. His voice seemed a little familiar, but I couldn't place it. I shrugged it off.

Chapter 29

Rockwell Does the Impossible

"We got issues Bean," Ezra said urgently.

I looked at his head. There was a bandage over his right eye and was holding his arm. "What the heck happened to you?"

"I ran into some trouble, okay," Ezra explained quickly.

We all met up in the cafeteria/main room after arming all the C-4, the base was ready to be blown to bits. My suit armor was severely damaged. I could feel bruises all over me and was sure I had some bruised ribs. Not only that, but I was out of all

Learning to Fly

missiles and low on M-4 ammo. Even some of my flight systems were compromised. Overall, I'd been better.

"What's wrong?" I asked, expecting the worst.

"Four Su-57s. Coming in fast. Five miles out. Be here in a matter of seconds." Ezra said quickly.

"Are you sure?" Hunter asked.

"I watched the man radio for help," Ezra assured.

"You just sat there, watching him?!?!" Hunter asked incredulously.

"I had just walked into the room, okay." Ezra defended.

I sighed, annoyed with all these problems. Couldn't things just work out as planned for once? I did kinda plan on this, but not *that* many aircrafts. I thought there would be one or two. Rockwell was our air support but wasn't good enough to take on four planes at once. No one could do that. And what's worse: I couldn't help him. My flight systems were compromised.

"SAM, how are we looking?" I said to SAM.

"Armor compromised, sir. Flight system issues."

"Tell me something I don't know," I said harshly. I took a deep breath and calmed myself down. "Can I fly?"

"Not for long, sir. Quick maneuvering is impossible. The suit is not combat-ready, sir."

I grunted. It was more of a yell. Just as I did, Eli jogged in. "Bean! Rockwell is closing in!"

This was not part of the plan. Rockwell wasn't our best pilot. But he was the only one who was in the air. The helicopter had air-to-air missiles, but the helicopter would just be a sitting duck against 5th-generation fighters. But what other choice did we have? We had to get out of here.

"Bean, what are we going to do?" Ezra asked, bringing me out of my thoughts. I looked down at everyone. They were all looking at me to know what to do. I had to think of an answer. That's what leaders were for, wasn't it? Improvise, adapt, overcome.

I looked at everyone confidently, "We do something called a tactical retreat. The plan: we blow the base, get in the Kitty, and go. We just have to hope, pray, and believe that Rockwell can escort us out." I hoped my fake confidence convinced them. I was scared out of my wits. Rockwell needed to pull through.

"So, let's go!" I ushered everyone out. They all started running out of the base towards the helicopter. I told SAM, "Get me Rockwell on the radio."

"Yes, sir," SAM responded.

Eli had gotten to the helicopter first and started the engine. I screamed after him, "You filled her up, right?"

"Of course, Bean. Who do you think I am?"

Hunter reached the helicopter and helped Ezra up. I jumped on after him. Hunter turned to Ezra with his hand outstretched, "Detonator?"

Ezra passed him a square box with several dials and a button with a case over it. As he did, the helicopter started gaining altitude. Then I heard Rockwell come on the radio.

"Bean?" Rockwell's voice came through.

"Rockwell, how close are you?" I said quickly.

Learning to Fly

"I'm literally coming above the base right now,"

"Good. We've got four Su-57s coming in hard and fast from the west. We need you to escort us out of here." I said while sticking my head out to look for the F-35. I heard the roar of the F-35's engine as it flew above us.

"Wait, what?! Four of them?!" Rockwell asked, shocked. "I can't take on four of them! I need your help."

"No can do, my suit's severely damaged, and I don't have any rockets and very little ammo," I said while watching the F-35. Then I saw the Su-57s coming from the west, flying in formation. I turned to Eli, "Bogies! West of us! Hurry up, man!"

"I'm going as fast as I can, Bean," Eli shouted back. "Yelling won't make me go faster.

I radioed Rockwell, "Rocky look west. Take 'em out. We believe in you." I hesitated before adding, "*I* believe in you."

"Ok," Rockwell said, clearly breathing hard. "I can do this."

"Yes, Rockwell, you can," I said calmly, betraying my feelings.

Eli was now high enough to blow the base. I turned to Hunter, "Blow it, Hunter."

"On it!" He responded. Hunter pushed the button. The entire base ignited in a ball of flame. Rubble started flying all over the place. One piece even passed right under the helicopter.

Eli turned the helicopter to the east, heading back. As he did, I heard a second explosion; this one was behind us. I looked back to see an F-35 flying past a destroyed Su-57.

"YEAH!!" I heard Rockwell scream into the radio.

"Good shot!" I exclaimed.

"That was sick!" Hunter said with emphasis on the "ck," as usual.

I watched the F-35 banked right, heading back towards the other Su-57s. Two broke off to attack Rockwell while the other started heading for us.

"Rockwell, they split!" I screamed through the radio, "Two on you, one on us."

I turned to Eli, "Can you do anything to stop them?"

"What am I supposed to do, shoot backward?" Eli yelled back.

"Hey, that's a good idea!" I leaned out and fired my M-4 backward. The bullets didn't reach the aircraft. I was just wasting ammo.

"It didn't work!" I yelled back.

"No duh, Sherlock!" Hunter chuckled, despite the situation.

"Shut up." I snapped as I put my gun away. "You would've done the same thing."

I looked back at the F-35. Rockwell was struggling with two Su-57s on him. He was banking left and right but couldn't seem to shake them. The Su-57s were stuck to him like glue. One fired a missile, but by some stroke of luck, the missile was defective and just fell to the ground. Then one of the planes peeled off and pointed its nose up. The plane was going to try and dive down on Rockwell.

"Rockwell, one peeled off." I yelled into my radio, "He's going to try and dive down on you. You've got to get behind that plane!"

"Bean! The plane is gaining fast!" Ezra shouted behind me. I glanced over at the approaching Su-57. Ezra was right. That bad boy *was* gaining fast.

I took a deep breath, trying to be calm, "Rockwell, we've got a pretty big problem over here."

Then I saw Rockwell do something I didn't think *anyone* was capable of. His engine turned hot red as he turned on his afterburner. Then he banked left hard. And I mean *hard*. That turn was at least 14 G's, probably more. The max I had ever pulled was ten. Let alone 14. And he didn't even have a G-suit on. But here it was. I saw his entire plane shuddering under the G's. I thought for sure it would break apart. But it held strong.

"Holy cow." I gawked.

The plane straightened out, and Rockwell powered towards us at max speed. The other two jets trailing him were left in the dust. I heard a loud beeping coming from the cockpit.

"BEAN!!! He's got a lock!!" Eli screamed at the top of his lungs.

I turned and looked at the Su-57. It had gained more distance than expected. My eyes widened. At that moment, I was truly terrified. More terrified than I had ever been. There is no other way to describe it. Total and utter fear. And I was helpless. I watched as the air-to-air missile came off its holding as the rocket ignited its engine. And then, in one swift swoop, an F-35, and I'm not kidding here, flew through the Su-57. At least, that's what it looked like.

The F-35 fired a missile, connecting with the aircraft, blowing the rocket coming for us along with it. But the F-35 was right behind the missile, and it looked like the F-35 went right through the Su-57.

I had to blink several times to make sure I wasn't dreaming. I patted myself down to make sure I was even alive. And then exhaled. And I laughed. It was more like exhaling. Not really a laugh. I mumbled to myself, "Oh my gosh. Oh, my gosh."

Hunter was going berserk. Screaming things like, "Did you see that?! That was crazy! The man is insane! He was *NRRRRO* and then like *BCKCKCKC....*"

"I am thoroughly astonished, Rockwell." I couldn't take my eyes off where the Su-57 had been.

Rockwell was catching his breath, "You liked it?"

"Ohh, I loved it!"

"Hey, Bean!" I turned to see Eli talking to me. "The other two jets are turning around."

"What!?" I looked back to where the planes had been. He was right. The two remaining Su-57s had turned around. They were going away from us. I was suspicious. Why had they turned around? It didn't make sense. Nothing made sense. They had their chance. Why didn't they take it?

"They were scared of us!" Hunter said proudly.

"I don't kn-" I started.

Learning to Fly

Ezra interrupted me, "They saw what Rockwell did and ran off!"

"I really don't tha-" I started again.

I was interrupted by Eli this time, "They sure were scared!"

I gave up trying to talk. I'd bring it up later. I was sure those guys did *not* turn around because they were scared. But sometimes, you need to let people have their happiness. And I felt happy too. Proud. My plan had worked. The mission was a success.

Britton Bean

Chapter 30

Repair Work

"Easy Bean. Easy." Eli said, almost in a whisper from over my shoulder.

We finally arrived home after refueling another four times on the way home. Helicopters really were a pain to transport. We had decided that we were going to bring Bit Kitty in a C-5 from now on, or just not bring him at all. But on the last refuel, I had asked Eli if I could fly the helicopter. Let me rephrase that. I *pleaded* with Eli to let me fly Big Kitty. He relented. Now I was trying to land this Kitty.

"I've landed before, you know." I kept my eyes fixed ahead.

Learning to Fly

"I want it to be soft this time, though." Eli patted me on the shoulder.

"You're dumb." I chuckled as I pulled back slightly on the stick, easing the helicopter down to the ground. The helicopter jostled as it hit the ground. At least it was smoother than last time.

"That stupid luck of yours, Bean." Eli groaned as I turned off the engine.

"I'm telling you, it's the hat. You should thank Harry." I told him as I got up from my seat. I was in a good mood after the mission's success and the helicopter landing.

"I am not thanking an inanimate object," Eli said sternly.

I gasped, grabbed my hat, and put it towards my chest, "He doesn't mean it, Harry." I gave Eli a stern look. Eli just rolled his eyes and jumped off the helicopter while taking his headset off. "And I'm the crazy one?" I heard Eli mumble.

I chuckled, put my hat back on, and turned to SAM, who stood like a statue in the back of the helicopter. It was kinda creepy. "Hey, SAM, loosen up a bit. This isn't a military inspection."

"Yes, sir," SAM responded a bit uncertainty. "Sir, if I may, what do you mean by 'loosen up a bi-'"

"SAM, it's a joke." I knew SAM didn't understand. I jumped off the helicopter to the ground, and SAM followed me. I heard the sound of jets roaring down as I did. I looked up to see Rockwell coming in for landing in his F-35. There were two other F-22s behind him, ready to land. The F-22, painted pink and green, started doing party tricks in the air, like barrel rolls and spins. I turned around to SAM, "Tell the rest of the guys to meet us at Narnia. I'm starving!"

"Yes, sir," SAM responded.

I started walking towards the road to grab a car when Eli pulled up in an orange McLaren P1. He opened the falcon-wing doors and patted the passenger seat. "How about a victory drive, Bean? Only one rule, you can't use that Bean Luck."

I chuckled and yelled, "Which means I can't drive, right?"

Eli shrugged, "Well, that depends. How dangerous are you going to be?"

"I'm not driving then." I smiled and jogged over to the car. I grabbed the door and pulled it closed.

Eli punched the car into gear and put the pedal to the metal. The cars ate the pavement as it gained traction. The vehicle started accelerating fast. Two seconds later, we were at 60 miles an hour. We were flying down the road. I grabbed the seat belt and clicked it in. I didn't want to die like this.

You know, it's a lot scarier in the passenger seat. When you are the driver, you know what you will do. You can feel the car better. You know the limits of the vehicle. When you are in the passenger seat, though, you feel helpless. You don't know if you will make that turn or hit that tree.

Eli turned hard and drifted around a corner. I could smell burning rubber. I gripped the seat hard as we turned. Eli straightened out and I felt the car accelerate. Adrenaline shot through my veins. I loved this!

We took more turns like that and sped fast on the back streets. We speed through Santa Clara and onto the highway as

Learning to Fly

fast as possible, at 215 mph. We drove around for about an hour before we headed home.

It was fun. It felt like we were kids again. And to think I was only 19. I felt way older and like I had lived such a long time. My life had changed so much. I had grown up so fast. Like I had skipped some part of my life. If the nuke hadn't dropped, I would probably be getting ready for college.

Back then, I was so young, so innocent. Back then, I was just trying my best to survive Biology. But now…time was no longer on my side. One of my friends was dead. Now I was a fighter and a leader. My greatest fear was that another person would die. And it would be my fault, just like last time. I just felt annoyed. Why bother fighting when it's unfair? Russia had more resources. The probability of winning was one in a trillion. I had so much more to worry about. And was this battle even worth it?

There was one thing I did know. I had to finish what I started. I had promised my friends I would keep going many years ago. That I would never give up. So that's what I was going to do. Never give up. Winston Churchill once said, *"Never give in. Never give in. Never, never, never, never—in nothing, great or small, large or petty—never give in, except to convictions of honor and good sense. Never yield to force. Never yield to the apparently overwhelming might of the enemy."* So that's what I would do. Never give in. And never give up.

Britton Bean

***

After getting food in my body, I just wanted to sleep. I was so exhausted, tired out of my mind. All of the guys slept too. As the sun was rising, I woke up and wondered what those Russians were doing right now. Probably picking up the pieces of their destroyed base. I smiled at that.

I looked at my watch. It was 8 a.m. I grabbed breakfast and tended to the chickens and our garden. Chores were still chores. I rubbed my neck and back. They ached badly, but my ribs hurt the worst. Those bullets the man in black shot at me really hurt. I was still worried about that man, more so than the other ones. But I had more important things to worry about at the moment.

I walked over to the research lab and walked downstairs. There was SAM, standing like a statue as always. I turned on the lights and sat in a chair. Taking the computers out of sleep mode, I opened a program connected to SAM. The program showed a holographic picture of SAM and showed where the issues were. His right leg thruster was damaged along with the armor in that leg. I rubbed my own leg, feeling the bruises. The frontal armor was also destroyed. A red warning came in a text box next to it. "Radar systems destroyed." It would be a pain to get those parts.

There was also a text box in the upper right-hand corner that showed my ammo situation. All of my rockets were gone. I was totally out of M-4 ammo, but that was easy to replace.

Learning to Fly

We saved all the special foldable ammo we could from Area 51 and foldable rockets. Good thing we grabbed them.

I got up from my seat and chained up the suit. I put the chains under the suit's armpits and connected the chains to a hydraulic lift. Then I walked over to the wall and pulled a lever, lifting the suit up off the ground. I walked over to my desk and grabbed my toolbox. I opened it and pulled out a drill, along with a wrench. I looked over at the suit and rolled up my sleeves. I sighed and mumbled, "Time to get to work."

***

I was just replacing the right leg armor when Rockwell came in. I turned when I heard him come down the stairs. "Did you sleep?" I asked.

"Yeah." Rockwell muttered through a yawn, "I did."

"Nice shooting up there yesterday," I said, focusing back on putting the armor in.

"Eh, I had a good teacher." Rockwell smiled at me.

I chuckled, "Still, you have to be a good student to pull a 14 G turn. I meant to ask you, how'd you do that? The best I've ever hit is 10 G's, and I think I passed out."

"I really don't know. I remember seeing you guys helpless in the helicopter and knowing I had to get to you. I remember hearing the entire aircraft start creaking. It was as if the aircraft was falling in on itself. And then, one second, I was pulling on the stick, and then I blinked, and I was heading straight for you."

"You should have died, though." I shook my head. "That many G's would prevent blood from reaching your brain. And you were in that turn for at least six seconds, more than enough to kill you."

Rockwell chuckled, "Guess I got some of that Bean luck."

"Maybe." I contemplated. I opened my mouth to speak and then decided against it.

"What?" Rockwell asked.

"Never mind." I motioned to the computer, "Could you check if the armor is fitting correctly."

Rockwell walked over to the computer and checked it. He held up a thumbs up, "You're good."

"Perfect." I drilled the cover back on.

"I'm going to get a drink real quick. Do you want anything?" Rockwell started walking towards the stairs.

"Sure. Just get me some water. Thanks." I replied, putting the cover over the screws, making the suit seem seamless. Rockwell walked up the stairs.

I thought about what Rockwell did today. No luck could protect you from 14 G's. There was only one thing that could – family. And while that does sound cheesy, it's actually science.

People have been known to lift entire cars when family members are trapped. Your body seems to gain twice the strength when this happens. It's part of your fight-or-flight response. Scientists can't really measure it. So, the only way that Rockwell could survive that many G's is if his flight or

Learning to Fly

fight response kicked in. I grinned as I watched him walk up the stairs. Deep down, I knew that he knew it too.

I worked until noon on the suit, restoring the armor and reloading ammunition. That stuff was easy. The radar, on the other hand, was completely destroyed. I removed the pieces the best I could, but the radar was unrepairable. I checked our supplies and even asked Eli. We didn't have any spare radar parts hanging around. I guess I should have expected that.

It was frustrating, but the radar wasn't a necessity. The targeting system could handle the radar within a five-mile radius. So at least I had *some* radar.

I finally went to the main house and saw everyone talking over noodles. Rockwell and Ezra were over at the table while Hunter was at the bar, turned towards them. Eli was over by the stovetop and saw me come in. He held up a plate, and I nodded. He scooped a chuck of noodles onto the plate. I opened the fridge and grabbed a container of leftover watermelon. Homegrown watermelon was amazing.

I grabbed the plate Eli had left for me and sat next to Hunter at the bar. I started listening to their conversation.

"And then you just turned and came after us!" Hunter jabbered as he picked through his food.

"Dude, that was literally the coolest thing I'd ever seen." Ezra complimented. Rockwell shook his head.

"That was quite the show," I commented as I shoved a fork of noodles into my mouth.

"Ahh, guys." Rockwell sheepishly said, "I'm pretty sure everyone here would do the same thing. And better."

"Hmm, sure, whatever man…" Hunter nodded. Rockwell smiled sheepishly and looked embarrassed.

I decided to change the subject, "I need to test out SAM. I just fixed him up and need to ensure everything works as it should. Anyone want to come?"

"I'll come!" Hunter reached over and put his plate in the sink.

"I'll come too." Ezra stood up.

"Nice." I nodded to Eli and Rockwell, "Eli? Rocky?" They both looked at each other and nodded.

"We'll stay here," Rockwell said.

"You're clearly not a mind reader." Eli grinned, "Because I kinda want to go with them."

"Well, you nodded at me like you wanted to stay." Rockwell shot back.

"Why would I nod if I wanted to stay here? You might be able to pull 14 G's, but you clearly can't read basic human expressions." Eli chuckled sarcastically.

"Fine! How about this: we flip a coin. If it's heads, we go; if it's tails, we stay." Rockwell suggested.

"Alright." Eli agreed, "But good luck finding a coin."

Rockwell reached into his pocket and pulled out a 2023 shiny American quarter. "Found it."

"What!?!" Eli yelled, "You're telling me that you just happen to have a coin in your pocket?"

"It's my lucky coin."

"No such thing."

Learning to Fly

"Bean has a hat he takes everywhere, and no one says he's weird."

"Hey, leave Harry out of this." I shot in.

"Well, we already know he's a lost cause, but I didn't know mentalness was contagious." Eli looked at Rockwell in disgust. "How long have you had it?"

Rockwell coughed, "Five or six years."

"WHAT!?!" Eli threw his hands in the air.

"In my defense, I found it on the ground in the bunker, which is pretty lucky considering the fact that I never found any other form of money in the bunker."

"So, you've been carrying around that quarter this entire time!?!"

"I mean…"

"Oh my gosh!" Eli looked genuinely worried, "I'm living with a bunch of mental patients." Eli suddenly turned to Ezra, "Did you know about this?"

"Of course, I did." Ezra said simply, "I was there when he found it."

"Oh my gosh!!" Eli looked like he was going to die, "You knew that your brother was mental, and you did nothing! You lived with him all your life!! I can't believe it. What's next, drugs, smoking, or heaven forbid," Eli sniffled dramatically, "Brussel sprouts!!" Eli collapsed on the ground. "This is your *older* brother we're talking about Ezra."

"By two minutes," Ezra exploded. "Two minutes older than me, guys! Not a big deal."

Britton Bean

"Best two minutes of my life." Rockwell looked on longingly.

After that comment things kinda escalated and the brothers tussled for a while. After separating bruised bodies, we decided it might be good to cool off. So, Hunter and Ezra raced to the airport while I got the suit ready to test.

As for Rockwell and Eli, they had a long... *conversation* about the coin.

Learning to Fly

Chapter 31

Entering in Style

I decided to take a spin in the suit to look over the area surrounding the airport and spied Hunter and Ezra talking below me. They looked like they were arguing, probably about who won the race. It was funny how petty they could be.

"Alright, SAM, let's enter with style." I proclaimed.

"What are you thinking, sir?" The autonomous voice responded.

"Hmmm. I heard there is an ejection system on this thing." I started plotting.

"Yes, sir," SAM confirmed

"Alright. I've got it. Switch to vocal recognition. I don't want this headset on me." I said, still thinking everything through. I wouldn't have thought this much about a simple thing a few years ago. Or even a few months ago. The headset lifted off my head.

"Vocal Recognition is on, sir."

"Perfect." I paused, making the calculations in my head. "Here goes nothing." I sighed, "Eject SAM."

There was a rush of wind as I felt a powerful push. I shot out of the suit like a bullet. It surprised me, and I lost where I was for a second. I quickly collected myself and positioned my body like a bird with my arms stretched out. The suit recognized this and flew over to catch me. The suit's back opened. As I got closer, I screamed, "Don't catch me till the last second, SAM!"

I took all my willpower to say those words. I didn't have much faith in a computer. In all the movies, this is where the robot betrays the owner. But I had a feeling about SAM. The suit heard me and fired its boosters to match my speed.

I stole a glance at Hunter and Ezra. They were looking up by now, with their hands above their heads to shield the sun. They definitely looked surprised.

I was breathing hard. Every breath was shorter than the last. I watched the suit below me. I was getting closer to the ground by the second, only about 500 feet now. The suit didn't show any sign of moving. I kept falling.

I could now see the facial features of Hunter and Ezra clearly, and was at about 300 feet. At this point, I was three

Learning to Fly

seconds away from hitting the ground. Then the suit came flying towards me. I braced for the impact, clenched my teeth, and closed my eyes. I suddenly felt myself slow down and then stop. The next feeling was getting pulled upright and I opened my eyes.

There I was, hovering five feet from the ground, with Hunter and Ezra gawking at me. I exhaled several times harshly. I chuckled and smiled, "Thanks SAM."

"I could have gotten closer, sir. Apologies." SAM replied in his monotone voice.

"No, that was close enough." I exhaled again.

"That was sick!" Hunter yelled.

"That was definitely something." Ezra nodded.

I lowered myself to the ground and stepped out from the back of the suit. "Do you want to do it, Hunter?"

"Do I?!" Hunter grinned.

"I was thinking we would do it with both of us," I explained.

Hunter looked confused, "What?"

"I call it juggling. I ran the calculations. I just needed to test the response time of the suit." I motioned towards the suit. "It's good enough."

"Wait…What?" Hunter said, still confused.

"Yeah, you're not making any sense right now, Bean," Ezra added.

"Okay, so here's what you're gonna do." I tried to explain. "I'll start in the suit. We'll start at about 5,000 feet up. You'll jump out of the helicopter, and I'll eject from the suit. When I do, the suit will fly over to meet you. It will catch you and hold you for about two seconds. Then the suit will eject you again and come for me. This just repeats until we get to the ground."

"Wait, that means that someone will land without the suit." Hunter pointed out, almost like a question.

"The suit will catch the person closest to the ground right before they hit the ground. That person will only have to land from like ten feet up." I tried to explain again. Hunter was still confused. I sighed, "You'll see. You just gotta trust me."

"If I had a nickel for all the times, I've heard you say that," Hunter mumbled. I pretended not to hear him.

***

"Britton, I hate this idea," Hunter said over the radio, looking over the edge of the helicopter.

Ezra had flown a helicopter with Hunter up to 5,000 feet, where we would try the experiment. I passed about 100 feet below them.

"If I had a nickel-"

Hunter cut me off, "Britton!"

I chuckled off the radio. Then said to Hunter, "Ready when you are!" Off the radio, I mumbled, "Say your prayers."

"Would you like me to switch to vocal recognition, sir?" SAM asked.

Learning to Fly

I yelled, startled by the voice. "Ahh! You scared me, SAM. Yes, do that." You'd think I would be used to SAM surprising me like that. Apparently not.

"Apologies, sir. Switching to vocal recognition." The headset lifted off my head, along with the eyepiece.

"Alright, Britton. I'm ready." Hunter came on through my earpiece.

"On my count," I said, getting serious. "Five...four...three...two...one"

The suit ejected me hard, but I was ready for it this time. I used the energy from the ejection to swing my body around, doing a barrel roll in the air. I caught sight of Hunter falling and the suit rushing under him. I watched as the suit caught him and threw him back in the air.

Hunter wasn't prepared for the power. He started spinning as he came out. I was looking right up at him, my head as far as it could go. But my head could only go so far. I lost sight of him. I turned to look straight and was surprised to see the suit right under me. My eyes widened in surprise. I quickly spread my arms. The suit adjusted speedily and caught me. I had just gotten in when the suit ejected me again.

I wasn't as prepared this time and went spiraling out. I quickly adjusted as I saw the suit adjust to catch Hunter. Suddenly, Hunter came flying past me. I had just stopped going up as the suit caught him. I continued falling and flew past the suit. I was getting closer and closer to the ground.

I craned my head to watch Hunter as he ejected. This time he spun into the ejection, more ready for it. He did a barrel roll and spread his arms. I looked down to see I was approaching the suit. I was caught and then ejected seconds later. We were in a rhythm now.

We continued juggling three more times. As I fell, I did the calculations in my head. Hunter would be landing without the suit. And concrete isn't soft. Hunter was caught and ejected from what looked like three feet. I didn't have time to see if he landed softly. The suit came in and caught me. I activated the thruster even before I was fully inside. I heard a loud humming coming from the suit.

I immediately looked over where Hunter should have landed. There he was, crouched on the ground panting. I let the suit fall to the ground. I stepped out of the back and ran over. "You alright, man?"

Hunter looked up with a huge smile, "No, I'm dead." I punched him in the shoulder, and he started laughing.

Learning to Fly

Chapter 32

Our New, New Plan

We all gathered in the war room. Everyone was seated, with Eli eating some cantaloupe out of a container. I was at the front of the room. I looked at the empty seat. There was a plaque built into the seat with Porter's name in it. But there was no Porter to sit in it. I sighed and shook my head quickly, trying to shake the moment from my brain. I had a job to do and had been calculating this plan for hours. It *had* to work.

"Here's the deal. Russia knows that we struck. And they're going to prepare for a counter-strike. And what's worse is that they know where to attack." I started. "We can't fend off an entire army. So, the best defense is offense. If we strike again, the Russians will have to regroup, delaying their attack even more."

"That doesn't sound like the best strategy." Rockwell muttered, "We are going to attack to *prevent* the Russians from attacking. We can only move so fast. Eventually, they will catch up with us."

"Yeah," I said solemnly. "But hear me out." I clicked a button on my computer and a map of Russia was pulled up on the wall. "Look here." I pointed to a red dot in Eastern Europe.

"If we attack Russia's base in Ukraine, Russia will have to divert its forces from here." I pointed at Nagurskoye. "All the way over here." I pointed at the red dot.

"Russia's size is to our advantage here. Their forces will take at least 24 hours to help defend their western front. What's also to our advantage is common sense. Russia is going to be thinking that they are being attacked on two fronts. This will divide their forces even more. And maybe."

I took a deep breath. "Just maybe, Russia might think that we are unimportant. They may even forget about us completely. In their eyes, we're just a group of kids with some military aircraft. Why would they ever think we were doing this? And they won't believe that we can coordinate an attack of this size. It's the Russian stubbornness that will lead to our victory."

"So, wait, what's after that attack? I mean, what do we do next?" Hunter said.

"Great question Hunter." I clicked a button on my computer. The screen now showed a series of red dots all over

Learning to Fly

the middle of Russia. "Then we hit all of their bases in the middle. With their aircraft now divided on two fronts, the middle will be wide open. That's when we bring in our good ol' friend, the B-2."

"What's that?" Eli asked with his mouth full of cantaloupe.

"It's an American Stealth Bomber. With a payload of 20 tons, this bad boy *will* annihilate the rest of the bases."

Hunter's mouth fell open. "20 *tons!* That's like one bajillion pounds!"

"Hmm, not quite, but yes, it is a lot." I smiled.

"So, after we bomb those bases, what then?" Ezra asked.

"Then we asked for their unconditional surrender." I proclaimed proudly.

"What if they say no?" Eli asked while sticking another piece of cantaloupe into his mount.

"Then we assassinate one of their leaders," I said calmly.

"WOAH!!" Ezra yelled.

"That escalated quickly," Rockwell murmured.

"Alright!" Hunter smiled.

"Guys, calm down," I shouted over everyone. "Everything will be fine."

"You literally just said you're planning on assassinating a Russian leader." Ezra retorted. "And we're supposed to be calm?"

"Well, guys…" I started. I didn't really know what to say. I looked over at Eli for help. He was slouched in his chair with a big grin and eating the cantaloupe like popcorn. He was definitely enjoying this. "Eli...Help me out here, man."

"Hmmm. I think I'll stay here on the sidelines for this one. I really want to see how this turns out." Eli said, almost giddy.

"Eli!" I barked.

"Ohh, feisty." Eli smiled as he pulled a blanket over him. "Play, please." He held his hand up like he was pushing a button on a remote.

"Bean, we are not going to assassinate a Russian leader. It's a war edict." Ezra emphasized.

"Is it war edict to nuke an entire nation?!" I challenged angrily

"Bean, we fight for military advantage only!" Ezra retorted.

"This *is* for military advantage!"

"How?"

"If we kill one of their leaders, that will push them closer to surrender. Their bases will be destroyed, and their military annihilated. At those odds, they *have* to surrender."

"What if they don't, Bean?"

"Then we destroy them."

"With what?" Ezra challenged. But as he said it, I think he knew.

"Ezra..." I grimaced, thinking about it.

"We are not using that."

"Ezra, in WWII, America was forced to–"

"Britton Bean! We will not be using that weapon." Ezra said firmly.

Learning to Fly

"Sometimes, people have to do things that they're not necessarily proud of. But they do them to make it so people *can* be proud. So that their citizens can have their freedom and liberty. So that life can be lived."

I shook my head, "So you have to ask yourself: Is this one of those moments?" I stormed out of the room.

***

I sat on the roof, with my feet hanging over the edge. Ezra never agreed with me. And now that I was thinking about it, he might be right. I thought about the plan that I'd come up with. I'd calculated for the worst of the worst-case scenarios. And yet, I was still uncertain. And I didn't like it. I was supposed to be confident. Why couldn't I feel confident? Why couldn't I feel sure of myself? I didn't understand. I heard the crunching of the roof tiles behind me.

I glanced back and saw it was Hunter. I turned around to watch the sunset. Hunter came and sat down next to me. "You never told us when we would leave for Europe. I really want to see the Eiffel Tower. You know, I heard somewhere that it was built by wolves. I don't know how they did it without them opposable thumbs."

Hunter did a thumb war with himself to show me. I couldn't help but chuckle. Sometimes Hunter had some good one-liners. I sighed, "Hunter, I'm not sure this plan will work. I've been thinking—"

Hunter cut me off, "Well, there's your problem, Britton. You're thinking."

"What?" I asked.

"Britton, you're someone who doesn't have to think. Ever since we first met, your first instinct was always right, right?"

"Well…"

"For the sake of the argument, just say yes."

"Fine, yes."

"Your best plans happened when you *weren't* thinking. When you didn't second guess yourself. When you knew just like that." Hunter snapped. "Britton, you don't need to think about your plan. It will work. And it will succeed."

"But what am I going to do about Ezra?" I motioned down towards the research base.

Hunter patted me on the back, "Why, learn from my advice." Hunter stood proudly, "Focus on the present, learn from the past." He framed the words with his hands.

I guess Hunter was right. The more I thought about it, the more I realized how correct he was. For how dumb Hunter could be, every once in a while, he would say things that not even the smartest people in the world could say. I was glad that I had him as a friend. Everyone needs a friend like that.

I stood up to join him, "For the record, I came up with the first part."

Hunter started walking away, "Did you really though?"

"Hunter, I will push you off this roof."

Learning to Fly

Hunter brought his arm around my shoulder. "Ahh, Britton, this is a good moment; let's not ruin it." And then Hunter smiled that smile. And I smiled back.

Britton Bean

Chapter 33

I Become a Magician

It was early morning when we all loaded up in the C-5. We decided that we didn't want to take Big Kitty. I took Harry, though. He was the most important member of our team. I also took SAM, of course. He was pretty important too.

This was going to be a long flight. A 13-hour one. And it wasn't like a C-5 had the most comfortable ride.

We grabbed some MREs that we found at Nellis. About 100 of them. We were set for at least two weeks. We snagged plenty of ammo, along with C-4. If there's one thing I've learned, you can never have too much C-4. We would also be picking up a B-2 in Missouri. Or what was *left* of Missouri. We

Learning to Fly

just hoped that one base would have a B-2. We had the bombs for it which we'd picked up in Hawaii, and loaded those on the C-5. It wasn't the safest thing in the world. The C-5 fit all the supplies and was only halfway full. That thing really is huge.

Sadly, I lost rock, paper, scissors and would be flying the first shift. Everyone else wanted to sleep. And frankly, so did I. My part would be flying to Missouri. Then Rockwell and I would take the B-2 and follow the C-5 to an island above Sweden. We knew there was an abandoned base there from our satellites. We also learned that the base had some old Harriers.

Harriers were British planes. They were single-engine multirole-fighters. They could also land and take off vertically, which would be useful. They weren't the biggest, but they would do. We also hoped that the base would have a helicopter or something.

This would be our base of operations for the mission. We planned to strike the Ukraine base, then wait 24 hours for Russia to respond. We needed them to divert their forces. We also hoped to take down some of their fighters. We were pretty sure that Russia didn't have many planes because they ran away from Rockwell. I just hoped we could handle the fighters.

We took off at 5:30 a.m. And let me tell you, I was exhausted. I felt like I was falling asleep at the controls. But there was always something about watching the sun coming up over the horizon. It was beautiful. Something so simple, yet so beautiful.

It was about 9:00 a.m. when we landed at the B-2 base. Luckily, it looked good. We taxied the planes next to each other and hopped out to stretch our legs and explore. We quickly found a B-2. It really wasn't that hard to spot, there were only three of them left. We chose the one that looked to be in the best shape. We named it Pitch Perfect. We thought it was kinda ironic. It was also a good play on words because "pitch" is the up and down of a plane. I had to explain it to Hunter. I wanted to stay longer and see what else I could find, but we had a schedule to keep.

After we refueled, we took off at about 10 a.m. I finally got caught up on my sleep while Rockwell was at the controls. We were just over Great Britain when Rockwell woke me up.

"Bean, it's British Air Traffic Control. They want to speak to you."

"Five more minutes." I groaned, tired.

"Bean!" Rockwell said more urgently.

I groaned and sat up. I yawned and put on a headset. I clicked the mic button and said, "Hello, this is Britton Bean; trust me when I tell you, we are only passing through. Over."

A man came on with a British accent, "We do not have you on our scheduled routes. You are also flying American military planes. Over."

Thinking on my feet, I said, "We are caring refugees from America to Sweden for an organization that uses old military planes. Over." I was starting to get nervous. But I didn't show it.

"Why did you not file a flight plan? Over."

"Ohh, I think we did. Maybe uh, someone didn't transfer it. It should be under uhhh...." I looked over at Rockwell desperately for help. He just shrugged. "Uhh, give me a second here." I looked around for anything to give me an idea. I brought my hand to my hat in frustration. Then I got it. "It should be under *Harr*ison Refugees. Over."

Rockwell covered his face with his hands and shook his head. I waggled my finger in the air and smiled. Rockwell mouthed, *We're dead. We are dead.*

Then the man came on again, "I thought they stopped delivering years ago. Over."

Rockwell's eyes widened, and he mouthed *No way.*

I laughed hard and started jumping up and down in my seat. Then I held down the mike and said, trying to hold back laughter, "No sir, we started again." I giggled, "Over."

"You guys repurposed a B-2? Over." The man sounded skeptical.

I nodded, "Yes, sir, we repurpose anything here at Harrison Refugees. That's probably why you didn't see our flight plan. We'll get that to you right away. Over." I looked over at Rockwell. He was still shaking his head in disbelief.

"Alright then, umm, safe travels. Out." The man ended the conversation. That's when we went crazy.

"No shot!" Rockwell yelled.

I started laughing and laughing. "Let's go! Let's go!"

"What are the chances!?! What are they?!? How? How? What? How does that work?"

"That was awesome!"

"That darn luck of yours, Bean. That darn luck!"

"That was awesome," I repeated.

Britton Bean

"That was dumb. Dumb luck!" Rockwell said with his head resting on his hand.

We just went on laughing and laughing for what seemed like forever. It seemed that luck was on our side. But apparently, Harry didn't have any more luck to give.

Learning to Fly

Chapter 34

Hunter Makes us Laugh

We landed on the island at 8 p.m. At least, that's what our watches said. Really it was like 4 a.m. We could see the sun rising to the east. We didn't worry about it too much, though. We had all gotten plenty of sleep on the trip. We were ready for the battle.

As I had predicted, the base did have some leftover Harriers. Sadly, there were only three. Which would mean we would have to figure something out. There was also a helicopter, but it was only a utility helicopter and nothing you could strap any missiles onto. We had plenty of missiles, even the mini ones that went in the suit. Our supplies could last a month.

Britton Bean

We started arming the Harriers as soon as possible. Hunter was cold as usual, complaining every once in a while, saying things like, "Why is it so cold!" or "This is why I live in St. George." or "My hands are like blocks of ice!" It was actually pretty entertaining.

We loaded up three Harriers. They were for Ezra, Rockwell, and Eli. Hunter and I would be trying out our juggling tactic. Eli approached us about it.

"So, how many times have you done this?"

"Enough." Hunter proclaimed.

"As in?"

"Once," I murmured quietly.

"You've only done it once?!" Eli raised his voice.

"Hey, it's pretty simple, alright. We're good at it." Hunter assured him.

Eli rolled his eyes, "So how do you do it?"

"The suit senses someone falling and automatically ejects the person inside," I explained.

"So, the person inside can't control the eject," Eli said, almost like a question.

"Well...yeah." I sheepishly answered.

"That seems dangerous, don't you think?" Eli asked.

"Well, when will we ever eject someone without making sure no one's inside first? That's right, we won't." Hunter happily explained.

"Yeah, that'll never happen." I agreed.

"Alright," Eli said. "Well, you guys better survive. I need someone to tend to the chickens." Eli grinned.

Learning to Fly

I scoffed. Then I turned to everyone, "Alright, guys, let's get going before there's too much light."

Rockwell gave me a thumbs up from a Harrier and slid the cockpit closed. Ezra jumped into his. Eli jogged over to the last Harrier. I motioned to Hunter, and we jogged over to the helicopter. I hopped into the pilot's seat, and Hunter jumped beside me. I put on headphones and turned on the rotors. I watched as the Harriers took off vertically. I watched as they slowed down as much as they could to wait for us to catch up. I tipped the stick forward, and we started barreling toward them.

***

We were over Poland when I gave the announcement. "Let's go over the plan one more time." I started.

I took a deep breath. *This is it, Bean.* I thought to myself. *You can do this.* I began, "First, I will fly ahead and take out their air-to-air missiles and guns. Then the Harriers will come in and lay some cover fire. After that, Hunter and I will drop down and place the C-4. This is when Russian air support should arrive. Now it's up to the Harriers to take them down. The fighters are going to be cautious. If I'm assuming right, they don't have that many fighters left. You guys gotta give it to them. I'll come up if I can. While you're doing that, I need

Britton Bean

Eli to land to pick Hunter up. Once you get him, I'll leave in SAM, and we'll blow the place. Any questions?"

"Hey, Bean, why don't we put SAM in drone mode after you land." It was Rockwell. "This would give us a third person on the ground."

"Yeah, that's pretty smart." I realized. "I'll make sure to do that. Anything else?"

"Hey, who's got the detonator?" Eli asked.

"As always, I do," Ezra answered. "I'll blow it when you guys are clear."

"Cool."

"Alright then," I started. "Let's do this thing."

We flew for another 30 minutes before we began our plan. I readied myself. I took several deep breaths. I stood up and took off my headphones. I plunged my ears over the noise and walked over to the suit. SAM was standing like a statue, as always. The back of the suit opened as I approached and walked in.

The sound instantly ceased as the back closed. The suit tightened around me. The headset fell down, and my heads-up display came on online. The suit automatically connected to the radio.

Well, Bean, this is it. I thought. *Same as last time. Let's end this.*

"Alright, boys, let's change the world." I jumped out of the plane and powered east.

"How come I never get to say things like that?" Eli asked.

"Yeah, didn't you say that a few years ago?" Rockwell said.

"Guys," I said. "It's semantics."

"No, it's not," Rockwell commented through a yawn.

"What does semantics mean?" Hunter asked.

"You know what, Hunter, I've given up on you." I chuckled.

"It's an honest question!" Hunter defended.

"Hunter, you're 19, going on 20; you should know that word," Eli stated.

"I'm not going to pretend like that's a word everyone knows, okay," Hunter complained.

"Hunter, we all know it." Ezra chimed in.

"Oh yeah, what is it then?" Hunter challenged.

"Hunter, it's pretty petty to argue over semantics," Rockwell remarked.

Everyone laughed.

"Ha ha ha." Hunter mocked. "Just tell me what it means!"

"No, I don't think we will." I giggled. "You'll go to your grave not knowing what that word means."

Everyone laughed again.

"This isn't funny, guys!" Hunter sneered.

That just made us laugh harder. I think that was the last time we all laughed.

Britton Bean

Chapter 35

I Jump Off a Building

I flew for another three minutes at Mach one before I reached the base. It was in Ukraine. Just outside Kyiv. I remembered when the country was putting up a fight, when it was Russia versus Ukraine. It was a simpler time back then. I hoped life would be like that again. But here we were. Fighting in the same place.

    I struck fast and hard, destroying AA guns before they could fire. The surface-to-air missiles got off the ground, though. Three of them came at me fast. I broke left to avoid one. Then I centered on another and fired my gun. The missile exploded.

Learning to Fly

I banked left and fired a missile at the last one. It quickly fell, then exploded. Then I turned and fired another missile toward the surface-to-air missile holder. The entire thing exploded into a fireball, followed by a secondary explosion.

I looked down and saw Russians filling the courtyard, all with AK-47s. They started firing at me. I banked right and fired three missiles into the courtyard. I saw a Su-57 start to taxi toward the runway. I could not let that happen.

I flew up and then killed power. As I started to fall back down, I engaged thrusters, heading straight down fast. I fired a missile at the aircraft, blowing it to pieces. I only had six left. *I've got to use these sparingly.* Said one part of my brain. But the other...*You should just go and fire all of them at the runway. Do you really need missiles?* I listened to that one.

The runway blew up in flames. I could see three more Su-57s. The Harriers would take out those boys. At least they couldn't get off the ground. Then I heard Hunter over the radio. "Britton!! We're here!"

"Coming!" I turned quickly, straining under the pressure of the G's. I saw the Harriers and the helicopter coming out of the clouds. The Harriers promptly sped up to fire on the ground and base. I flew past them and under the helicopter.

"Ready, Britton?" Hunter said.

"Ready, Hunter," I confirmed. Then I watched as he jumped out of the helicopter. I said quickly into the suit, "Change Vocal Recognition." I didn't get to hear the answer as the suit ejected me.

Britton Bean

I was prepared for it and spun into it, spreading my arms wide. I watched as Hunter flew past me and into the suit. Everything was working perfectly. The juggling was repeated five times. On the fourth time, I realized I would land without the suit. So, as I went into the suit, I said quickly, "M-4!"

I popped out with an M-4 snuggly in my grip. The suit had ejected me at little-to-no power. I was only six feet from the ground. I hit the ground and rolled. I came to my one knee as I heard shots all around me. It was a miracle that I wasn't hit. Hunter had landed in the suit and wasn't holding back. I looked around me to gather my surroundings.

I saw the Harriers circling us and firing their cannons. There were what looked like hundreds of Russians coming right for us. More than I had anticipated, more than I had planned. We were surrounded, and we didn't have much ammo.

I looked to the entrance to the base, which was heavily guarded, but quickly realized that the entrance was the only way to safety. I watched as Hunter came out of the suit with his own M-4. He put his back to the suit and fired. He had the backpack on that carried the C-4. I started firing back at the Russians, but they were endless. For each one that fell, there seemed to be three more coming at us. The suit went into drone mode and started firing with a machine gun.

I assessed my supplies as I fired. I had only two mags of ammo, a full mag of .50 caliber ammo, a Desert Eagle pistol, and some C-4. Hunter had the rest of the C-4. We knew that the only way for cover was through the base, despite it being heavily guarded. I turned to Hunter, "We need to head for the entrance!" I screamed as I motioned that direction.

"Are you crazy?!" Hunter said between shots.

"It's the only way, Hunter!" I screamed as a bullet whistled past my ear. "SAM, cover us! C'mon, Hunter!" I started running in the direction of the door. SAM flew over my head and fired.

"You're crazy, Britton!" Hunter yelled from behind. I would have to agree with that. But Hunter followed me anyway.

I pushed the button on my radio, "Cover us!"

"On it!" Eli said. I saw what must have been his jet turn and fire down in front of us, shooting up gravel only ten feet from me. He sure was confident that he wouldn't hit us. I wasn't, but kept running anyway.

As the dust faded away in front of me, I saw that the entrance had dramatically cleared out with only five Russians between me and the door. They leveled their guns at me. I was faster, though. I fired at them first, but had only gotten three shots off when my gun clicked empty.

Only two Russians had fallen. Taken aback, I ducked to avoid the shots. But it was too late. One of the bullets grazed my left arm and I felt blood start to run down my arm almost immediately.

Luckily Hunter was a better shot than me and had a full magazine of ammo. With three shots, the way was cleared. Ignoring the pain in my arm, I sprinted towards the door.

Britton Bean

I rammed my shoulder into the door, breaking the lock. But man, that hurt. My shoulder felt like it had been broken. I gritted my teeth against the pain as Hunter ran in, closed the door, and deadbolted it. Just in time too. I heard the metal door creak as someone ran into it.

We kinda just stood there for a second, catching our breath. I heard our enemies banging on the door, but the bolt held. Then I listened to a spray of gunshots, and the banging stopped. I squeezed my shoulder where the bullet had grazed me. The cloth and mesh on my arm was ripped and covered in blood.

Hunter looked at me and said between breaths, "I told you, Britton…you're crazy."

I chuckled, "Thank Harry." I pointed at the hat as I reloaded my gun.

Hunter just gave a half grin and said, "Get yourself together and take the second floor." He took off his backpack and handed me some more C-4 along with a bandage for my arm.

I groaned as I moved to grab the C-4 and applied the bandage quickly. It definitely wasn't a pro job, but it would help the bleeding. "Alright." And just like that, we were back on the run again.

We ran down a hallway until we came to another open area. It was a mess hall. Tables were set up in rows with a walkway through the middle. There was a service counter on the south side and I could see the kitchen behind it. There was a staircase on the far north side as well. But there was no time

Learning to Fly

to take in the scenes. The Russians were probably heading to a second entrance right now.

Hunter broke off into the kitchen while I headed for the staircase, my weapon bouncing on my chest the whole way. I hadn't had time to put my C-4 into my pack, and I didn't strap my gun onto my chest.

I reached the stairs and started up, three at a time. I placed a piece of C-4 on the railing. I got to the top and came into the main room. There were five doors leading into rooms all around the main room. The main room was filled with a pool table and there was another table with cards and chips neatly stacked on top. It looked like a Poker table.

I placed C-4 on the pool table and some C-4 on a window looking over the compound. I looked out the window. I looked at where Hunter and I had been. The courtyard was empty now. The once-packed area was now nothing but littered bodies. And that scared me. I didn't know where all the other Russians were.

I quickened my pace and headed into all the rooms. The first one was empty, the second one too. The third one had a bunch of machinery in it and the fourth was full of boxes. In all of the rooms, I left two C-4.

The fifth room I came to was different, though. It looked like an office and a bedroom had been smooshed together. In one corner was a laptop open with several cups around it. All with coffee stains. There was a bed in the far-left corner. There was a window in between the bed and the desk and I could see the sun rising on the horizon. The window also opened up onto the roof. But I didn't have time to look around any longer, the Russians would be here any second.

I placed my last C-4 on the computer and opened the door to run out. But that's when I saw Russians running up the stairs. They started yelling in Russian when they saw me.

I quickly shut the door behind me and locked it, but that lock wouldn't hold forever. I glanced out the window and saw Hunter was running for Eli's Harrier. But then I saw Eli jump out and run away from the Harrier. Hunter stopped, confused. Moments later the Harrier exploded. I looked up and saw a Su-57 pull up. The air support was here. And it wasn't anyone friendly.

I turned back to the door and the violent banging behind it. The door started to bend. I held my gun to the door. My earpiece started exploding with conversation. I couldn't pinpoint who was saying what.

"Incoming Ezra!"
"I got him!"
"Get SAM up here!"
"On your six, Rockwell!"
"What the heck happened?!"
"Su-57 happened!"
"We need SAM!"
"I've got him."
"Wait, what am I supposed to do?"
"Survive. I'm coming up there, guys."
"I count four!"
"Two on me!"

Learning to Fly

"Bank left Rockwell!"

I was occupied with my own problems. The door was about to break open. So, I did something bold. I stood right next to the door hinges, then unlocked and opened the door. It swung open, and one man rushed in. As he did, I slammed the door on his head and he collapsed. I jumped out from behind the door and fired. Bodies started falling. I knocked down several, but many found cover.

I flipped the desk and went behind it. I leveled my gun at their cover and fired. Plaster chipped away from their cover area. My gun clicked, and I quickly reloaded my last mag and pulled back the hammer to cock it. I knew I couldn't do this forever. I glanced at the window again and executed a plan.

I slid over to the door and closed it. Then I sprinted over to the window. The door burst open with gunfire. I shot back as I ran. Bodies fell to the ground, but more kept coming. My M-4 clicked empty, and I took out my Desert Eagle. I fired as I rammed my M-4 into the glass window. The glass shattered. I turned and jumped out.

I landed on the first-story roof with the tiles cracked where I landed. I ran towards the edge while tapping the bottom of my watch twice. I heard gunshots whizzing past me. Suddenly something exploded below me. Fire erupted. The C-4 had blown.

"Please, SAM," I begged. I jumped as the roof below me exploded. As I fell, I could feel the heat of the fire. I looked down and saw the destruction. SAM flashed below me. But his back was already open, open too early.

Britton Bean

That's when I saw Eli. Time slowed. Almost to the point where it stopped. I saw Eli grasping at the air. Trying to grab onto something. Falling towards the flames. He had been in SAM.

My mouth opened in surprise. I couldn't believe it. It was unreal. It was a nightmare. Eli continued to fall slowly, trying to grab hold of something. But there was nothing but air. And then I saw his head turn.

We locked eyes. The look in Eli's eyes broke my heart. There were so many emotions in that gaze. It seemed to be mining a hole into my heart. My soul. He understood and he cared. He was determined. He wanted *me* to be determined. He knew me. He believed in me. And then, he was engulfed in the flames. Consumed.

I never looked at fire the same way again.

***

The suit came around me and turned upward. And I did something that really scared me. I laughed with shock. I couldn't believe that had just happened. I thought to myself, *what just happened? He'll be fine. He's down there. We'll laugh about this someday.*

I knew I was lying to myself. I couldn't believe what had just happened. My stomach seemed to be fighting against itself. It was like something was tearing up my insides. And I knew. I

Learning to Fly

knew it was my fault this time. Truly. I had given the order. I pushed the button. I had said the words. And what's worse, I saw it happen. I knew what happened. It was my fault.

"Incoming!"

"On your six!"

"Eli, we need you!"

Eli's name brought me back to reality. I was suddenly aware of the world around me. I looked around from the suit. Four Su-57s were swarming all over my friends. They couldn't last much longer. I would not lose another soul today. I clenched my fingers and fired my thrusters as hard as I could.

I flew toward one of the Su-57s at full speed. I would ram into it if I had to. And that is exactly what I did. I dashed head-first towards the plane. At the last second, I pushed hard on my front thrusters, putting my feet in front of me. Then I killed the power.

I powered my feet into the cockpit glass with all my hate. Hate did not adequately describe my anger. My feet blasted through the glass. But they didn't stop. My feet flew into the pilot's face, through the fabric of his chair, and through the armored metal, into the open air.

I powered back toward another jet only milliseconds after making it through the metal. In the corner of my eye, I saw the Su-57 spiral to the ground. Warnings started to pop all over my display. SAM even said, "Sir, the suit's armor is damaged in several areas. Continued flight is not recom-."

"Shut up, SAM!" I said quickly. The alarms suddenly quieted. I flew after the second Su-57. I could hear radio chatter in my ear but couldn't make any of it out. My ears were filled with my heavy breathing.

I caught up with the Su-57 and grabbed onto one of its tails. I pulled hard. I could hear whining as my suit struggled with the strength of the metal. I clenched my teeth hard. Suddenly, the tail came loose. I flew backward into the other tail. The other tail gave way as the plane suddenly started spiraling downward. I went flying off of the aircraft. I quickly regained my bearings and headed straight up.

That's when I heard an explosion to my left. I looked over and saw plane wreckage falling to the ground. A Harrier came flying through the falling wreckage. I flew over and grabbed two pieces of scrap metal from the falling destruction. I flew to the last jet.

The radio chatter in my ear was going crazy. Cheering. I still couldn't make out any of it. That's when I noticed the last jet was turning east. *Not this time. You don't get to run, you coward.* I thought.

I was approaching the aircraft fast. I saw the engines turn hot red and orange as the afterburners started. But I was too fast. I felt a shudder as I broke the sound barrier. I flew past the jet and turned to face it. Then with two flicks of the wrists, the scrap metal flew into the engine intakes. The aircraft exploded. And I watched it. That's when my ears started to work again.

"Eli! What are you doing?!" Ezra screamed. "He was running away!"

"What were you thinking, Eli?" Rockwell yelled.

"Eli." I sniffed. "Is dead."

Chapter 36

The World Becomes a Lot More Real

"Idiot, Idiot, Idiot!" I growled to myself while pounding my fist against the wall.

We were back at the abandoned airfield. We'd picked up Hunter from the wreckage of the base and headed back. We searched for Eli but couldn't find his body. Only ashes.

I was on the second floor by myself in what looked like an office. I had let Rockwell stitch my arm, but it still hurt like heck. Everyone else was downstairs. I'd smashed everything in the room. When there wasn't anything else to smash, I pounded the walls, trying to break them too. That didn't work too well.

I groaned and fell to the floor. I looked at my hands, sticky with blood. I started remembering it all over again. I remembered Eli. I remembered Porter. I remembered Kai. I wondered if I was causing this world more harm than good.

"It should have been me," I said softly. "I should be in those flames. I should be ashes." I looked at the ceiling, begging, "Trade me for him. He's better. He's the one who should be down here. Not me. Please. I'll give up everything. I just want him back. They need him." I motioned downstairs. "I can't do this anymore. I can't lose another."

After a while, I must have fallen asleep. I woke up to the creaking of a door opening.

"'Sometimes, people have to do things that they're not necessarily proud of. But they do them to make it so people *can* be proud. So that their citizens can have their freedom and liberty. So that life can be lived.' You said it yourself." I looked towards the door. Hunter stood there. He looked out of place. Like he was trying to play golf with a baseball bat.

Hunter looked at me sternly and more confident than I had ever seen him. He smiled, "*We* knew what we were getting into when we signed onto this. Porter and Eli would want you to continue. To push on. Through pain. Through loss. Through challenges. And *we,*" Rockwell and Ezra came up behind him, "will continue. *We* will push forward. But right now, it's up to you."

I was surprised. Astounded. Hunter had done something that I didn't know he was capable of. He looked at me in the way only the best of friends could. I realized that Hunter and I had switched places. I should be where he was, helping my friends. Not the other way around. Hunter knew that too. I

Learning to Fly

looked around at all of my friends. They looked funny in a way. Like they were in the wrong position. Like they didn't know what to do.

Come on, Bean. I thought. *You're a leader, so act like one. Push on, and don't quit. Keep moving.*

"Bean?" Rockwell encouraged. "*I* believe in you."

I nodded. I knew what to do. We were going to end this. "Let's do this. We are going to succeed. And we will not lose another person. We *will* account for every possible situation."

"You got it." Ezra agreed, "We'll go and continue your plan. Bomb their bases. We can even scout it out."

"No," I said. "Scouting it out is just an extra risk of being attacked. We are not doing that."

"Bean, we can't attack a base if we don't know the exact locations," Rockwell commented.

"We've got satellites. They can see the locations." I said, annoyed.

"We don't have satellite visuals of some of eastern Russia," Rockwell muttered.

"What?!" I blurted.

"Remember the satellites we lost? Some of them were over Russia," Rockwell explained.

"Can't you just move them?" Hunter suggested.

"That's not how it works." I groaned. I took a deep breath to calm myself. "We are not putting anyone in any aircraft!" I said louder than I intended.

"Britton…" Hunter put his hands up to calm me.

I glanced at him, then continued more calmly, "It's way too much risk, guys."

"Fine." Ezra exhaled. "We'll bomb blind."

"No way!" Rockwell said, "There's got to be something that would make this easier. We'll just be wandering out in the open, looking for places to bomb? That's stupid. The Russians are bound to see us and send up some fighters. And we're in a freaking B-2. Hate to tell you, but it's not the most maneuverable aircraft. We'll be sitting ducks."

"He's right about that, Britton," Hunter agreed.

I bit my lip. There had to be something. To every problem, there was a solution. But whenever I thought of something, they just seemed to shut it down. Didn't they see I was just trying to protect them? Why couldn't they just see that? I looked around the room. There was broken glass all over the place. An indentation in the wall where I had punched. Then something caught my eye. A broken monitor. I knew it. I chuckled at the simplicity. Why hadn't I thought of it sooner?

"Radar," I said simply. "We'll monitor you guys through radar. We'll see them coming from miles away. And with you guys flying at your top speed, it should take at least 15 minutes for the fighters to reach you. By then, I'll be in SAM right next to you. I'll guide you home."

"Wait, can't you just take SAM up there with them?" Hunter asked.

"Radar. SAM has a huge radar cross-section." Rockwell said with a side grin.

"Meaning..." Hunter said, gesturing with his hands.

"Meaning that SAM would be easily visible on radar. The B-2, on the other hand, not so much." Rockwell explained.

Hunter finally got it, "So that means that the Russians won't even see the B-2, to begin with. And if they did, Britton would be there to take them out."

"And we'll go at night to prevent them from seeing you with their eyes," I added.

"Genius!" Rockwell exclaimed.

"Wait, wait, wait," Ezra said quickly. "If the B-2 is so stealthy, how will you see us on the radar?"

"The transponder," Rockwell said, like it was obvious. "I noticed it the other day; the plane's transponder is different. It's encrypted and can't be picked up by other signals unless they have the password."

"So, what's the password?" Ezra asked.

"Man, you just went straight to that." Rockwell said, "Not any, 'Wow, Rockwell, that's really interesting. I'm glad we have you on our side. You're really good at what you do!'"

"Dude, just tell me."

"Fine! Give me a sec." Rockwell turned and ran down the stairs.

I turned to Hunter, "We need to get some radar equipment. It should be around the base somewhere. I'll clear a room."

"Alright." Hunter agreed. He turned and quickly followed Rockwell down the stairs.

"Bean, are you sure this will work?" Ezra said.

"It's gotta." I said under my breath, "Gosh, it's gotta." I jogged out of the room and towards the room across the hall.

Britton Bean

Chapter 37

I Tried

"Finally, what took you so long," I mumbled as Rockwell handed me a piece of paper.

"You know it's not easy to *decrypt* something, right?" Rockwell retorted.

I was sitting at a desk with four monitors all around me. Two of them showed a radar screen, and another showed a satellite view. The satellites were connected to the B-2. At least it would be connected when I got the password in. Of course, there were certain spots where we lost visual. But satellites didn't have the best visual anyways. This monitor was just supposed to show the general location of the B-2. The last monitor showed a password box. This monitor would show the status of the aircraft. It's fuel, engine temps, speed, altitude, etc. All I needed was the password, and it would all pull up.

"Remember to keep radio silence unless absolutely necessary." I reminded Rockwell.

"You bet." We fist bumped. "You know we're not leaving for another five hours, right?"

"Yeah, but it's still good to have everything set up," I said. "Don't want any hiccups."

"Alright…" Rockwell said, not fully convinced. I think he wanted to say something else but held his tongue. Rockwell walked out of the room.

I slid the paper across the table, "Type this into the box Hunter."

"Huh! Officer, it wasn't me!" Hunter exclaimed as he shot up in his chair. "Oh, sorry, I was asleep." He rolled over to the desk, still waking himself up.

"No, duh," I said under my breath. I brought my hands to a keyboard and did my final checks on everything. I even checked things that I knew were fine. This system would not fail. I would not lose another friend. Not today. Not tomorrow. Not ever again.

Everything in the system was fine, and the transponder was working perfectly. Even after putting it through rigorous testing such as flying the plane at max speed, making 7 G turns, and such. We even flew the plane upside down for a second. The transponder wasn't fazed. Even when we shut off the engines, the transponder was still on, using its battery power. I was confident in its abilities.

Britton Bean

Everything else was perfectly fine. In fact, it was better than fine. It was exceptional. The satellites were working even better than expected. Without the transponder connected, the plane was virtually invisible. I even slept. A dreamless sleep, though I didn't sleep for long. I was woken up by Rockwell.

"Alright, man, it's time," Rockwell said above me. I jumped up to my feet.

"Alright." I turned to my left and yelled, "Hunter!"

Hunter screamed and fell off the row of chairs he had set up as his bed with a thud. I smiled and thought *That'll never get old.*

"Man!" Hunter grimaced on the floor, "You have got to stop doing that." He got up and walked over to meet us.

Ezra walked up behind Rockwell, "You guys will hold down the fort, right?"

"Yup." I said, "You guys are going to bomb those bases, right?"

"Heck yeah!" Rockwell exclaimed. "Let's see how they like it!"

"Ohh baby!" Hunter high-fived Rockwell.

"Remember." I told Ezra and Rockwell, "Radio silence unless absolutely necessary."

"Yeah, yeah, yeah. Don't activate the radio." Rockwell said impatiently. "We're good, Bean. We know what we're doing."

"Okay." I took a deep breath. "Just don't die."

"I got you, Bean." Rockwell gave a small smile. "To the ones who died." He motioned a salute with his hand.

Learning to Fly

I gave a side smile, on the verge of tears, "and to the ones who survived."

"See you soon, Bean." Ezra nodded.

"Guide us home, Bean," Rockwell said. And with that, they walked out of the room.

***

Hunter and I watched out the window as the B-2 powered down the runway, loaded to capacity with Russian bombs from Hawaii. I had a bad feeling in my stomach. A feeling that I should go to the radio and order them to come back. But I didn't. I'd checked everything. I'd made sure that nothing was wrong. But that feeling wasn't going away.

We took three-hour shifts each. Hunter took the first shift. I took a nap while he was watching the screens. I was emotionally drained. Hunter woke me up right at the three-hour mark. That was just like him. Nothing had changed.

I sat down in the chair and looked at the screens. The satellite view showed that they were over eastern Russia. The transponder showed everything was fine. All systems were online. Everything was working just as planned.

Things continued favorably for several hours. It was during Hunter's shift that he called me upstairs. I had just been making hot chocolate to wake me up. I walked upstairs with a mug in my hand. I walked into the room and asked, "What is it?"

"I just lost the transponder signal," Hunter said, moving the mouse over the transponder screen. It just showed a box that said, *Transponder Disconnected.*

I set the mug on the table and forced Hunter out of the chair. I scrambled to find the problem. As I ran a scan to check for issues on our end, I asked Hunter, "Last known satellite location?"

"We lost visual hours ago," Hunter said from behind me.

"What about radar?" I asked as the scan was completed. The screen showed: *No issues found.*

"Right there." Hunter pointed to one of the screens.

"Did you see any aircraft?" I said as my voice raised.

"No. I would have told you." Hunter said quickly.

"There's got to be something wrong on our side," I said as I started another scan. Same result as the last one. I refreshed the radar. Nothing. I rebooted the whole system. Nothing changed. I finally gave up and jumped up from my seat. "Keep me up to date. If anything happens, tell me immediately." I sternly told Hunter.

"Okay," Hunter said as he jumped into the seat. In my hurry to get out, I knocked over the hot chocolate mug. It fell to the ground with a shattering crash. The sound seemed to pierce right through my skull. And that's when I knew. I stopped as if I had been hit by a dump truck.

I shook my head and sprinted downstairs and out the door. I tapped the bottom of my watch twice. Suddenly SAM flew

Learning to Fly

around the corner and stopped right before me. I basically fell into the suit.

I already had a feeling in my stomach. I could feel the dams in my eyes start to break. But I reinforced them and kept going. I rocketed upward. I would not give up yet. This was simply a misunderstanding. That's what I told myself. I could hear the Spark start to hum under the sudden increase in energy consumption.

I powered through the night. Fighting through the feeling in my stomach, I headed for the last known location of the B-2. I felt the suit shudder as I broke the sound barrier. I continued gaining speed. I could hear my breath come out ragged. I was struggling to hold back tears. *Everything's fine. You're overreacting.*

"Anything yet?" I said over the radio, more panicked than I wanted to.

"No, sorry," Hunter responded.

I thought about sending a message to Rockwell and Ezra. It would compromise their mission. But it was the only way. I decided to do it.

"Rockwell? Ezra? Are you guys there?" I said quickly.

"Bean?" Ezra exclaimed, shocked.

Relief flooded me. I exhaled a breath that I didn't know I was holding. "Thank goodness!"

"What's wrong, Bean?" Rockwell asked.

"Your guys' transponder got turned off," I said, gathering my breath.

"Umm, no. It's still on."

"Wait, what?" I said, confused. "Where is the signal being sent?"

"Wait a minute. That's weird. It's being sent somewhere in–" Rockwell got cut off. Static filled the air.

"Rockwell? Rocky? Ezra? Someone!?" I started to panic again. Then I caught a glint of metal in the moonlight. "SAM engage targeting system." I began to get scared again. The eyepiece came down to my eye. In the eyepiece, a light blue grid expanded over the entire area. Then an object became outlined by the grid. It was in the shape of an airplane. It was too small to be the B-2. It was a fighter, a Su-57.

My eyes widened as adrenaline shot through my veins. My eyepiece got a target lock, but it was too late. Two rockets shot out from under its wings. But it wasn't fired toward me. It seemed that the jet fired them into the distance. I dismissed this and quickly shot a volley of missiles. The missiles hit true as the plane exploded in flames.

But there was another explosion. A bigger one. In the direction the Su-57 had fired. A fireball flew into the air. There was a secondary explosion, this one sounding like a bomb. I was blinded by the light and closed my eyes. Just before I did though, I thought I saw a parachute appear below me. But when I recovered from the light, I realized there were no parachutes. There were no survivors. Rockwell and Ezra were gone.

I felt numb. It was as if there were no more tears to cry. No more dams to break. Every ounce of feeling was gone. I

Learning to Fly

had lost so much that there was nothing left to lose. I could only shake my head and look at the fireball.

Fire was interesting. So peaceful, yet so violent. It had taken everything from me. My home, possessions, family, and lastly, it had finally taken my friends. And yet cavemen would all go crazy for it. I didn't see the appeal.

While I hovered there, I thought of my life. Had I done enough? Had I finished my duty? Had I completed my mission? Was this "mission" even worth it? I was this far in. I can't stop now. There are times to turn back. Times when it is best to call it quits. I ran past those times. I was going so fast that I didn't even notice them. And now, when my luck finally ran out, I realized I wasn't afraid to die. I didn't fear it anymore. Once you see so much of what you fear, you become unafraid.

So, I turned and headed back to the base. While I did, I said over my radio simply, "Get C-5 ready."

"Are you talking to me?" Hunter asked.

"There is no one left to talk to but you, Hunter."

Chapter 38

I Make Hunter Mad

"Britton Bean!" Hunter ran towards me as I stepped out of the suit. "What are you thinking?!"

"We are going to wipe Russia off the map," I said as if I had said, *I love puppies.*

"I regret to tell you, but we don't have enough bombs!" Hunter said, his anger growing.

"Yes, we do," I said simply. "The Sparks."

"What happened to assassinating a Russian leader, huh? Did we just skip that step?"

"Plans change, Hunter. My plans have done nothing but change. I have to make a new one after every single mission!" I

Learning to Fly

was yelling by now, "So I'm done making plans! I'm done trying! It's all or nothing; it always has been! You said it yourself, Hunter; I work better when I don't think."

"Britton!!" Hunter said, grabbing my head and shaking it hard, "You're losing your mind!"

I took Hunter's hands off my head, "You can join me or not, but you can't stop me, Hunter."

Hunter stepped back from me in utter disgust and shook his head solemnly, "You're not Britton. I don't know you."

I just looked Hunter in the eyes and said, "At least one of us is thinking logically." Hunter just shook his head and solemnly walked towards the open back of the C-5. I turned to SAM and said, "Drone mode."

I continued to the back of the plane. The back was already open. I walked in and looked at all the supplies we had. All supplies were in huge crates. There must have been at least 50 boxes. Eli would have known the exact number.

Hunter had walked straight to the cockpit and shut the door. I heard the engines start. I pushed a button on the wall to close the back. Soon I felt the plane begin to taxi towards the runway.

I opened the crate labeled *SPARKS* and looked at the devices. There were 100 of them. It would do. To one side, there was a remote with several buttons on it. A big red one was covered by a plastic case.

I picked up the remote and turned it on. I flipped a switch, and all the Sparks' LEDs lit up. I flipped the switch back. The lights turned off. I nodded and placed the remote back in the crate.

I walked towards the cockpit door and opened it. As I did, Hunter pushed the throttle forward, and the C-5 engines whined. The aircraft started moving forward.

I sat in the co-pilot's seat. The sun had just risen over the ground. I looked into the sunrise. It was hard to believe the things that had transpired, it was unbelievable. In 48 hours, I had lost three of my best friends. They were the only people actually keeping me sane. I realized that when the sun rose again, either I'd be dead, or the entire country of Russia would be. This was my final stand. My last hurrah. All of my battles led to this.

***

I caught sight of SAM flying on our wing in drone mode. I knew he would protect us. He was our only protection. He was our wingman. I thought of the power he held in his graphene frame. A Spark. An object that had such explosive power. And yet, if used correctly, it could power dozens upon dozens of homes. It seemed crazy that something so little could have so much power.

I looked at my own hands. I was that small yet powerful force. My team is that powerful force. *Was*. My team *was* that powerful force. But they were gone now. All that was left was

Hunter and me. I glanced at him, and saw the strong, confident, and powerful person he was.

He looked back at me. His eyes seemed to be full of disappointment. It cut through what was left of my heart. Then he took a deep breath, "We are not doing anything until we give them the choice for surrender." He was confident. It was non-negotiable.

"They won't surrender," I mumbled, reaching for the radio. I wanted to say more. I wanted to say, "What will that change? They'll still be there. They won't stop harassing America. Why do you think America hasn't reassembled? They can't. Russia will make sure of it. They'll knock us down whenever we try to get back up."

But I didn't say any of that. Instead, I grabbed the radio and spoke, "Russian Base come in. Over." There was a chattering of Russian, and then it stopped. I said back into the mic, "Does anyone speak English? Over?" There was a short silence, and then a Russian came in a thick accent and said, "What do you want, you scum?!" He didn't say over.

I replied calmly, "Get me online with Putin. Over."

"Don't joke with me, you dog!" Except he said something a lot worse than dog. "You killed him!" The voice replied. There was something else after that which I will not repeat either.

I looked over at Hunter, surprised and nodded. He was unamused and just looked out his window. I said, "Is that so? Over."

Britton Bean

"Don't act like you don't know! He was in that base you attacked in Hawaii! On vacation, mind you!" The man followed this with very harsh words. He was swearing like a sailor. I couldn't believe he knew all those swear words in English. He was not happy. And he sure didn't like my next sentence.

"While that's great and all, I need to talk to your leader to discuss your unconditional surrender," I said calmly.

I won't repeat a single word the man said after that. Needless to say, I don't think he would transfer us to his leader. I thought, *well, I haven't been cussed out in a while.* I finally just turned off my radio.

"I told you," I said to Hunter.

Hunter shook his head and said simply, "You have the controls." And then he walked out of the cockpit.

I decided to climb to 10,000 feet. It was as high as we could go before, we would need oxygen. And the only way to get the Sparks out of the aircraft was to throw them out the back. So that would be fun.

I remembered the first time I'd flown a plane to 10,000 feet, it was for skydiving when I was only 14. Wow, I felt old. I was almost 20 now. Had it really been six years? I wish I could've gone back and told my younger self how stupid he was. I wish I could stop him from taking on the mission. I wish I could go back to St. George, get in a car, and put the pedal to the floor. I wish I could do more paintball battles again. But now, I don't even have enough friends to do that. Man, I wanted to go back to those times.

Learning to Fly

After an hour, Hunter walked back into the cockpit. He looked at me and, surprisingly, smiled. I gave a quick, suspicious smile back and then looked at my radar. We were just about to enter Northern Russian airspace. I slowed the C-5 as much as possible. I'd have to, or else we would get blown out of the plane when we opened the back. I slowed it to 70 knots. It felt as if the C-5 was hovering.

I looked over at Hunter, "Ready."

Hunter looked back at me, "It's been leading up to this moment Bean."

"Bean?" I asked, surprised he'd used that name.

"Yup." He smiled.

"Alright, let's go." I put the plane on autopilot. I took one more look at SAM. He had slowed to our speed and was still next to our wing. Hunter and I walked out of the cockpit into the cargo bay. It instantly got a lot colder. Despite the cold, I made my way to the box labeled Sparks. I made sure they were strapped in. The straps were tight and secure. I motioned to Hunter and said, "Get a good grip on something." He nodded and walked over to the wall.

I walked over to the opposite wall to the button that would open the door. I looked at Hunter. He nodded his assurance. I grabbed hold of a pipe for stabilization, then clicked and held down the button.

Alarms started blaring, and there was a sudden rush of air as the back opened. The sound was deafening. Even though we weren't going too fast, I still felt a yank on my arm. But I held strong. Soon the air equaled out, and the force pulling me stopped. But the cold only increased. I let go of the pipe and met Hunter by the Sparks.

"So, this is it," Hunter said.

"Yup," I confirmed. This was it. Millions of people could die today. Or just two.

Hunter looked at me, "Bean, this is the moment. The moment that will change history. So, I need to ask you one question: Will you drop these Sparks on innocent Russians to fulfill your own desires? People who are living their lives peacefully, people who will die because of someone else's decision?"

I simply looked him in the eyes and with confidence I hadn't felt in years said, "I'm not perfect. I know that. I've made errors. I've made mistakes. And what I believe may not be right. But it's my belief."

I stopped and took a deep breath, "While the leaders of this nation and its citizens could have been good, they chose not to be. They made that choice. No one forced it. I believe *the people* should be responsible for their nation. And these *people* have chosen to destroy *our* nation. All actions have consequences. Believe me, I know. And these people have chosen their actions. So, they will suffer the consequences."

I didn't wait for a response. I just opened the box and handed Hunter a Spark. As Hunter grabbed the Spark, he looked me in the eyes. I looked right back at him confidently. We stared at each other for what seemed like an eternity. I saw the disappointment turn to respect. And then Hunter gave the signature Hunter grin.

Learning to Fly

He took the Spark in one hand and grabbed my hat in his other. He turned it so it was facing backward. Then he said with a kind of chuckle in his voice, "Let's get that Harry luck going."

I gave him the biggest grin I could muster. And, grinning ear to ear, Hunter threw the Spark out of the airplane.

The moment seemed to slow down, to stop even. I watched as the Spark flew into the air. It seemed to glide majestically. It looked like an airplane.

I pictured my team as that Spark. Glided up and up, flying towards our goal. And having fun along the way. My life seemed to flash before my eyes: capture the flag with the gang, intense paintball battles, drag races with my friends, Monopoly and Risk board games going way too long, and insanely dangerous bets.

But that was only the beginning. I saw the wonderful memories come flying in. I saw us learning to love and care, learning to act now and think later, learning to have fun, learning to accept each other's struggles and talents, learning to look past our faults and see the good, learning to trust yourself and rely on your friends, learning what family really means…and one more. It is the one thing that no one is ever finished with, the one thing that everyone is still learning. It will never be mastered. Everyone will always, and forever will be, Learning to Fly.

Chapter 39

We Have Some Issues

I put my arm around Hunter, and we walked back into the cockpit. I increased the aircraft's speed slowly to equal the air pressure in the cargo bay. I finally reached max speed after half an hour. I looked at my fuel gauge. It was three-fourths full. I did the math in my head. We wouldn't make it back to the base. We wouldn't even make it back to Ukraine. This was a one-way mission.

I decided to throw another Spark out right after we reached max speed. It would take about eight hours to get all the way across Russia. That would mean we would need to throw out a Spark every ten minutes. We put the plane on

Learning to Fly

autopilot along our planned route. Our route cut a slice right through the middle of Russia, moving to hit key cities and bases.

  Hunter and I waited in the cargo bay with some blankets. It was freezing now, with the speed at 520 miles per hour. But we stayed in the cargo bay anyway, braving the cold. I still don't know why we did it. It seemed stupid, and it probably was, but we did it anyway.

  After about an hour of flying, I heard the first Su-57s come up behind us. I quickly grabbed an M-4 as soon as I heard them. I hurried to the edge of the huge cargo door. I considered walking down the slope of the door but decided against it. I aimed my gun into the air, searching for the jets. Hunter joined me shortly after. We both looked into the scattered clouds covering the area. I steeled my nerves against the cold and gripped my gun tighter.

  Then I saw SAM fly past us into the clouds. It honestly scared the daylights out of me. I fired off a burst of shots at SAM before realizing he was on our side. SAM was too fast for me anyways. I heard Hunter say beside me, "Chill, Britton."

  "What happened to Bean?" I said with my eyes glued to the sky.

  "You're Britton, not Bean," Hunter said simply.

  "Man, that's cringy."

  Hunter was about to respond when a Su-57 came tearing through the clouds, its sights fixed on us. I pulled the trigger on my gun hard. A burst of shots flew out of it, aimed towards the ceramic glass of the cockpit. Hunter also opened fire next to me. Hunter was a better shot than me and hit the pilot through the glass. But as the plane dipped, we saw the aircraft was already on fire. It had already been hit.

A second Su-57 came out of the clouds. It was also on fire. Then a gold suit flew in, pumping lead into the metal frame. The pilot tried to evade, but the more agile suit eventually was right on its tail. The Su-57 was doomed. With one last burst of a .22 caliber machine gun, the Su-57's tail came free as the plane plummeted to the earth. SAM then took what would have been a *very* high G turn and flew right in front of our noses. The force of the thrusters knocked us over.

When we regained our footing, SAM had disappeared again. I looked through the clouds trying to spot him. He was nowhere to be seen. Suddenly there was an orange explosion in the clouds to my right. Then a few seconds later, there was an explosion to my left. Explosions started appearing faster and faster, all over the place. Suddenly a giant ground-to-air missile flew through the clouds. But just as suddenly as it had appeared, it exploded. And like a serpent slithering through the waves, SAM appeared above the clouds for a split second and then dove down to meet what I thought must have been more missiles.

The barrage of ground-to-air missiles stretched on for six hours. Four more planes even appeared to take us down. But these were older model cold war Mig 31s. SAM quickly dealt with them without us even firing a single shot. They never got close enough. Explosions seemed to shake us every second.

Learning to Fly

They seemed to never stop. While this happened, we kept throwing out a Spark every ten minutes.

After what seemed like forever, the explosions stopped. "Finally!" I exclaimed. "Did they learn their lesson yet?" I was sitting against a crate with earplugs in my ears. I took them out and rubbed my ears.

"I think they'll be back," Hunter shouted across from me. "I think I'll keep my earplugs in."

"You're probably right, but those things hurt my ears." My watch vibrated as a timer ended. I stood up and walked over to the crate that held the Sparks. I walked to the edge of the aircraft and threw the device out. I didn't even watch it fall. I turned back to Hunter and shouted so he could hear me, "I'm going to check on our route and our fuel."

I opened the cockpit door and saw SAM flying next to our left wing. I looked at our route, and my eyes widened. We were only 30 minutes away from the edge of Russia. We'd made great time. We must have had a tailwind behind us. I glanced at our fuel. We only had an eighth left.

We would have to drop the last Sparks and head south to escape the explosion. We could possibly make a landing in Mongolia. China wasn't an option. They would not like us there. Countries really don't like it when you wipe their allies off the map. That's if we even survived. I glanced out my left window, expecting to see SAM. But he was gone. I sighed. They must have sent up more missiles.

I walked back into the cargo bay and looked into the Spark crate. I counted five left. I saw the remote on the floor of the crate. I reached in and grabbed it. I examined the buttons. It had been made by Rockwell. I should be able to operate it easily enough. There was a switch and one big button covered by a plastic case to protect against accidentally hitting it. I decided to show Hunter how to operate it, just in case.

I walked over to Hunter and motioned with my hands to take his earplugs out. He rolled his eyes and relented. "Ohh, calm down, will you. This will be quick."

"It better be. Unlike you, I don't want to lose my hearing." Hunter said as he stood up and stretched.

"I was just going to show you how to activate all the bombs. But since you really don-"

Hunter cut me off, "Oh no, I want to." He said eagerly. "How do you do it?"

I showed him the remote. "First you flip the switch, activating the Sparks." I flipped the switch. Then I motioned to the Sparks. Their LEDs were on. "See?"

"Yeah, and then you click the big one. I'm not stupid, Britton." Hunter said.

"Are you sure about that?" I asked as I flipped the switch. All the Spark's LEDs turned off.

"Can I hold it?" Hunter said, ignoring my comment.

"You say it like it's a cat," I grumbled. Hunter just looked at me, confused. "Yes, you can," I said quickly. "Gosh," I mumbled. I stretched my hand out to give it to Hunter.

Just as I did, there was a sudden explosion on the plane's left side. I was unprepared for it and was knocked off my feet. The remote clattered to the ground. The aircraft banked harshly right. I slid across the floor and hit a crate. The plane corrected itself and leveled out. Then the aircraft dipped right again, executing a right bank, heading south.

Disoriented, I got up and looked around. Almost all the crates were against the right wall. I saw snapped ropes all around the area. They had snapped under the stress of the maneuver. It was by pure luck that I wasn't crushed. I found Hunter getting to his feet to my right. He looked fine. I felt around myself, looking for any wounds. I found a few bruises, but that was it. That's when I remembered the remote.

I glanced around quickly, trying to find it. If that remote had fallen out, all of this would have been for nothing. I searched around frantically. I let out a breath of relief as I spotted the remote against a crate, unharmed.

I picked up the remote and quickly ran to Hunter. "You, okay?" I asked.

"Yeah, you?" Hunter brushed himself off.

"Yeah, I think we were hit," I said quickly.

"Definitely." Hunter agreed. Then, reading my mind, he said, "You check the cockpit, and I'll shoot at any planes I see."

"Alright." I pivoted and ran towards the cockpit door. I slammed my shoulder against it, breaking the seal of the door. *That was stupid.* I thought. *You could have just opened the door.*

Ignoring the pain, I ran to the controls. Alarms were going off everywhere. I had lost engine one, and engine two was quickly losing power. I glanced out my left window and saw that engine one was on fire. I shut off power to engines one and two. The plane lurched farther right as I did. Then I tried to restart engine two. Engine one was lost. Engine two surprisingly came on at full power. I yanked the yolk to the left to level out the plane. My left wing was badly damaged, but I managed to level the aircraft. I lowered the thrust in engines three and four and increased the thrust in engine two to keep the plane headed straight. It reduced my speed but would keep the plane from plummeting out of the sky.

I adjusted the autopilot to keep heading in the same direction. My speed drastically decreased to 350 miles per hour. I heard a rattling as bullets tore through our fuselage. "Come on, SAM," I muttered.

I ran into the cargo bay and set the remote on a crate. I picked up my M-4 and ran to meet Hunter at the edge of the plane. I aimed my M-4 towards the sky, looking for any enemies. What I saw though, shocked me to my core.

SAM came around the plane, flames coming out of his right arm. He was quickly followed by three more Su-57s, firing all their guns at the small target. We opened fire on them, aiming for the cockpit glass.

Soon my gun clicked empty. I grabbed the extra mag on my waist, pushed it hard into the slot, and pulled back the hammer within a second. I continued firing on the planes.

I watched as a bullet hit SAM straight in the chest. It went right through him. SAM's thrusters sputtered and then came on again. While struggling to stay in the air, SAM slowed. As the Su-57s flew past him, he grabbed one of their tails and clung

Learning to Fly

on. And then, with one swift move of his fist, he punched the right engine hard.

The engine nozzle bent left and down. The plane's nose suddenly pointed straight up. SAM clung to the metal tail of the aircraft, dangling over the open air. Then the plane stalled, and it started to sway to one side. It fell like a rock to the ground.

I ran to the side of the cargo bay and looked over the edge. The plane fell down fast. I saw SAM, now clinging to the wing, raise his fiery hand. And saluted. Then, he plunged his fiery hand into the Su-57's wing. The fuel tanks in the wings exploded.

The entire wing tore off from the plane. I saw the pilot eject as the plane plunged into an uncontrollable spiral. I saw SAM jump off and his sputtering thrusters turn on. He flew hard and fast toward another Su-57 below him. This time he aimed right for the engines. He struck them, and the plane exploded. But Harry's luck was not with SAM. He did not reappear this time.

I bowed my head and saluted. I would miss that guy. He saved us. I couldn't have done any of this without him. I felt a tear fall down my cheek as I thought of all the things, I did to make him the successful companion and military resource that he was. You always feel more attached to something you create, and SAM was no different. I would miss him.

Britton Bean

Chapter 40

My Final Hurrah

Another rattling of bullets through metal woke me from my thoughts. There was no time to mourn now. I had a job to do. I sprinted back to Hunter. "We lost SAM," I said.

"I liked that guy. Now we only have one good shot." Hunter smiled at me, despite the situation. I couldn't help but smile back. Typical Hunter.

I looked out into the air. I counted at least half a dozen Su-57s. And now they were all targeting us. There were too many. We couldn't win this fight. While Hunter was fighting, I quickly found the crate that held parachutes. I got two and started to run back to Hunter. I was only five feet from him when he yelled, as he dived to the ground, "INCOMING!!"

Learning to Fly

There was a huge explosion in our tail, and the plane's nose suddenly pointed up at a 45-degree angle. I slipped, and the parachutes fell out of my hands and slid down the ramp into the open air. *Shoot!* I thought.

Crates started to slide out of the aircraft. I caught onto a metal bar on the wall and held strong.

But Harry flew off my head. "NOO!!!" I tried to grab him, but it was too late. I felt a tear stream down my face. I knew he was just a hat, but he was my hat, and we'd been through so much together. And as Harry left, our luck went with him.

I quickly glanced at Hunter to see him holding his own bar across from me. I saw crates continuing to fall out at an alarming rate. *There go all our supplies.* I thought miserably.

Suddenly I caught sight of a certain crate. The crate I had put the remote on. The remote was gone. I looked around frantically and found it sliding towards the opening next to Hunter. But Hunter saw it first.

He let go of the bar and jumped towards the remote. I did the same thing instinctually, avoiding crates as they flew past. Hunter slid across the floor and grabbed the remote. But he didn't have any good handholds.

I saw him scrambling to grab something. But the ground was too slippery and at too sharp of an angle. I felt a box nick my feet as I started spinning. I placed my hand on the ground to steady myself. But that slowed me too much. I saw Hunter's legs start to dangle over the edge. I dove towards him. I watched as his hands tried to grab onto the rim. "Britton!" I heard him scream.

Britton Bean

I was so close. Mere inches away as Hunter's left hand tried to grab onto the edge. He couldn't, though. He fell out of the plane into the air. I dove off the plane, searching for his hand.

I caught his left hand with my right and the edge of the plane with my left. I heard a sickening pop as I grabbed Hunter's forearm.

Hunter screamed in pain. "Oh gosh! Oh, man! Okay, that hurt. Oh gosh!"

I looked down at his left arm. His left shoulder looked sagged, and his arm seemed a little longer. I'd popped his shoulder out of the socket when I caught him. I saw him gritting his teeth against the pain. I could feel my own muscles burning from holding him. I was fully extended like a man on a cross. I could feel the stitches on my right arm start to come undone. Blood started pouring down my right arm from the wound.

"I got you, Hunter." I groaned, breathing heavily. "I got you." I heard the whine of engines as Su-57s came in for another attack. This time though, they fired at us. Bullets whizzed all around us. I turned my head and closed my eyes, waiting for just one of their bullets to pass through me. But none did. I heard the planes pull away.

My arms burning, I tried to pull Hunter up. But I couldn't, I was too weak. I said a quick prayer and tried again. I screamed as my arms felt like they were on fire. I kept trying to pull him up, but I just couldn't. It was impossible. Deep down,

Learning to Fly

I knew it. But I wouldn't let myself believe it. Hunter knew it too.

"Britton, this is a fight you can't win," Hunter said, remarkably calm.

"I got it." I cried as I tried another time to pull Hunter up. "Try to climb up my arm Hunter."

"I can't move my arm, Britton." Hunter motioned to his left arm. I looked down at Hunter again. He just shook his head. His eyes held…pity.

"No," I whispered, knowing what he would do. "No."

"Britton, we've lost so much. We've lost our families. We've lost our friends. But through it all, I knew one thing for sure: you would always keep moving. No matter what happened. You *knew* that life wasn't easy. But we had to keep moving forward." I saw tears start to streak down Hunter's face,

"There are two types of people in a war, Britton. Ones who sacrifice their lives so that a better future can come to pass. And then there are people who sacrifice everything, fight to the bitter end, and then go *build* a better future."

Hunter's breath became shaky. "Whatever you do, Britton, remember yourself, remember that others rely on you. Remember that others look up to you as an example. And most of all, remember you're not perfect, that you make mistakes. You've given so much, Britton, more than anyone else could, and I'm sorry. I'll miss you, but you will always be my brother."

Britton Bean

"You can't go." I sobbed. "I won't let you. You're my only friend left, Hunter. Please."

Hunter looked at me, shook his head with tears running down his cheeks, "Something is not beautiful because it lasts: it is beautiful because one day, when life is going terribly, you will remember that times can and will be beautiful. All you have to do is see it."

Hunter stopped speaking. He looked up at me with more pride and confidence than I thought possible. Then he just smiled and said in a way only Hunter could say, "See ya around, Britton." And with tears running down his face, Hunter let go of my hand. I didn't have the strength to hold him. He fell through the air towards the ground below.

And as he fell, he turned on the Sparks, opened the plastic case, and clicked the red button. And with that, I'd won. It just depends on your definition of won. To me, I'd lost.

Learning to Fly

Chapter 41

John

Britton rested his back on the uncomfortable seats of economy class. Britton was 23 and president of NUSA. He was frustrated and angry at life. And it didn't help that the attendant didn't even try to get Britton in first class.

Britton was on a flight back home after adding yet another state to the Union. They were popping up like flies now. Almost every refugee camp wanted to become a state.

Britton was supposed to be flying in Air Force One, but after one of the engines failed, his vice president Gage Hanson booked him a flight on a regular plane. It was supposed to be first-class, but the attendants couldn't find his name in their system. Britton had tried the "I'm the president!" card, but without any identification on him, the attendants' just thought Britton was trying to get an upgrade for free. Eventually, Britton gave up.

So here was Britton, in a middle seat, in an airplane bound for St. George, Utah. A man came and sat at the window seat next to Britton. The man smiled and nodded politely. Britton tried his best to smile back, but he really wasn't feeling it.

Britton felt empty without his friends. He had dreamed that one day, the world would stitch itself back together. The world was doing better than it had ever been, now that Russia was gone. America was regaining more of its former glory every day. And yet, there was only one problem with this world: Britton's friends were not in it.

The airplane finally taxied and took off. Britton noticed that the man next to him looked nervous. The man looked middle eastern. He had short, black, combed hair with deep blue eyes. He had some peach fuzz on his checks. The man looked young, yet his eyes told a different story. Like he had seen terrible things.

The man noticed Britton looking at him and explained, "It's my first time on a plane."

"Oh no…it's fine." Britton stuttered. Something about this man intrigued him.

"What about you? How many times have you been on a plane?" The man asked.

"Oh, many times."

"They're pretty cool, aren't they?" The man said while looking out the window.

Learning to Fly

"Yes, they are." Britton still loved planes more than anything. "What's your name?" Britton didn't know why he asked that.

"My name's John."

"Good to meet you." Britton wanted the conversation to end, but John kept going.

"How's life going?" John asked.

"Ohh, it's fine. How about you?" Again, Britton didn't know why he said, "How about you?" It just popped out.

"Ahh. I've seen many, many places. I have seen miracles. I've seen terrible things that I wish I could unsee. I've been better, and I've been worse. I've struggled, yet I always seem to get through. My life isn't easy, but life isn't supposed to be, is it?"

"Wow." Britton nodded respectfully, "Well said. I used to be able to speak like that."

"Yeah, well, when you're as old as I am, you become quite good at speaking." John laughed.

"If you don't mind me asking, how old are you," Britton asked.

"Ohh, I don't know, like 2,000."

Britton chuckled, "It certainly feels that way sometimes, doesn't it."

"Yes, it does." John stared at the seat in front of him.

"So, where are you from?" Britton asked. He had started to like this man.

"Ahh, I travel a lot. I don't really have a place I call home." John shook his head. "Where are you from, Britton?" Only later did Britton realize that he never told John his name.

"St. George," Britton answered.

"Ahh, I've been there. Nice rebuilding going on there." John commented.

"Well, I try."

"Are you involved?"

Britton chuckled. "Of course, I am. I'm the president. I thought you had figured that out by now."

"Well, I don't really pay attention to politics," John said, like he didn't even know that Britton had formed an entire country. Britton didn't mind this. He hated being recognized in public, and people around him started whispering things like *"That's Britton Bean!"* or *"I don't believe it!"* He just wanted to talk to someone normally. Instead, everyone who spoke to him ended every sentence with "sir" or "Mr. President." It reminded him of SAM.

Their small talk continued until the plane eventually landed and taxied to the gate. They talked about life and all the terrible and wonderful things they had seen. They talked about how humans could be cruel, and yet, most of the time, they were wonderful creatures. But soon, the seatbelt sign went off, and everyone started shuffling towards the exit.

"Well, I guess I better get going," John said.

"It was good talking to you, man." Britton smiled. A real smile. Not one of those fake ones that he put on for the cameras. He liked the man. And for a second, he forgot about

Learning to Fly

his worries. He forgot about losing his friends and his family. Because this man seemed to make him feel at home. And home was where they were.

Britton started to get out of his spot when John said something from behind him.

"Just remember, Britton: everyone has struggles in life. Some are harder than others. Some struggles may seem impossible. But there is always someone who cares about you." Then he paused as if someone was whispering something in his ear, "See ya around, Britton."

Britton was so taken aback that he could only turn and open the overhead compartment. When he came to his senses a few moments later, he turned back to the man.

"Hey–"

But John was gone.

***

Britton asked around, trying to find the man. He asked the airline if they knew any information about him. The airline said that the seat was supposed to be empty. They also told him that no one named John had bought a ticket on that plane.

Britton interviewed people on the same flight. No one ever saw him enter or leave the plane.

Britton Bean

Britton got the FBI and CIA to try to track him down. They never could. They claimed that the man Britton had described never existed.

As Britton thought about it more, the more he realized how mysterious the man was. He never told him his full name. John knew Britton's name and said that he didn't even know Britton was the president. He said that he was old, and yet he looked so young.

But what Britton did know is that he was never the same again. He looked at life differently. Britton became a new man, someone dedicated not to what he had lost, but to what he could gain. How he could rebuild and do better. How he could become someone to rely on again. He remembered what Hunter had said many years ago, "I think that we should focus on the present, but I also think that we should learn from the *past*."

The FBI and CIA told him that the man must have lied about everything. But Britton didn't think so. Britton had a theory of his own.

He believed that the man's name really was John. That man was old. That the man knew what Britton needed most in that one moment. And Britton knew how the man had disappeared. He also knew that no one would believe him if he said something. So, he decided to keep the experience to himself from then on.

Learning to Fly

Epilogue

Britton looked at the reporter. It had been three days since Britton had given the reporter his story. Britton had asked for an advance copy of the article, and the reporter agreed.

They sat in Britton's office. It was a refurbished room in Narnia. Britton had declined all efforts by the government to move out of the house. The government wanted to make it a historic site.

Britton was sitting behind his desk with the reporter's tablet in hand, reading the article. The reporter, Justin Woodwind, sat silently across the table. The article's title was

Britton Bean

The Untold Story of Our Nation's Hero. Britton almost laughed at the title. He thought it was way too dramatic.

He read about his own life. His own struggles and tribulations. Of course, the "untold story" took up most of the article. In the end, it talked about his life after the Great Flash.

Britton began to read.

There was a period of six months in which we don't know exactly what happened to Mr. Bean. He did not feel obliged to share what happened in those six months. What we do know is that Britton Bean landed in St. George, Utah, in a Chinese Xi'an Y-20 cargo plane. We also don't know what happened for one week. Mr. Bean would not elaborate on this either. It is suspected that this was when the iconic Silver Pillar Cemetery was built. The five unknown graves are now suspected to be Rockwell Dansie, Ezra Dansie, Eli Stucki, Porter Butterfield, and Hunter Haws. A stone pillar sits at the head of them. The pillar is famously engraved: "To the people who died, to the people who survived, to families broken, we give you this token." This exact cemetery now spans 1,300 acres and holds the remains of 1.2 million people who died in the Nukes of 2023.

Mr. Bean is then reported to have gone to Idaho Falls, Idaho. This was the biggest refugee camp from the Nukes of 2023. According to numerous eyewitnesses, an F-22 with a green body and pink wingtips landed at the Idaho Falls airport. A small young man climbed out of the F-22. A hunter in the area said, "When I looked at him, I saw a powerful yet battered

Learning to Fly

young man. He looked as if he had been to war." Little did that man know how right he was.

The man who greeted him was surprised. "He walked towards me and asked simply, 'I need to see your leader.' He spoke with so much power, I didn't think to question him."

Mr. Bean met with Gage Hanson. Gage Hanson had come from Montana and was about Britton's age. Mr. Bean was taken to Gage, and a long conversation, lasting three hours, commenced. Britton would not elaborate on what was said, so Gage Hanson provided the details.

"He approached me while I was fixing lunch. When he walked in, I knew he was different. He looked powerful, proud, and determined. And yet, his eyes looked tired and exhausted. He told me he was rebuilding America. I told him I'd already tried in Meridian, Idaho. But when the Russians saw that, they bombed Meridian to smithereens. I also told him that other areas had tried the same, to the same result.

He gave me a side smile and said, 'That won't be a problem anymore.' He then told me that he had destroyed Russia. He didn't elaborate on how. He just asked me to trust him. I was suspicious of him and questioned him for three hours. Eventually, he told me, 'Come, follow me.' He said it in a way that wasn't threatening, it was caring."

Mr. Bean then took Gage Hanson to St. George, Utah, and showed him Narnia. Bean shared his plans with Hanson. "I remember thinking they were pretty smart." In the interview, Hansen stated, "Then he asked me to join him in recreating the USA. And I simply said, 'You betcha' and that was that."

Britton Bean

Britton then visited refugee camps around the USA, in Nashville, Tennessee; Baltimore, Maryland; Palmyra, New York; Little Rock, Arkansas; and many others. He gained support from around the country.

Representatives from nationwide camps met in St. George, Utah, on September 12, 2030. They formed NUSA. The New United States of America. Or as known by the public, the USA. The representatives made a constitution that very closely resembled the old USA constitution. St. George was named the capital, and Britton Bean, President. 32 states were organized, but only six years later, that number would grow to the original 48, excluding Alaska and Hawaii.

Britton Bean instituted measures to greatly increase the economy. He formed an Air Force, Army, and Navy. Bean started mining oils and minerals all over the United States. Weapons began to be produced for the military. This had a huge butterfly effect. Companies were created to produce supplies. People were hired to build and work in factories. People were employed to run those factories. Colleges were rebuilt to educate the citizens. Professors were hired for increased education. Engineers made and executed plans to rebuild cities and communities. Overall, the nation's economy skyrocketed quickly.

Population increased as impoverished countries like Mexico and other countries in the Yucatan Peninsula saw job opportunities in America. The nation saw record-breaking immigration, with over 27 million people immigrating in a single year.

Learning to Fly

With the increase in population, trade between countries exploded. Trade renewed with England first, then included France, and then to all of Europe. Africa and South America, who were relatively unharmed by the World War and had become quite wealthy, and America was soon trading with all nations in all the continents except China. The world entered into a time of global peace.

After eight years, Bean stepped down as president. He got married and had three kids. He became a commercial pilot.

Technological advancements were made at an amazing rate. Cancer was greatly decreased with a type of new injection that contained nanobots. Great leaps in Fusion technology were made, making it extremely close to becoming a viable option. But nothing was ever found resembling the Spark.

Some hackers did find a top-secret folder labeled "Spark" in old Russian files. But mysteriously, the files were wiped beyond recognition and recovery. There were only four words, "It isn't worth it." No one knew what it meant.

In 2043, China started getting protective over the Alaskan Area. Overly "protective." China controlled Hawaii and Alaska. Chinese troops were placed on the edge of Alaska, beginning to encroach on Canadian territory. Gage Hanson, the President at the time confronted China in a public address, famously saying, "If your men move one more inch into Canadian soil, the full might of the NUSA will hit you harder than we did to Russia." China did not listen. And the country entered into its first war of the era.

Britton Bean

The NUSA went in guns blazing and pushed China back to the tip of Russia. Sadly, in the first battle, the United States five-star general, William McMullan, was shot and killed. Instead of promoting within, *all* generals unanimously voted for Britton Bean to take McMullian's place. Mr. Bean agreed.

Bean firmly believed in the Air Force. He won his battles through surprise. And he flew alongside his men in his inferior F-22 painted green and pink. Yet he had 23 confirmed kills by the end of the war.

China was pushed back to its own land. But by this time, England boldly chose to join the war. This was followed by France and then by all of Europe and even some South American and African countries. With all of this going on, a revolution started within China. A revolution for democracy. So, with the might of the world backing him up, General Bean pushed forward into Chinese territory, and China finally surrendered for peace.

The conditions of surrender gave back Hawaii and Alaska, returning America to its 50-nifty-United States. It also gave the Chinese Revolution control over the government. The Chinese Revolution made the DOC or The Democracy of China.

Fueled with inspiration from China, North Korea also suffered a revolution. With support from nations worldwide, South Korea was restored to its former glory. With countries at peace around the world, the world was finally happy.

The International Space Association, or ISA, was formed with the goal of traveling the Solar System. The organization made it to Mars in 2056. All nations had a singular goal in

Learning to Fly

mind. Fusion energy was finally considered a good investment in 2061. Energy was now no longer an issue.

In 2070, nations worldwide gathered at a convention in St. George, Utah. The issue on the table was a new world organization. It was called Nations United, or the NU. It was proposed to be a new world order. A singular earth. All the people and nations of earth working towards a common goal. There were many people for it, and many nations pledged their allegiance. Britton Bean was called to speak on the issue. Many people believed that, had not it been for him, none of this prosperity would have happened. They considered him the George Washington of the modern era.

Bean was 61 at the time, and he was aging fast. Bean spoke out about the NU. He was the only one that did. This is a part of his speech.

"I warn you against the dangers of this organization. Does this organization know what is best for the people of the entire world? Or does it choose to profit? This NU may start as a great government, but what will it become? Do not let history repeat itself. Look around this room. We are already united. Nations from Africa, Asia, Europe, South America, and Australia. We don't need a fancy organization to tell you that. The NU should be a promise. Not an organization. A promise that whatever happens, *all* nations worldwide will support each other and understand each other. A promise to good, a promise to success, a promise to the betterment of mankind. That's what the NU should be. Not an overarching power or supreme leader. A promise."

Britton Bean

There was a silence that came after that. And then, the France Ambassador stood up, nodded, and clapped. England followed, South Korea, then America, and then everyone stood up and clapped. Britton Bean nodded solemnly and walked down from the podium.

Two years later, the NU was officially formed. It was formed as a loose government that had little to no power. It was more of a...promise. The NU wanted a president nonetheless. Britton Bean was their first choice. But without explanation, he refused. It was simple "No."

People were shocked. Everyone questioned why he wouldn't do it. Entire campaigns went out to make Bean president. Nations around the world asked the simple question of why. Britton Bean never gave the answer. I asked him the same question in my interview, but all he said was "No." We may never know the answer. But the life of Britton Bean *will* be known.

* * *

Britton sat on the stone bench next to five graves. The graves of his friends. In the middle was the six-foot pillar. Everyone always talked about what was on the back of the pillar. The poem Britton himself had written. But what Britton really cared about was what was on the front. Inscribed on it

Learning to Fly

was John 15:13: *Greater love hath no man than this, that a man may lay down his life for his friends.*

Britton looked at the words solemnly. He knew his time was coming. That he would soon join them. Britton had gotten the diagnosis from his doctor just a few hours ago. Radiation poisoning. It was because of his exposure when he was younger. Many people had it, but it was curable through the use of nanobots. Britton had denied treatment. Britton was a dead man walking.

But Britton was hopeful. He wanted to go home. And home was wherever his friends were. He was happy to be dying. He had lived a good life. He'd done what he'd promised. He'd fought till the bitter end. And made a country from the ashes. He'd fought hard and listened to Hunter. He had built a better future. A future based on freedom and liberty. To him, he'd won.

Britton knew that there were things that he did not know. Who was the man in black? How had the Russian gunship gotten past the border of the USA? Who had blown the C-4 early that killed Eli? How had the Russians found the B-2? What did Rockwell say after he cut out? He could not figure them out, but maybe, just maybe, his descendants would figure it out one day. And then, they would know. Everything would be revealed. And it would be wonderful.

Britton remembered what Hunter had once told him, "Something is not beautiful because it lasts: it is beautiful because one day, when life is going terribly, you will remember that times can and will be beautiful. All you have to do is see it."

A woman came and sat down next to him. She slung her arm around him and gave him a side hug. His wife knew his death was imminent. That it was a matter of days. She understood him better than anyone else alive. She was the only one that knew the whole story.

Britton felt pride grow in his soul. He'd done it. Britton had fought the strongest nation on earth. But that wasn't his pride he felt. He felt pride in his friends. His family. He'd created something greater than any battle or war. A family. A family of friends. And with them, he learned how to prosper.

Britton died on October 7, 2074. In his will, he asked to go the way his friends had. By fire. Britton was cremated.

"He lived a life of success." His wife said at his funeral. The funeral was attended by millions around the world. It was the biggest social gathering ever. "A life that he was proud of. He fought for what he believed in, for what was right, and even if the odds seemed impossible, he fought on. He believed that no one would ever be perfect. That everyone *will* make mistakes. He loved his friends. The people he fought beside. The people that died right next to him. He considered them to be his home. To him, he had learned all he wanted. And now, I think he's up there with his friends, once again, Learning to Fly."

Made in the USA
Las Vegas, NV
13 September 2023